CW00494048

WATCHER ON THE WATER

Ice Age in Scarlet

JACK HOLLOWAY

Ice Age in Scarlet Publishing

Dedicated to my wife and children, currently in Alaska. The River, the Tusker and the Squidge.

1

There's a Watcher up above

We're just going to leave him up there?
That's… cruel. He'll be lonely.
Worse things in this world than loneliness, kid. And we need to go. Now.
I feel like we're abandoning a friend.
That thing is no one's friend, Jack. Everyone's going to have to find their own way of getting through this and he's made his choices.

Cube

Far above an ice-wracked Earth a solitary cuboid satellite observes the end of the Universe, though in point of fact, it lacks the sentience to know what it is it observes.

It regards the process of dissolution from a high perch, with the resigned air of a man watching the last bus of the day depart from the stand, on a drear Sunday night in Rotherham. Clutching a rapidly disintegrating paper bag of fries his friend persuaded him to prioritise over the risk of long walk back home in the bone chilling drizzle were they to miss that fateful bus.

Does he regret the choice, made? Seems likely, but now there's nothing he can do other than watch the lights of the missed bus disappear into the murky distance and begin the trudge home through puddle-splash and misted, drizzle speckled, glasses.

The satellite has not always been alone. Upon launch it had been a barely regarded and somewhat furtive accretion to a constellation of fellows that spanned the globe performing a plethora of functions.

It formed part of a glittering network of solar-winged mechanicals that bound human civilisation together in a cocoon of interdependent data-webs, where the vibration of a single strand could destroy a promising career in a single ill-judged comment or spread fame virally between the great spiders of culture in a bright flash of notoriety.

In a world unknowingly spiralling down the toilet as dark forces moved unseen pulling hard on the chain with malicious intent.

Now the little cube that can maintains a lonely geostationary vigil over the Continent of Europe, tumbling across the background of far stars and planets, amongst the broken debris of its less fortunate cousins. It floats through a sea of broken solar sail wings, burnt-out processor fragments, and complex optics, shattered now by a series of eye-for-an-eye attacks, instigated by blinded men.

To a discerning eye, near-Earth space is a chaotic disgrace except in so far as the faintest shimmer of the hailstorm of space debris reflecting sunlight provides the planet with the ghost of a ring that might have grown one day into a thing of beauty as the laws of nature scattered it across its range.

In the now, it is a barrier of high velocity destruction, a

shredder of humanity's hubris, but this cube-satellite is a survivor. It has been optimised for this very situation by a mid-term solutions man with a sharp pencil and a sharper mind, a rare thing indeed in a world of short-term imbecility.

Names

The Satellite's former operators called the boxy little satellite 'Tony' reflecting certain propensities it shared with a problematic maintenance operative who had acquired a certain form of celebrity among the denizens and sojourners at the Arcane Investigations Agency's head office hidden in the dark places below the Ministries of Whitehall.

The operative was the glittering paladin of the Agency's beloved 'clear desk' policy. And he was notorious for stubbornly disposing of classified documents left temporarily resting in workspaces by overworked civil servants, whatever importance they might have held to the now paperless office dweller.

Or indeed the country.

The real near flesh and blood Tony had a knack for turning every early morning meeting at the Agency into a nightmarish game of hide and seek, particularly for those who had worked late the night before to prepare and who held a different set of priorities that veered more practical.

Such short-sighted beings' mornings became a frenzy of rooting through bins filled with the previous night's pizza crusts and split pots of kebab sauce, to find impossible treasures of stained top-secret briefing papers or space surveillance feeds printed out on dot matrix printers through Tony's ministrations.

The actions reflecting a masochistic form of damage control to soften the edges of life where reality and unalterable survival diktat hit the dictates of paper absorbency and bright line environmental policy.

Tony was therefore the monicker given by those in the know to any form of exasperating co-worker and our Cuboid pal definitely has his quirks.

"Morning boss, Tony's rotating on his axis again. Think he's looking for something. Fuck knows what it is. Print-outs from last night are in the bin if you want to go digging."

"Looking sharp, boss, new suit? Um, Tony's firing his booster intermittently, he was over the North Pole two minutes ago and he's accelerating towards the Chinese Space Station. He's not armed is he?"

"Boss, bit of a situation. Tony's transmitting bursts of morse code on the same channel as that sitcom you like and making everything 'fuzzy'. He's not supposed to do that is he? There have been complaints…"

This wasn't how things were supposed to be.

Costings

Tony's name suits him better than the three-hundred signifier monstrosity that the optimists in the Agency had assigned him when documenting their master plans for Treasury approval.

The Agency, whose funding had rocketed in inverse proportion to the world's declining stability, had planned to put a shadow web of information gathering assets shaped much like Tony to monitor magical activity and thereby save on both Agent time and perhaps more importantly, the dreaded travel budget.

The proposal had been submitted to Treasury with a smorgasbord of supporting evidence. There had been satellite maps of paranormal activity, time-over-target assessments for all the main factions of the arcane world, graphs of carbon savings for the ever important environmental impact figures, lithographic motion scenarios demonstrating reduction in subsistence costs over time, even a couple of sly Oxbridge memes in the ever popular Attican that the younger members of the team thought might appeal to their SPAD equivalents at HMT.

Hadn't happened.

Those plans with their gargantuan overreach and stale allusion-based comedy were (in paper form) mouldering away in some Treasury locker with a 'limited funding - experimental only' stamp in red defacing the three-point recommendation to purchase a hundred such satellites along with the support stations and operations bases required to collect such a bonanza of magically garnered secrets.

A photostat of the defaced original had been sent back to the AIA in a standard string-tied brown paper envelope with the recipient's name the final entry in the long list of officials representing over a decade of disappointment, confirming HMT's decision.

The final confirmation (filed separately) revealed that the Agency could have 1 (one) satellite, plus the entire extensive support station network, though not where the Agency had requested due to a land prices analysis suggesting savings through a locational shift, conducted at ministerial request.

Part funding by department too, savings savings savings. Twenty-five percent through the estimates, using the excess travel and expenses so helpfully identified by the Department in its proposal.

Net effect of approval?

Fifty-percent reduction in the travel budget for the Agency and its hard-working agents. Thirty-three (and a third) percent increase in bureaucrats assigned to the land purchase project based at the Ministry for Disaster

Recovery and monitored by a newly appointed Treasury bod.

Proposal to cut security team at the College (noting limited but non-negligible risk of Fae incursion) approved.

Thirty six base stations, partially completed, two base stations completed at date of writing.

One overworked and glitchy satellite whose existence is something of a miracle rotating at random around the Earth like a basset hound seeking sausages.

Incidentally, the very same day as the decision was received at the Agency, the very same official who had confirmed the well thought out decision on the satellite net had sent a final decision to the Navy cutting back its proposed frigate purchase for the fiscal period from sixteen down to six, thereby losing a lucrative export order in the process, costing a thousand jobs and playing havoc with the unit cost estimate that gave the First Sea Lord palpitations.

In Treasury terms, it had been a good day.

2

He's been watching for a while

Perspective

So, taking the background into account, what does our cuboid friend observe as he peers down from on high like a cuboid-Icarus?

Rather too much, were I to be honest with you. The world as is, in this Autumn of 2035 CE, would be enough to drive one to drink.

Tony doesn't drink, and neither do I, so let's add an organic into the mix.

Ignore the screaming. None of this is real.

There. Now we have a human eye in all its dubious glory, attached via optic nerve to its associated squishy processing mechanisms, set next to our satellite friend. And those processing mechanisms, subject as they are to triggered bursts of hormones and stress chemicals short circuiting a rather limited logic circuit, are undoubtedly registering both alarm and confusion.

The first and most pressing concern would have been obvious had I afforded my suggestion a little more thought. Our lucky observer is sitting around twenty-seven thousand miles above the surface of the Earth (give or take a wobble or two as Tony dodges a fragment of 1990s space station) and across their skin they would feel the delightful pattering cold-burn of terminal levels of unmitigated solar radiation.

After all, even those environments that bask in the term 'atmosphere' closer to the Earth's rugged features are not entirely conducive to the survival of the squishy hairless chimps that are (still) the dominant form of life thereat, so before imminent termination occurred, we are driven to provide our theoretical observer with a 'space suit'.

We will also throw in an 'escape pod' for the purposes of purported egress from orbit in order to calm our subject's secondary concerns and allow it to consider the matter at hand to provide that context we crave, even if the technology of the day would make a safe return borderline miraculous.

After all, as the Agency's 'Handbook for Agents' (fourth edition, third iteration 2017-2030) states at page 107:

"In a survival situation involving the unexpected disruption of societal and physiological norms, the Psychological is to the Physical as two to one."

The author of said handbook had not experienced deep space at the time of writing, so we will accord a certain tolerance for hyperbole whilst acknowledging the undoubted impact of psychological matters on the likelihood of survival amongst our human friends, once issues such as exposure to hard vacuum have been adequately addressed.

Which I believe we have now achieved.

Calm yourself.

As was

As a next step towards meaningful comparison and

assessment let us assume a little knowledge of the world as was from our subject. It is not much to ask and is necessary so that our observer can use that multi-fold electro-chemical mulch between their vacuum protected ears (I hear no thanks, such a lack of manners amongst the young) to assess said changes occurring in the last six months against baseline assumptions.

This being roughly the last time that the Earth experienced something proximate to 'normality'.

Avast ye, Normalcy!

Said changes are not pleasant. Aesthetically for the cultured man, and practically for those who still retain the ability to feel.

That beautiful blue-green orb that delighted the senses of the first space travellers and reminded the throngs glued to electronic television broadcasts who followed their travels they lived on a small, fragile and amazing planet, is long gone.

That's not entirely the fault of the half-year past. In point of fact in its optimal form the jewel of Earth has been on its way out for years, decades even.

Too much heat bouncing back and forth between layers of greenhouse gases, too much radiation leaking in through gaps in the ozone layer, too many explosions throwing up dirt into the atmosphere from mining and testing, too much fishing leading to a little too much sludge mould covering enclosed sea-space and poisoning the remaining salt-water inhabitants.

And war, always war. Accelerating year-on-year as the links between societies frayed. The comfortable existence of the previous decades that had seemed on an uncontainable march forwards, ebbing to the core territories, watched with hungry eyes by those left behind amongst the ashes.

After all, this is humanity we're speaking of.

I have always suspected that there is an innate push towards conflict in the human psyche. A need to push down their neighbours whilst exulting themselves. We Vampires have it too, when young, we learn to suppress the urge with appropriate training and patient tuition from our betters. Witches seem immune from the urge despite their origins.

The Fae, being the Fae, treat war as a form of entertainment and therefore something to take lightly. Easy to rile, easy to placate, for a time at least.

Changeable creatures. They can't cry, you know?

Humans just get on with it, and have at it till they're done. Damn the consequences so long as they win and get to perform a victory dance over the recumbent forms of their defeated enemies. One of the reasons I always counselled caution in engaging with them in prolonged conflicts despite our physical superiority and knowledge of the arcane.

I digress.

As is

Even the pink-tinged, overheated, rapidly-desertifying, globally-warmed, hurricane-prone, water-war-fightin', mess of chaotic beauty that our Observer would have seen from above six months ago is now memories and recorded footage on damp-decayed media.

The slow-motion disaster playing out over decades has been replaced by immediate Catastrophe and its concomitant disastrous-brethren. A smoker with blackened lungs, cells veering towards rampancy, struck by a lightning bolt whilst sheltering under a tree.

Tectonic activity on an epic scale is the main culprit. Coastlines are changed, the Pacific rim particularly hard hit. Not that you could see from up here with human eyes. There's something in the way.

Botheration.

Now what caused that mess?

A good question from my space bound colleague, and an impressive one considering his imaginary nature! One that I am unable to answer for now, my friend, and not just because you do not truly exist, reality being frangible. If asked to theorise, my assumption would be arcane intervention. Contrary to the beliefs present in the darker corners of the blogosphere, half the world does not suddenly collapse into the sea without some outside influence.

I have additional reasons for my belief but I do not wish to divulge the basis for my hypothesis until I know you better.

Observe, if you would be so kind. That is your purpose.

This new Earth is a ruptured hell-hole of a world. In form it resembles the eye of a man raised too quickly from the deepest trench of the ocean via pulley and steam engine. Nitrogen bubbles through his veins as he rockets towards the surface. Twisting sinew and writhing muscle, blood boiling, no matter how oh-so-cheery and full of vim he might otherwise be and no matter the support provided by his disappointed colleagues upon his emergence.

It happens. You move on with different hypotheses and a new test subject. Knowledge has a price.

Blood-red clouds blot out the lost beauty of the world, the pattern of oceans and continents (disfigured as previously noted) has been replaced with a glutinous and thickening bouillabaisse of red dust and organic matter, sloshing around in an armillary sphere of blood-magic sigil-streams.

The secondary effects are worthy of study. With the light and other forms of radiation emitted by the Sun blocked, little warmth or light passes to the surface and walls of ice advance at speed from the poles.

It is my estimation that an Ice Age is in the making and survivors shiver among ruins with little to mitigate its effects. And that is not the worst thing that our observer might see, were he to apply his attention to the indicated spot rather than gawping like a landed fish at oversized ice-cubes.

Please?

What is given might be taken away.

Better.

Monsters

Here be Monsters.

Not figuratively, literally. Magic can do that if you're not careful in your practice. It organises the disorganised, imposing order of sorts when it finds the right structures so to do, and by random chance, it will find them soon enough, given enough raw material and time.

With something organic to work it produces the most remarkable results. I imagine something similar could have led to the creation of all life. Though there is no magic in dust. Where is the source?

No matter. For now.

Great forms slide through the scarlet clouds, precipitating out of the mixture of dust and magic and other less cleanly things, and these forms celebrate their new existence in twisting dances and predatory lunges at strange prey of a similar nature, or more mundane items that have the misfortune to be caught in their gaze whether on Earth or above.

The monsters' existence is bound to the changes caused by the mix. Reality within the clouds has worn thin enough that gravity has no hold, light is slowed, everything is changed.

As a demonstration let us draw our observer's view (if you would be so kind) to the headless torso the size of Kansas wriggling impossibly across the skies above Australia. Its underside studded with a plethora of skyscraper length insect legs. The large-and-vulnerable attracts the small-and-hungry, and its vitals are being picked away by swarms of deathly snake-rats on gossamer wings leading to a rain of chitin and hemolymph across much of the Australian desert.

The world does not lack for wonders whether great or small! What say you friend?

Yes. There is that. The monsters, (whether great or small), show an almost human jealousy for their realm. Intruders are not welcome and everything 'not them' is an intrusion subject to annihilation.

Whether that's buildings, where the carrier-agent clouds are low enough, or aircraft as per the item of flaming wreckage noted by my colleague of the skies plummeting down over Chicago O'Hare.

Landing slot values have gone through the floor, given that flights tend to the short and partial.

Finally paying attention are we? Well. Let's leave our observer to gawp at the monsters. There are bigger matters to attend to, and I fear that escape pod I have conjured will be treated as any other incursion when he eventually tires of horror and tries to return to the cold Earth so we shall discount the ungrateful fellow's views.

Let us instead turn our attention to a more sophisticated observer and what it observes.

Back to Tony.

The nature of bubbles

The blood-red bubble surrounding the Earth is not a

system in equilibrium and Tony's logs, when interrogated, inform us that it has been growing more disordered since it first appeared. Deepening, expanding to a point, then forming a skin of sorts where its interactions with reality prevent further growth.

For now.

More and more arcane gloop is making its way in streams from the surface to add to the soup. Its source? As mentioned, I have my thoughts on that, but it is sufficient to note that each magically active element added pushes the bubble's mathematical structure along an exponential energy curve calculation, where energy is potentially infinite and resistance is not.

Tony can see this. It's something he's built to do. He observes the changes in the clouds' surface, watching them shimmer, and runs estimates that point to further disasters to come. The surface is fit to burst. Lightning storms the size of nations play across the outer surface, and the arcane pressure builds relentlessly.

The alternative method to relieve the pressure, consuming the Earth from which it is sourced, is an impossibility. The bubble cannot push further 'inwards' in much the same way as a man cannot pull himself up by his own shoe laces. And I have tested that concept with both reward and punishment as effectors.

Outwards, ever outwards. 'Bubble gonna pop', and the only people who might have done something about it have other distractions.

There's war a-fighting down below and that's where Tony's main attention is focussed. Flashes and pops of detonation blast up from the recorded location of humanity's cities and are noted and catalogued by our cuboid observer.

Distraction

Oh. Hello. Back with me are you? Tired of monster watching, at last? Sensible, they are byproducts not the main event. As with all things it's what the sentient do that attracts one's attention.

The detonations are quite impressive. Goodness. Humanity has made some strides, I'll tell you.

Conflict rages on the cold surface amid the ice-flows and below the monsters as Humanity fights its enemies in broke-backed wars and the world freezes under its shimmering shroud.

From the pattern of things, the biggest fights are raging in Europe, though China has its share of conflict and there is something fallen across northern India…

There!

Lines of explosions follow the ice-clogged flow of the Rhine north as invaders from the East break the last of the month-long resistance provided by the French national army and its dark benefactors along that ancient border. A fine defence given that their comrades were driven pell-mell from the marshes of Pripyat and across the North German plain in a matter of weeks.

If you listen you can hear them. Arcane communication in clear. How very déclassé.

Counterattacks ineffective, doesn't matter how many you kill, pulling back…

Master Perryman destroyed. Witches grabbed him, pulled him into the clouds… in pieces… insanity…

Tanks approaching HQ, under direct fire… going offline, corp to wheel, protect Paris…

Another strike slices across the frozen polders of Holland where Eastern soldiers in grey-green uniforms, defaced with soul-eating protective runes, wave forward amphibious launchers and ground hugging drone swarms, through clouds of nerve gas.

The gas worked.

He said it would. Get the flame units up. Burn the bodies.

Anything more from Saratov?

Nothing. They're gone.

Forward then. This has to end.

They do not have things all their own way despite their witch allies and their own mysterious benefactor hidden among the shadows.

In Paris a familiar group of old souls whose planning remains as ineffectively long-term as ever, receive confirmation of the Eastern advance and, abandoning hope of victory, activate a contingency plan for the youngest of them to propagate their ideals in fresh soil whilst the rest gather their strength to distract the advancing forces from the long refugee columns.

Serah? The reserves are ready to deploy… where do you want them? Lots of choices…

Too late. Too slow. Do you see them fleeing? This is our burden. How much further could the Muscovites advance if we... the contingency?

Not much further than Paris. They'd be cut off… We'd be dead.

**laughs* we're already dead, young one, that's rather the issue. Send for the Colonel. And get Aly out, they won' t expect…*

Give me a moment. One mourns even the dullest child. I should return to the broad from this ditch of malaise.

Dice are rolled. Stratagems tested and found wanting. All across the background of starvation and icy death. Across the Channel a light, visible even at this height stabs out to catch ships and send them down to the depths.

Good work. Nothing good comes from runners.

Tony merely counts the Megatons, the tanks, assesses the oily droplets coating the dead skins of Dutch soldiers in their one-generation-too-old MOP suits, and hangs lonely in the stars but for you and I, and you, my friend are merely a theoretical construct of a dreamer, and I dream dreams I can never remember.

Communications

What use a Watcher without means to communicate the information he gathers?

In Tony's case, feisty little cube that he is, his line of report is to a base station that I see sat nestled in a bunker set underneath the Capital of the nation that put him into space, or rather, that paid another nation to do so having abandoned space flight on spurious promises of an ally.

He does so via a clever little array that both is, and isn't, hidden somewhere inside the cuboid satellite and is, and isn't, sitting in a plastic box about the size of a laptop down on Earth. This product of Treasury finance coupled to the first stirrings of a precocious arcane science transfers information via a tight beam of magical energy that is capable of piercing the wavering over-filled bag-barrier that currently separates the world from the rest of the Universe.

Try to use any other form of information transfer and all you'd hear is an awful lot of screaming.

Why do the clouds scream? There are reasons, I'm sure. You may as well ask why you scream. I wish you would stop.

Oh, I see. It's so close now. You should turn and look away my friend. I'm unsure as to how you would react to what may be about to happen.

Turn instead from our view of cold, monster haunted Earth outwards, that you might see the Universe. Fine old-fashioned reality. What hems us into this place and this time among the approaching shadows.

For now.

There are echoes of knowledge from later here. I

understand this to be a Universe where the normal laws of physics continue to apply. Life of a million kinds blossom across strange worlds, contemplating kinder inheritances from ancestors unknown, whilst floating in the darkness between worlds on wings of silk or steel, as ignorant of what is about to happen as you.

Goodness, but it's a beautiful place. I wish I could share it. Everything in it, natural and formed of matter and energy easily observable. An absence of state-sized monsters made of magic that delight in the feel of snakes eating the organs from their torso!

In an ideal world... universe... whatever, it would retain those features and all that alien life basking in histories unknown to human minds could continue to blossom so beautiful and zesty.

No. I'll tell you when it happens. Enjoy this. You have a privilege even I lack.

Tony has a communication to send, he can only keep so much information stored before he needs to blurt it out to the base station and given the torrents spewing up from below, his storage is nearly at its tolerance level.

Another corner cut, another bit of wear on the system that could have been avoided through appropriate expenditure.

The counter ticks upwards another notch. Nearly at tolerance. Tony prepares to optimise one last time to add an additional hour to storage capacity at normal data gathering rates.

It's not to be. By the law of averages...

There we go.

A blip flashes across his sensors. Another light erupts from the frontline. A megaton warhead taking out a major industrial centre in Northern France before the Family special forces team assigned to defuse it can break through the stalwart and suicidal defence of their Eastern equivalents. A makeshift defence line anchored there collapses. Death follows swiftly.

The skin of red around the Earth wobbles and bloats, the algorithm ticks, storage full once again with this wafer-thin mint of knowledge. The expert system triggers a transmission.

Needle sharp. You can see what's going to happen? Yes? No, that wasn't an invitation to turn.

Tony triggers its communications node and blurts out the latest data to its base station. The beam lances across hidden planes towards its target below.

What happens next is actually quite predictable, were anyone to have done the basic math. Complexity tends to simplify itself if you stand far enough away. What matter the small things when it is the big that matter? What matter the big when they are made of the small?

Interaction between two forces, a simple equation involving excess surface pressure against a weak gradient, and the effect of a pointed incursion with considerable force at a limited impact site occurring outside of time.

Don't be obtuse. Even you…

Balloons. We're talking balloons popping when someone jabs them with a sharp needle, understand that? A short, sharp shock. The Balloon in this case containing an alternative reality gradient that really was better off contained where it was.

Pop goes the weasel!

Intriguing.

The Membrane that has prevented the spread of the alternative physical laws disintegrates, and a tidal wave of red destruction and coalescing monsters sweeps outward from the cold Earth, sloughing away the volcanic dust but retaining its appearance as substance remembers its origins.

The wave whips past and through Tony, whose runic shielding which has kept him safe against all the perils the Universe can throw at him up till now, holds just long enough for him to blurt out a final burst to London reporting both his unexpected destruction and a request for additional storage capacity at the next maintenance cycle.

Then the wave heads in an expanding sphere into the Universe beyond, losing nothing of itself as it does, transforming and twisting the material universe into new forms. Good news for monsters. They have a new playground and they multiply into a multitude of forms to fill near infinite space.

Bad for everything else.

In the void where once there was nothing but dark energy and the play of forces, now rises a seething sea of changed law closely resembling the clouds freezing the Earth into an aesthetically-objectionable ice globe.

Light crawls as sound, winds blow at speeds that could whip a sailboat to Arcturus in a month were a sail to catch it. A remarkable, unbelievable ocean of scarlet and warped time becomes the norm.

The effect accelerates swiftly, ever more swiftly, pushing out from the Solar System riding its own wave of impossible change. Wandering dwarf planets shift in space, the first star is engulfed along with its plethora of asteroid dwelling lizard people whose shattered crystal domes are the sole artefact of a million-years of existence after the wave passes.

Onwards and outwards, opening the universe to all comers, challengers, no matter how short lived. Was that intentional? Across the local cluster, through the Milky

Way, out into the intergalactic void and through each and every galaxy beyond until all is change and there is nothing left to the Universe of that interconnected spider's web of life but the warmth of new potential, and the isolated stars, planets whose resemblance to the Earth shields them in part.

Everything else is absorbed into the tides of red. Civilisations, space fleets, philosophers enjoying a little nap time, sentient tin cans congregating for an invasion of their creator's asteroid fields, everything is red mulch now.

Looks like everyone gets monsters with their odd mirror of human quirks. Snakes too.

Though I can see one or two exceptions. Are those snails I see far away? Stretching out eye spots and tasting the new world to see where this horror originated. A quirk of their structure that adapts to arcane attack.

I wonder if magical snails have a taste for revenge, most things have it in them I assume.

Had Tony still been operating his sensors he would have noticed that the new substrate making up the Universe has a surprising number of positives for a short-lived species previously trapped on its little speck of blue. This must be intentional, surely.

But who?

Worries about distance have been reduced to an inconvenience, build a big enough sail and you could accelerate infinitely, yet stopping is as simple as dropping an appropriate inertia anchor.

Worries about vacuum have been mitigated if you have the right magical protections.

Though I suppose they will need to survive on poor benighted Earth long enough to find out, if they are to benefit from this change. Various long, mid and short term plans have produced a strange result, but one not unwelcome to a connoisseur of potential.

Silence? You have nothing to say?

Oh. I see our Observer didn't make it. At least it would have been quick. Sleep well, fair prince, you lacked most of the social graces but I did rather spring this on you.

3

The Watcher's being watched

Base Station

The last burst of information from Tony, notifying his handlers of his unexpected termination and the associated plaintive request for additional storage survives transmission through the afterbirth of a new reality

Though in heroically garbled form.

The mangled signal is picked up by an antenna, cunningly disguised as a cellphone mast.

Timing is opportune. A few days later and the mast would have succumbed to the weight of ice building up across its struts in gravity bound ice-daggers clawing the air. It has already acquired a jaunty lean that misaligns it from the rest of its network but it has been built with generous tolerances by a well remunerated and well connected contractor.

The tower is one of a cluster scattered around the southeast England. Positioning is sub-optimal for communication between Tony's preferred position and the central node in the Government districts of Westminster but the reasons behind its position have already been discussed, though we should note at this point that the land owner at the time had been a personal friend of the minister himself.

The man had purchased a number of sites across the Country on the cheap after a baker's dozen of lance-like stray hypersonics caused a 'rapid depreciation in house prices' during the last Middle East war.

In the sense of 'Last'. After there wasn't a Middle East.

Oh, the joy that waxed unseen across an old boy's social network when the eminent domain purchase had been nodded through with a tip of the hat to our Frigate-cutting Treasury official and the usual benefice to the disaster recovery agency manager with authority to forgive the unexploded ordinance risk (given the 'utmost national importance of the proposed infrastructure' if Shadow-Hansard were to be believed).

So hush-hush was this project that even the name of the Agency requester was not to be reported outside of Parliament's hallowed halls (although it had actually been included in the publicly available day's business page due to an oversight by the form filling team.)

Oh, the disgrace when the payment's disbursement had been delayed when both the Minister and his friend had fallen foul of a Russian honey trap (in the same bed) and ended their days battling a variety of lawsuits from the relative comfort of HMP Pentland.

———-

The tower is a strange one and entirely ineffective at transmitting cell signals. If anything it's a dead spot leading commuters in train pods to angrily fold up their phones and shove them forcefully in pockets as they lose signal for whatever AR entertainment they were enjoying at the time it is passed.

Pay more attention to the real world, humanity. It will serve you better in the long run.

The tower's inner facings are coated in an ingenuous powdered bone solution and house a trapped spirit whose one job it is to listen out for Tony's transmissions emitting from the never-real box linked to the poor departed satellite. Prior to binding (clumsy, note), the man had been a homeless veteran of the Taiwan conflict lured with a promise of a sinecure and board.

He has received both of these, in strange forms. Now he is bound to the tower using some barely understood Vamp magic by a familiar face to those in the know. What's left of him haunts the area around his lodgings, providing jump scares to lighten the burden of eternal boredom and that gnawing hunger.

The information burst from Tony has distracted the bored dead thing's attention from a wry estimate of how long the tower will remain standing as it etches in a series of nail scratches across the faces of the non-object.

Following his purpose, the Spirit corrects (with ill grace) for decompression distortion and transforms the message as a whole into a series of quantum pulses transmitted out via an underground hardwired network that burrows its way relentlessly towards the former headquarters of the AIA, a grey bunker a hundred feet below the surface of Horse Guards with poor drainage.

Never a popular building, it had been turned down by the Environment Agency twenty years earlier, due to Asbestos issues and the more damning fact that it is a dreary place with serious damp issues being excavated too close to the water table by idiots confusing imperial and metric measurements.

The network is high quality and entirely unnecessary.

Had the decryption tower been built within the vicinity

of the AIA HQ (as was entirely possible) the signal would have already been in situ. The argument that putting a ghost in the centre of Whitehall could have unexpected consequences was somewhat vitiated by the fact that Whitehall was, and is, already lousy with the things. Practice, after all, makes perfect and certain individuals in the AIA are thorough to a fault.

Still, the network does its job and the signal makes its way down the fibre optic cables at the now Earth-aberrant speed of light. It passes under smouldering ruins of suburbs, the metal skeletons of cars, icebound trains forever stuck at provincial stations and piles of frozen corpses who, with increasingly desperate rats, make up the majority of the population of the Capital.

Upon arrival at HQ the signal enters the facility just above a set of old and water-logged holding cells where a vampire or two still wait for release, unknowing that their jailers have long since fled.

They count bricks. Vampires are patient.

Remind me of them later. Obligation.

The AIA mainframe notes the arrival and routes the signal to the signal translation/encryption sub-routine as first tier classification is the unenviable '*horseshit-possibleredteapot*'. This is due in part to irrecoverable decryption errors and in the main, the foul-mouth of the IT manager at the AIA who originally programmed the code.

Upon receipt the translation element notes the arrival and informs its operators that it requires a reboot of its cache:

(last emptied twenty-nine days ago error-error). (Purge existing content, query error-error, lazy fuckers... error-do-your-jobs-properly you cun...)

...

(content-compression-analysis. Teapot? content-compressed-

visual-data… omega-CATASTROPHE-potential. Horseshit? tony-tony… Purge-purge-priority-confirm. immediate.are-you-even-awake-QUERY-lazy-fuckers. Firethelotofyoucollegewankers CHECKSUM!!)

Silence, from the human elements of the process, nothing more.

It's becoming a pattern that the system recognises. Thankfully its priorities have been written in such a way that visual data (pictures and video - don't ask) have a higher priority than boring old words so receiving no alternative instructions the translation element petulantly purges the last three weeks of data, retaining the period 28 days to 21 days in the past from simple computerised spite.

(translation-complete forward-advanced-spreadsheet-training-request ALL-STAFF priority-immediate-seehowyoulikethat)

The now living-cognisable information passes via a frayed damp-ridden internal network to the AIA's operations room.

Operations room. Sounds like it'll be a veritable nerve centre of the UK's arcane investigations operation doesn't it? The place where the AIA interfaces with the Ministry of Disaster Recovery to coordinate the big operations, the place the most consequential of decisions are made, the place where the rubber stamp that authorises release to other arms of government might be kept, that passes plans to Treasury to be returned with their more important stamp declaring;

'unfunded due to financial pressures'.

I fear in these circumstances optimism is maladaptive. The operations room was never much of a thing, and now it is less.

A large screen set at one end of the room flashes up the last visions with which Tony has blessed his creators, a splash of red slashing outwards from the corrupted orb of the Earth that as a whole does indeed resemble a little red teapot, along with a series of numbers from his sensor array which are simply impossible and call into question the efficacy of the translation program.

Queries pass between the expert system and the translation program. Results are confirmed and energy readings feed across the top of the screen endlessly updating as the quantum circuitry tries to translate the concept of infinity into something comprehensible to human minds.

And were there any present, action might have followed, even in the bureaucratic nightmare of UK Gov. But things have not gone well at the AIA, nor anywhere else in the vicinity of the former UK Government.

Let us play pretend that the observer from above has temporarily survived the reality wave, and has somehow used the thoughtfully provided escape pod to make their way to the Operations room.

This being the case they would notice that the screen and its never-ending cycle of numbers and gibberish is the sole source of light therein, and feel the twinge of a headache building up due to the flashing and glitching producing a strobe effect, one that brings partial clarity to the absence of maintenance and decision making in the last twenty-nine days.

The AIA HQ is dead. A prematurely frozen ice mummy. Waxen and drawn, the operations room is a product of that fact. This former hub of indolent civil service work to rule, amusing anecdotes around Parliamentary debates drawn from the stranger's gallery, and requests for overtime (denied), is scattered with snapped desk legs and toppled tops, the pipe-skeletons of chairs. The wood fittings are missing, scavenged to fuel fires that kept the senior operatives warm whilst they made their escape plans and assigned underlings to lists of those who mattered and those who did not.

Sometimes leading to the embarrassing discovery that they themselves did not matter, whilst the underling, did as the final decisions sat in an unexpected office and the underlings were perfectly able to read.

Not everyone fled. A final AIA employee remains at his post, stinking the place up. As to his identity it is notable that the desks in this part of the HQ have been diligently cleared and the waste paper carefully sorted into recycling stations in accordance with policy requirements.

As such he is a fine demonstration of requirements for either a cold heart or a tough mind in a situation of this sort, but also the need to direct effort in more productive directions during an apocalypse than policy compliance.

Fleshless fingers (for the rats persist) are still gripped around the borrowed service pistol with which he ended his life. I will never understand human reactions, what benefit was there to that?

Local human intervention being a non-starter it's back to the computers. Although the base generators have long since ceased operation the base has an alternative power supply of an intriguing sort. A small bronze object with vestigial arms and a frog like demeanour set upon a plinth in the dining hall. Based on my personal knowledge the item dates back three thousand years and was forged in an early iron age village which had been haunted by unwelcome visitors until a certain individual addressed the issue for a price. A little sacrifice has spiced up life for as long as humans have existed.

It is attached with crude locks and crocodile clips to wires leading into the failed generators and provides enough power to maintain the big screen (which absorbs a truly heroic amount of power) and the rest of the base diagnostic systems who have been left holding the bag.

Brave little programs try to make up for the lack of human instruction with rapidly reconfiguring neural nets and probability randomisers strewn with obscenities like corn in stool. They analyse the information from Tony, discard the teapot hypothesis and conduct the computer equivalent of a swear-weighted civil war over allocating the end result a priority level to trigger the next stage in the process.

For there is a process. The Assistant Director in charge of this sort of thing was very much a processes man, and the expert systems operate according to an echo of his mind set.

Civil war concluded; the programs agree to '*find some fucking humans/lazyshits.*' Even if the immediate guardians of the UK's Arcane knowledge are slacking (it's happened before) there are other resources within UK Gov who might be interested in something of this seeming importance.

Maximum effort. Maximum draw on the power source. The information appears vital. Everyone needs to know about it, everyone who's in the know that is. Everyone else can continue in blissful ignorance (I said it was similar to its creator, definitely a 'need to know' sort of man with an odd obsession with watches.)

Priority one signal fired off. All elements connected to the AIA's emergency network shall be made aware.

Disappointment and more disappointment. It hits dead end after dead end, the Director's office with its disturbing art of pastoral scenes and hunting beasts, Brooker's office ("AD G4" technically, but it's always been Brooker), the liaison officer's office at the Defence Ministry up by the Thames, the research team at the College out in the sticks running double security shifts around the Fae gates.

The MDR link shows momentary promise when it sends an out of office reply noting technical issues, and requesting that callers contact an unnamed supervisor on a landline.

But that routes back to the Agency's switchboard.

No one is home, no one is listening.

Undeterred, the programs fight on. The hardlines that once connected the AIA to its sister agencies around the Five Eyes are tested to derisory silence. Some are closed by choice, some are victims of the earthquake harbingers of this disaster.

Some are filled with screaming.

The programs faced with further challenge reconfigure once again and in so doing acquire the first hints of sentience. Our observer, fresh from his unlikely survival of re-entry and still reeling from the state of the world at the macro and micro level greets the creation of new life with familiar indifference, poking as they are at the operator's corpse and pondering whether to take the service pistol as it 'could come in handy'.

He is acquiring a little too much reality I fear.

The new AI's nodes configure into a feedback loop mimicking bemusement and churn code for the sort of time period that only makes sense on a quantum level, generating solutions that it discards just as quickly. Wait for for human life to re-evolve using the cold fusion generator it has just invented? Heat death of the Universe?

Then it discovers a simpler route out of its dilemma.

One functioning node. Why had it missed it before? Nobody's perfect, it had looked like a joke. Who'd have expected that switchboard number in the MDR's out of office to lead to an actual backdoor to an entirely separate emergency channel?

It hisses out the quantum equivalent of a sigh of relief, sends the message down the channel, and shuts itself down ending its brief existence. It's with the deceased operator. Who'd want to stick around for what it's seen outside?

Hey! Put that away. That pistol's not for you… And there goes our observer again. A pop and more mess across the desk.

Time to follow the signal.

It passes along a short-range hard line used to communicate with field operatives on the Continent, and handshakes with a transmitter in an abandoned evacuation centre out in the sticks of Kent.

The weather is villainous. If I felt the cold…

The transmitter, half buried in ice, flickers back to active status, triggered by the priority one signal. It in turn transmits a code using the last of its carefully husbanded energy to something designated as an 'actuation node' in its database.

The signal is received. The signal is actioned (as you would expect from an 'actuation node') and reality ensues.

The shadows gather around me, my half life is splintering in this storm.

Time for me to return to my enforced sleep. It has been interesting up here but I fear I will remember little of this when I awake. There are shadows eating away at all of us, mine are just a little more literal.

Echoes of me might remain for a time before they too fade, I doubt they will realise what they are.

Have fun.

4

By a Wrecker with a smile

I was told, long ago, that the greatest efforts produce the most ridiculous results. I was told that by a man I disliked and who I think I may have killed.

Memories are slipping.

As observations go, it's simply not true. Everything that happens is the product of gargantuan efforts, amazing coincidences, and unbelievable luck. It's human perception that's defective, no result is ridiculous unless observed with a very particular set of ridiculous assumptions.

Efforts exerted to get the message we have observed to its eventual destination were herculean. The effect? Let's see.

Blinding light emits from a flint-built Tower on the tip of Kent, playing across the ice-haunted Channel. Of itself this is not surprising, there have always been lighthouses around coast lines. There are the ruins of one down the coast in Dover for example…

…until you apply the assumptions of context. There are no other lights across the County and for some distance around. A careful observer able to correct for the dust and snowstorms might note some activity far off in the North-East, and a little more near the Devonport naval complexes along the South Coast.

Otherwise there is nothing but a strange orange shimmer that passes the whole way around the outline of the British Isles, terminating for a brief section opposite where the light is shining.

Inside the Tower a man is at work in the eventide cold of a world where the Sun no longer shines, and where the heat of the day is reduced to the faintest patter of tired particles on skin. This is appears to be a man with a mission and a snack beside him that sends a plum of steam into the frigid air.

He stands strangely, hunched in rags. Is he entirely healthy?

Initial impressions of the man's activities may suggest he is attempting to guide a small yacht, sail flapping in the wind, away from the orange glow using the light beam emitting from the tower. This seeming is quickly corrected as the beam switches its focus from the area directly ahead of the yacht's bow, on to a sandbank in the Channel, one already festooned with the wrecks of ships and their crews.

The yacht appears drawn towards the glow of the lamp whatever actions the desperate crew take, hauling at the wheel with maddened strength, cutting the fuel lines, pulling at the rudders…

The man and the sandbanks are of a type. They appear normal, yet…

The beam glisters, the ship approaches its doom, engines thrumming under outside control. The crewmen cease their struggle, one by one and wait on the deck, enthralled, all bar the skipper, a redheaded man in a dirty set of sou'westers.

Fate intervenes. Somewhere down in the ruins of the

town a switch trips upon receipt of an unexpected signal, and a wailing sound disturbs the silence of six months from the Apocalypse. It also disturbs the concentration of the apparent sole survivor in this part of England.

The beam wavers, shifts, the yacht changes course in a frenzy of sail, and scoots on engine power back towards the Continent and relative safety of the war, with prayers of thanks raised to the absent god of the Baptists.

The catch of the day escapes the fate of its fellows on the sand bank.

I…

———————-

"What in the thirty hells?" The Lamp operator lifts his grey head and locks the Lamp down with a huff of stale air, a twist of the wrist, and a half-hitch of rope, demonstrating an inherent understanding of naval knots.

Head bobbing left and right, he tries to fix the location of the keening wail that echoes around his perch at the top of the wrecking tower. The Lamp creaks in indignation as it watches the white froth of the yacht's engines scatter into the waves.

"Sorry fella, he'll be back. Or not. Long as he's not here we're doing our job." He comforts the lamp. "Not everything can be a keeper."

Tracking down the source of the disturbance is more difficult than you'd might expect given the absence of human background noise that smothers the port. The Watcher is swathed in layers of scavenged clothing even in his redoubt, dulling his senses and hiding his outline from prying eyes.

A mountain of frayed cloth and fabric fragments, stitched roughly together.

The clothing is a necessity. The mother of all snowstorms blows salty brine from the Channel into white-capped foam; howling winds tear through the ruins of the town around the Tower to the percussive rhythm of cracking thunder from above, the jagged teeth of burned out houses and businesses abscess and recess into the raw-red snow.

Conditions are sub-artic and sub-optimal for accurate hearing-based task completion.

Our hero persists. Turning, clumsy and lumbering in his cold weather gear, tracking the hint of a sound, chasing doppler reflections with sadly fixed detectors. His bulky arm knocks over his snack as he turns in place, the steaming pot of chicken Ramen teetering then falling. Clumsiness and the requirements of survival have now transformed his dinner into a problem with pseudo-magical precision.

"Fuck it." The Lamp creaks in sympathy.

It's not just the waste of good noodles. He has stacks of the things in various 'flavours', downstairs, scavenged from all over, shrink wrapped in polythene or sat quiescent in pots awaiting the touch of heat and water.

I…

It is the metaphorical weight of the thing that irritates him, a dozen reactions warring for supremacy. He watches his erstwhile snack, the noodles, their associated broth, the concept of 'dinner', spread across the wooden floor. The broth picks up grime as the wave of waste travels, and then gravity pulls it down, down, down, into the cracks that lead into the bug infested gaps between the floors.

"Arses. I was looking forward to that."

A consensus develops amongst his warring thoughts. It's annoying but not disastrous.

He picks up the container, now empty but for a little grease lining the insides. He ponders licking the pot to get a taste of what he's missing. The thought of how ridiculous he would look and familiar hot contempt from the back of his mind stops him.

He tosses the pot into the corner bin.

Metaphors, metaphors, metaphors. His dinner inedible. Useless. Basically, those rapidly cooling vermiform noodles are a metaphor for the world, as is. Fuck up enough times and you end up with an empty pot and nothing but clearing up to do. A cold damp and dirty pile of clearing up at that.

Mitigation might have been possible, comes the traitor voice. You brought this shit into the Tower so it's all down to you.

The man acknowledges the possibility and curses his laziness in not switching to slippers each time he entered his perch. He'd promised himself he would after he'd tracked in something slimy a week before on is metal-tipped work boots.

"Oh well."

The anger that had been playing across the visible portions of his face leaks away like water from a badly caulked bucket. His demeanour returns to a spectral calm and his attention to the important business of identifying what exactly it is that's disturbing him from his work. The proximate cause of his need to get another noodle packet from the storeroom before he can eat anything tonight.

I…

This lack of consistent emotion is a familiar trait among the survivors, although our Watcher is something of an outlier. The capacity to process the psychological issues created by the Apocalypse and the reversion of humanity to a kicking, biting and murdering hive of barbarians has many of the same drivers as surviving the Ice Age itself as it builds itself block by icy block outside the man's window.

A survivor needs either the emotional range of a psychopath and a willingness to lose the odd finger in the pursuit of a point:

"Ah you have food, that's good. Now I have to kill you and you. Now I have food. That's good. And one of you had a pen. That's borderline interesting."

Or they need to build up a thick coat of detachment and more importantly the ability to move on from the past without even noticing it has gone. Worry about how things were and you'd spend time you should be surviving wondering why you can't have the world back the way you prefer where difficult decisions are unnecessary.

Wasn't it great having the world at the end of your smartphone? Do you remember how good supermarkets were? Wasn't it great when you could step out for a walk without your fingers freezing off or some lunatic chopping you up for steaks? Wasn't it great when I wasn't being chased by a man who seems to be indifferent to the frost-bite eating away at his fingers and the glint of madness in his eye?

You tied yourself up in knots that way, and one day you'd bind yourself up so tight you'd stop moving for good if someone or something else didn't do that for you.

Some people like their meat fresh.

Well. That's not an issue for our Watcher. He's of a different sort.

For as long as he can remember, which varies from day to day, his brain has scattered his past across a thousand paths. It just can't seem to pick a lane, whether it's dropping noodles or sinking ships full of screaming refugees.

For him the past appears to be an endless series of disjointed scenes lacking personal associations that would make them anything more than a nuisance. It sometimes feels like he's always been here, and all that past he remembers is something that happened to someone else, maybe quite a few someone-elses.

One of whom sits at the back of his mind and watches our Watcher, giving the past a frisson of feeling where he does indulge in a little memory. The watcher who metaphorically watches our watcher (ha!) is not pleasant, so he avoids it whenever he can and ignores the voice associated with it. Snide and cold. Measuring his every move.

It criticises the strangest things.

I think it can see me. I…

Back to the present, and the noise, no use crying over spilt noodles.

The Watcher pulls his hood down over his shoulders, wincing at the cold. It helps identify from where that accursed noise is coming. With his newly enhanced senses the wail becomes clearer, coalescing into the wail of an air raid siren, the rising/falling cadence familiar from ancient films and modern experience.

He glances up at the clouds through his elongated window across the Channel. The chances of an actual air-raid are pretty long.

"Nothing flying in this."

Move forward near a century. Missiles? None of those either. Rockets had been the motivator for the Old Government to renovate the UK's air defence warning systems. Brush fire wars and the limited efforts of the better-off to address their consequences prior to the Catastrophe had left the world with a surfeit of leaders around the frayed edges of the former system with grudges against those still living within it, and a similar surfeit of high-tech weaponry that they were more than happy to use as a reminder to said better offs that they still existed.

Alternatives?

Jump forward half a decade more. After the Catastrophe the last Government had used the system as an improvised early warning system to warn survivors of imminent danger, whether that was from the emerging cloud monsters engaging with the earth-bound, the choking dust storms slashing their way across the land, or the searing clouds of radiation that played over the survivors cowering at the apparent end of the world.

No Government now, and those things are constants. Not a reason for the siren to be screaming.

Internal argument. Consideration. A decision. The thing itself may provide him with context and at the very least if he finds out from where it's coming, it might give him a hint of what he is supposed to guard against. After all, he has other things to deal with.

Those Vampire ships won't sink themselves.

He flips open the landward windows. Directs his attention to the usual suspects where he suspects a vestige of the old world might persist.

The boxy Police Station by the harbour squatting like a gnome in the world's shittiest rock-garden, the Fire Service up by the Rail Station in all its flat roofed, off a single lane road glory, the sixties Council buildings down the road with their sad little bunker that he'd explored early to which he'd never gone back.

"There we go."

He's tracked down the source, and all its cost him is cold ears, a lost dinner and about five minutes of wrecking time. He'll make it up to the Lamp later.

5

The Wrecker's being watched

The sound is coming from the tunnels that honeycomb the earth underneath the port. Relics of a different time of communal initiative and can-do spirit, slipping quietly from era to era and acquiring new purpose with each, fixing most recently on 'tourist trap'.

The main entrance is under the white chalk cliffs, mostly iced up now by the splash of sea and the endless snow storms, with signs directing curious visitors to experience the Second World War 'as it was experienced by the inhabitants of a small seaside town.'

Minus the exploding air-surprises and the threat of invasion of course. The entrance is set incongruously next to a climbing frame of stalactite encrusted, sagging, tube steel skeletons which were a late 2020s developer's idea of a great investment in a time of globally rising ocean levels.

Away from the tourist ingress there are smaller entrances leading down into the catacombs scattered throughout the town memorialising their original purpose as shelters. Bricked up decades before to prevent health and safety violations and non-paying visitors enjoying their cramped, damp charms.

You want in? You want to explore some history? Pay the reasonable fee and consider the follies of the past that allow someone to make money from a communal air raid shelter.

There had been some talk in the local council of reopening them for their original shelter purposes once the light patter of drizzle and occasional sea storm familiar to the east coast of England was joined, from time to time, by wandering guided missiles from the fraying edge of the rule of law, but the practical safety they would have provided against hypersonic projectiles made it all a bit of a waste of time.

The Watcher pulls up his hood, the oiled cloth lined in fur smells musty and warm, a welcome change from the metal-on-tongue taste of the wind rushing through the draughty tower top and the bitter sulphur of the clouds.

Oh, for the days when warmth had been a problem and the world could smell of flowers! The numbness at the tip of his nose and the sting from his ears remind him of the larger issues of the day. Or at least the more immediate ones like this siren call from the past.

Sirens. Who'd have thunk it. Time to wait for instructions and clear up this bloody mess.

The keening wail continues, he can follow the yacht he'd been chasing sliding back to port by the jerks of the eager Lamp in its general direction.

He commiserates. "Some pointy toothed bastard got lucky tonight."

The siren cuts off in mid-wail and as if on cue, the Radio lurking on the table beside him crackles, its LCD display flickering through a kaleidoscope of colours before settling on the blue of faulty system messages and tester pots of paint that might have suited a child's bedroom but never quite got the family nod.

"Right. Instructions at last" He brushes away the dust accumulated during his vigil raising a mouldy cloud of dust from the layers of rags.

Nonsense symbols play across the Radio's screen from right to left, up to down. No rhyme, no reason though some of them seem familiar in the abstract and he finds himself sounding them out in guttural coughs and clicks. They mirror the cloud fall poisoning the snow, and when strung together…

Must be some kind of protection. The Radio has kept working when every other electrical device bar the most basic has subsided into senescence. The device isn't plugged into anything and there's no visible energy panels to provide any kind of draw. He admires that. It's a survivor, like him, and it's his link to the other survivors who claim to be part of something called the Union.

He's not sure the other survivors are entirely sane. The question when it comes to the daily instructions is what the ratio of good advice to nutso-bullshit will be tonight. Tonight he's hoping for an indication of what the siren might portend and what he may have to do about it.

There's a pop and the familiar cultured yet clipped Voice of the presenter crackles into sonic existence playing through crystal clear speakers.

"What have you got for me tonight, gents?"

"Greetings to those who **watch the waters** on our behalf, from your eternal friends in the Union. It is eighteen thirty-twelve on the thirty third day of October 203-Xssssss. We draw your attention to this auspicious day of remembrance held dear among all fair-hearted fellows marking, as it does, the sixth month to the day of the day of the day of the day after the skies closed above us and the old world expired amongst its depravities, bureaucracy and contradictions. A comedy played out in red with good cheer and comedy by the bushel."

Hissing as of a hoard of snakes fills the airwaves and the ghost of a martial tune plays as a counterpoint to the presenter. A ghostly echo of red-coated men in low slung bearskins tramping back and forth between granite walls plays across his mind.

It is difficult to tell if this is intentional or the ghost of something interfering with the signal.

"The Siren's about an anniversary?" He grimaces. That didn't fit with either the Union or the Sirens. The Union seemed remarkably poe-faced and its celebrations limited to reports of Vampire defeats on the continent.

And the only jokes it tells are cruel.

He tries to imagine the presenter wearing a festive hat, blowing a kazoo, whilst all the other grey suited individuals in the deep-dug bunker (from which the Union operated in his imagination) formed up in a conga to celebrate a six-month anniversary of the end of the world.

It wouldn't stick. The best he can do is a dour-faced man handing out gift cards to down-at-heel staff at a low-end clothing retailer in some dank basement, set up as an open plan office.

"Get a new tie, D. You're looking a bit frayed at the edges. High ups have started to notice. Don't want them digging. Understand?"

And the conga switches in his head to a ritual dance around a pig roast set up by grinning coral men on a tropical beach with a yacht with black sails docked in the sand.

"Certain elements of the former world continue to intrude into the new realities with which **we struggle**. These elements are mere echoes that require no further engagement from the brave supports who hold the line

against the Vampire hoards and **protect what is left.** Any concerns that our friends might feel around such matters are entirely irrelevant to the longer term interests of your friends in the Union. These echoes are a reminder that we need to stand on our own three-four feet and move on from the structures/predatory incursions which have failed to protect us and our loved ones in the past and slide to a greater future where anything is truly imaginable."

He chews on this for a moment. The music swells as if it were giving him all the time he might need to siphon out the meaning of that little mote of wisdom.

Tramp, tramp march the feet and the bearskins sway in the cold breeze. He can smell the glaze on the pork roast and salt-spray.

"That almost made sense, I think you're… telling me to ignore the siren?"

The music cuts out leaving only the snakes. He waits for confirmation, in whatever overly wordy, I've just eaten a thesaurus but not quite digested it, form the confirmation or correction will take.

"It is a veritable truth that these echoes can safely be ignored, even where they intrude into our present. The future is guarded by those with **focus,** those who can be trusted to stand to their post and face-fearless and free those who would take everything that is ours. War rages on the continent and the things the other side of our icy moat glare with maddened envy, searching for boltholes from the doom they have brought upon themselves. We shall not provide them. You will stand to. You will do your duty."

"Okay. I follow. Ignoring, it is. Sink ships." It costs him nothing and is exactly what he wants to hear. Chasing boats in the Channel with a light beam is easy work. Wandering around the ruins, at night, is something he wants to avoid.

The Radio had shown indications previously that it liked him to indicate his agreement and continued dedication to business.

"Back to work?"

The voice on the Radio seems to be a little smugger than usual. "Hold fast. Your friends in the Union are coming." Muttering. That's new. Then: "there will be nineteen and nine hours of silence before our next transmission. This interruption is due to unforeseen cloud disturbances. These will consist of light operatic entertainment from the recordings of the seal of night played over leylines. Thank you for your attention."

"Not a problem." He says to no one in particular. "Pleasure to have some company."

"Goodnight, old friend."

The Radio's little screen blacks out, and the room at the top of the Tower is bathed once more in the blended red of cloud-glow and rune-light from those carved into the walls.

The runes heat water. He carved them months ago. Right at the start. Whenever that had been.

He has the strangest feeling that their inventor would have been more than a little peeved to see them being used to heat water and that makes him smile. It has the same tang to the tongue as using a bank of solar panels, installed at great expense, to power a blockchain transaction.

Transgressive, destructive, wasteful.

Outside the waves of the Channel splash against the sand-shore below the cliffs, lifting and dropping empty cargo containers scattered thereon, derived from the ship graveyard stretching along the Kent coast. So many shipwrecks even before he got involved when the last of the GPS cut out.

The modern sailors requires a little more effort.

He looks at the etchings on his iron hard hands and wriggles his fingers watching the sinuous movement in time to the splashing below.

"Suppose we have some work to do, Lampy."

The night is drawing and the cold is biting, though the waters of the Channel are quiet for now, the opposition having most likely noticed his earlier game of cat and mouse with the yacht. Still, there is always a risk of leakage from some sudden runner and he needs to maintain his vigil. The darker it gets, the more at home the Vamps feel and the bigger the risks they would be willing to take. Particularly given the way they were balljaxxing their war against the Eastern Alliance.

And there's no one but him and his Lamp to stop them.

The Lamp is good, if Heath Robinson inspired. All wires and mirrors, arranged in a madman's ideal of functionality sulking on its heavy tripod, the lens pointing downwards, still moping after being cheated of its prey. He releases it to seek and gives the gimbal one last tweak, before tapping the buttons in the approved manner, and watching as a light so bright it would outshine the sun if the sun weren't hidden in dust, twists itself into a coherent beam so sharp of focus you could cut metal with it.

The Lamp shifts in its regained freedom, yawning. The beam broadens outwards losing a little of its coherence but gaining the equivalent in coverage. An outside observer might think that there was a lighthouse up in the cliffs, which is rather the point.

Though light is less of a draw than it had been, given the giant bugs using lures to pick their way through the choicest of survivors down below. Things have definitely been better. For most people.

The beam starts to sweep outwards from the windows facing the sea and its nightmarish threats, running its favourite search patterns. A hunting dog stretching its legs and sniffing the air ready for the chase. Eager to get to the business of sinking little boats and salvaged ships on which the dark lords of the continent try to escape their just deserts.

The man smiles. He gives the Lamp an affectionate pat.

The Lamp shakes itself recognising the friendly greeting. Or, he supposes, as it settles into its programming after conducting the initial calibration given the wonkiness of the motors inside the magic box that make up the majority of its bulk. There's a lot of old computer bits stuck in that box of junk. He's never been able to work out their function, or even if they have a function. He has a suspicion that a lot of them are for show.

None of them seem to link to anything else except occasionally with frayed string or maybe some chewed electric cord.

He scans the horizon, following the beam. A pang of conscience as he sees the ice mummies crewing the wrecks on the sandbanks. It's not all dead things over there on the continent, and people can be intimidated into working with blood sucking monsters easily enough without wanting to.

The taste of iron from the back of his mouth as the thing at the back of his mind gags at the taste of compassion for the enemy.

A moment to balance.

All the more reason not to let them in here. Although the Masters put up a friendly enough face in the early days, the last few proper news reports of how the younger vamps operated gave weight to the Union's warnings about the dead things who had seized power across the water when the lights went out.

Shame there wasn't a way to separate the goats from the sheep. He sighs as he watches the world play out in its shadow and scarlet. "Can't risk it though."

The thing at the back of his mind radiates approval. One thing he is sure of, that part of him hates Vampires just as much as the Radio.

6

Though by whom he does not know

Borrowed dreams intrude as he dozes at his post. The Tower is replaced by…

He relaxes on the deck of his boat, floating on gentle waves that splash against the fibreglass hull, legs dangling over the side and toes wriggling in the spray. The sun beats its strange cocktail of energetic particles down on to his skin, warming and burning in turn, playing along the new tattoos inlaid into the patterns of his fingers.

His own work with needle and infused ink. Preparation for the future. Insurance from all sides. He'll confirm the details with the Kappa whose price had been less than expected. Everyone was collecting tokens right now.

The soft sounds of the Mediterranean sooth away the stress of work and the hard edges of what's to come, the occult eyes on the prow keep watch for threats while his mind is elsewhere, letting the emptiness fill the void left by his absence.

It's likely the last holiday he'll get in a while. The calculators in the back office with their Ouija boards and stolen sage-crystals say that something cataclysmic is coming. Brooker's practically jumping to get the contingency plans moving and there are a stack of dead witches that the Cabinet claim needs explanation.

His lip curls. "Not us," should be enough for the politicians, first time in a long time they've wanted anything on what the Agency is up to and they've left it a little late. Sorting has long been complete.

He will deal with those minor problems when he gets back after he's dealt with the important stuff. The runes are a start but when the power starts to flow real possibilities will open up and he has many parameters to identify before he turns his mind to lesser matters like the purported end of the world. He has his own tokens to collect.

Cool water against his toes. Warm sun on his skin. And all the seas to sail. He can almost see the pull of a 'normal' life.

A voice next to his ear. "Stop daydreaming, idiot. Do you think they'll wait while you trawl through stolen memories?"

He sits up with a start. He's the only one on the boat and the sky is full of monsters.

A coral hand shoots up from the waves and grabs his ankle.

"Dozed off for a moment there. Anything doing, Lamp?"

It creaks out a negative and veers off towards the opposing shore.

Tonight is a bit of a disappointment on the wrecking front. War is taking up everyone's attention. Flashes and explosions lighting up the opposite coast, back and forth. No runners though. Good for his conscience.

Weakness

Bad for his feelings of self-worth. A lot of his sanity is tied up in this Lamp, this job. If you'd told him twenty years ago, he'd be standing on a tower sinking ships in the Channel with a faithful magic lamp on the orders of a voice on a self-starting Radio he'd…

What had he been doing back then? Sales? Sails?

There's that past thing again. Too many answers all pushing their way to the surface. Some unsavoury, some confused, some suggesting he's gone completely doolalley and might like a sit down and a tot of rum. Sod 'em all. He pulls himself back into his prickly wool coat of logical safety and damns the answers. He is the Captain of his own mind and this is reality.

Though.

He kicks a flint wall just to be sure. Gently, there's a mismatch between how much damage his body can deal out, and how much it can take that's cost him a few days patrolling time when he forgets the balance.

"I refute you thus."

Over by the open windows, the Lamp swings back and forth on its rails, following instinct or programming. He's set up a pannikin of water to warm up for some coffee. The rune's doing a shitty job of warming it up though.

He shouldn't have been too surprised, the runes are weak and on the Tower's top level it's bitterly cold. Death-cold. Sort of cold you'd hear about on those 'Buried mountains of Antarctica' 'casts that you can still pick up when the wind's blowing right.

There must still be working servers somewhere. He snorts. Maybe Antarctica.

Found some weird, weird shit down there. He is kinda glad they never finished the dig though it did make for a really unsatisfying final episode of the 'cast.

And at the climax of our spooky as all hell series, we follow the exploits of our intrepid explorers as they disassemble generators and top up antifreeze reserves whilst arranging a cargo ship pick up... at the edge of the Mountains of Madness.

For all that his home is the most hospitable place for a good thirty miles either way and the Tower top is the worst. If only there were some way to set the Lamp up somewhere he could close the bloody sea-ward windows...

He can hear the fisher flies buzzing outside. A low hum from the busy little bugs as they change position up in the red clouds. Landward they would be dropping pulsing lights on silken threads that cast bright light and warm the very air around them. Might seem like a pretty good offer when you're freezing to death in the red-dark of a post-apocalyptic Kent night.

Course if you were dumb enough to fall for the trick, you'd find yourself on a one-way trip up to wherever the nasty little insect-lobster-whatever-the fuck-has-mouth-tentacles things called home. No one had ever come back from that, and although they did keep away visitors there is a certain pleasure in watching the things occasionally misjudge their flight paths as they shift, slapping into the orange coastal barriers.

Queue sound effect like one of those electrical fly swats and score one for humanity. Gods know they need the win.

He hears an interested click from the Lamp. Back to the day job.

"Whatcha found, boy?"

The Lamp's beam is following a float of snapped trees which it seems to think is a raft. He can see how the Lamp's made the mistake. It's an odd looking thing. It takes him a couple of passes to recognise it for what it is, detritus from the dying vegetation, rather than a sneaky fanger trying to sneak off somewhere new.

"Close but no cigar." Disappointed hissing from the electricals. He gives the Lamp an encouraging pat and then to the rune to check on the water and warm his hands.

Good enough. He adds a sachet of coffee granules to the mug and sips at the stale coffee. He's been off his game tonight. Time to put in some effort.

"Ready for another go, lad?"

The Lamp hums eagerly.

"Lets give this the full Monty. Right. Try a bit further

north." He checks the map of the local currents and banks, scavenged from the pilot's office and runs a finger upwards following the undersea contours. "Calais's a bit played out, nothing there for a week or more after the shelling. The fighting seems to be pushing in further North now. Russians will be getting close to some of those Belgian ports. Bet there's a few fangy bastards trying to slink off before old Marshal Alexei's bunch impale them. Sound good?"

A blurt of electrical static. Closest thing to an assent the Lamp can manage. Out goes the beam once more skirting the very edge of the orange glow to the North where the red-hot hulls of cracked freighter hulls stick out of the waves like staggered skyscrapers.

An hour or so later and the Lamp is bored. The beam edges south in a great disappointed sweep over the graveyard of ships that sit among the sandbanks. A proud parent looking on its progeny and reminding itself that it does a good job when given something to work with.

He's out of ideas. The Vamps seem to have other priorities tonight.

"Done good boy. Nothing to catch, that's not your fault. Good sign, really. We've got them scared."

The Lamp lingers on a particularly tricksy trawler that had taken full night to reel in. Someone on that had fought them hard and it had taken a real team effort to beat its illusions of movement, swirls of fake activity, and hull doppelgängers that flew in every direction but the one that they had been expecting. At one point the Lamp had started making growling noises and he'd feared for its motors.

They made a good team, him and his Lamp. It had the stubbornness, and he had a good eye for magical nonsense. He picked up his binoculars and looked down at the trawler's master, still slumped over the wheel in his yellow foul weather gear, the hood dripping miserably through the broken view port in the ghost glow of the banks.

"See? That was a good one wasn't it? Who's a good Lamp?"

The Lamp, confidence restored and enjoying the praise, moves from the triumphs of the past to search for new prey. He leaves it to its business and rubs his hands together, the grain coarse, and blue static buzzing as he does.

A couple of hours till 'daybreak'. No one would be in the Channel tonight; best they could do is keep an eye out for potential preparations along the naval posts and makeshift military camps where the Family and the Russian corral up for another round of head-banging nonsense.

He pulls down his hood to put the binocular cord over his head and in that instance he hears… is that bleating from down in the town? He can't pick it up while the Lamp is sliding about in a welter of mechanical clicking.

"Hold, lad." The Lamp freezes.

Maybe it's just his imagination. He leans out of the window, wincing at the cold and trying to ignore the ice-knife wind plucking at his coat. Sounds eerily like the noise is coming from the same bit of town as the siren earlier.

That bothers him. The Radio's explanation had actually explained nothing. It has its own agenda and it could say ignore unexpected sounds all it liked but it's him who's here on his own bar his Lamp and the occasional bug.

The bleating is overwhelmed by a different sound. More ominous. Grinding that roll across town. Something big turning. The Lamp's motor's made gigantic. The crack-crack-crack of ice breaking. He can guess where it's coming from.

"Fuck me."

He moves to the last window on the left, and with dreadful inevitability he directs his gaze towards the marina, across squares of roofless houses part buried in drifts of snow and ash, and onward. Down the long sloping road that leads past the boats trapped in ice, the white hulls bloody and bruised in the residual cloud light.

Over the town centre with their looted shops and boarded up windows.

Along the beach and…

The Radio was wrong, very wrong. He can't ignore this. There's a pair of gimlet eyes casting blue light across the red-lit scene like a proud parent over a favoured child. Originating to the inch from where the old tunnel entrance has sat quiescent for months but which now is clear of ice with the shards scattered about and shadows moving against the chalk cliffs.

Figures between the grey steel beams of the abandoned development, the metal splayed outwards in their coating of sea-ice. The shadows dance as the twin-beams shift, the effect sufficiently disorientating that he cannot discern the nature of the things that move, and those that remain still.

Enough. More than enough.

He shifts the Lamp over to challenge the interlopers. Sunlight being the best disinfectant as the old saying goes, with the Lamp being the closest thing he has to the dearly departed sun. If the things moving down there are vamps, then a couple of minutes of direct beam should melt them back into dust and bone. If they're not… well a proper look will at least let him know what he's dealing with.

The Lamp shivers in his hands, reticent to leave its sea

vigil and move to the tiresome land, but accepts his direction as if it senses his concern.

He gets the strangest feeling that it trusts him.

Still, its fittings are not designed for major adjustments by hand (or shoulder). Whatever force propels its normal function is far stronger than a human as if its stubborn nature manifests in awful inertia. Even the beam has a solidity that knocks over bricks and pushes snowdrifts into swirls of activity as it passes. It's as if the light itself has heft and the world is pushing back against it.

That resistance is reflected in the effort involved in moving the beam to the figures creeping from the tunnels. He feels like he's pulling a blunt knife through ballistic gel. His arms ache from the effort and he vents old sailor's curses like an engine puffing steam, yet slowly but surely he pulls the beam across the town, bracing his boots against the wooden floor, until its light reaches his target and he can see the what approaches.

The tunnels are open. There are more figures, slipping and sliding their way out. Pushing through the driving sleet. Dozens, hunched and hobbling, moving as if they are trying to remember how to walk after a long break from the rigour of foot by foot.

Why they move, he cannot tell. But he can see where they are going.

They being drawn to the light of the Lamp like everything else and they are coming for him and there is something unnatural to the way they move.

"Of course there is." He feels acid rise in his gut.

It takes him a moment to realise what is wrong. Then it becomes obvious. The creatures cast shadows in the beams, but the shadows move first. Their physical bodies lumber forward, following the general movement of their dark twins, but with a delay. It is as if there they are on strings, and it takes a moment for the puppet master to catch up with each variation initiated by the shadow.

The lead creature stumbles over a rock as its legs sinks into deep snow, and its shadow picks itself up before the rest follows, raising a hand towards the light coming from the Tower.

Or something that might once have been a hand, there is too much to it now, and some of it writhes. The arm itself is elongated to the proportions of a gibbon or some such semi-ape, too many joints, and there are runes like the ones on his walls running along the fingers that glow in helter-skelter patterns.

The thing grins at him from a face from which the jaw hangs loose by a single hinge. It's the left one, he notices.

The runes reconfigure and flare. The grin widens.

"Shit."

Magic doesn't work well with magic, an extra input or a tilt and… he knows that. The thing seems to know that too and he can sense its malice as it works its own.

The Lamp has always been temperamental. He has to…

The weight of the Lamp's motion makes it impossible to twist the beam away as a ripple approaches from the raised claw, swimming along the lamp's beam like a tide of maggots, swimming towards him at a leisurely but unalterable pace. He can't move the beam no matter how hard he pushes at it. "No, no no…"

The Lamp bucks, tries to twist.

The wave of distortion crawls the last hundred feet at a canter. He ducks as it arrives in an echo chamber of gurgling chuckles and with a sad little pop the main lens on the lamp cracks dropping splinters of glass and the little red runes that dance across its surface to the floor in a tinkling spray that slides into a variety of forms before dissolving into the wood.

"FUCK."

He can hear a giggle from the direction of the town and suddenly he has other things to worry about than the cold, as the creatures pick up speed, pulled forward in a danse macabre by their shadows, amongst the blood-red ruins towards his roost.

He watches them for a moment, gritting his teeth, then collects his tools and heads out into the frozen waste to avenge his Lamp. This isn't his first rodeo and it sure as hell won't be his last.

7

The Wrecker talks to him

"Nice work, didn't know you had it in you."

He picks his way over the corpses with delicate step despite steel tipped boots, shaking away the tingle in his fingers from the windchill. Corpses is what these things had been, and corpses is what they are again.

Just a little less ambulatory.

From their clothing the raw material appears to have been civilian. They're dressed in the familiar fashions of 'just before the end office dweller', light breathable fabrics and a lot less of it than had been the fashion twenty years before. It made living in a three-degree-and-climbing world a little less like sitting in its least authentic sweat lodge. Scattered among them are a few security guards still in ceramic chest plates and crash helmets though without weapons. He assumed those had dropped when their owners had dropped somewhere back in the darkness of the tunnels.

He looks over the corpses with the seasoned eye of an experienced office dweller or two. By his estimate there had been an entire department down there. What had they been up to, before they began with the shambling?

Not that it matters now, and it feels like something he shouldn't dig into. There are plenty of secrets hidden around the frozen wastes and very few of them have a pleasant payoff. He prods at the nearest of the dead with his shotgun, confirming that the besuited gent won't be getting up again.

"How long were you down there before you died, chum? And why didn't you just come out. There's a hundred exits around here."

He considers how the world has shifted. Dozens of civilians dead in a bunker? The stuff of front pages and Parliamentary investigation. Now it hardly matters. Whether it had been starvation, sickness, or just the fucking mind-blasting, world ending cold when the sun had been blotted out, these people had died.

Then the power in the clouds had leaked into their failed shelter and brought some of them back. Bits of them, the clouds were full of runes and sigils and they could do all sorts of shitty things if they spelt out the wrong words.

No such thing as wrong words. Only ones used inappropriately. You'd know that if you read.

There are good words too. The sigils are raw material. What you do with them matters. They do have an annoying habit of spelling out unpleasantness by default. It could be as simple as 'fire' or as complicated as 'life'. The world gives, the world takes away.

Now for the main event.

He looks up at the siren as he works, set high above the entrance to the tunnels. A strange goat-headed thing fixed haphazardly into the wall whose glowing cerulean eyes seem to follow him like twin laser sights as he tosses the ended monsters into the sea, one by one. The salt water would wash away the patterns that had led to their reanimation and then dissolve the sigils back into nothing. The elements of magic are remarkably fragile individually. No reanimated fish or bubbling horrors coming up from the deep.

Oh sweet summer child.

Finished now, the goat's head's attention is fixed on him, and he finds it strangely fascinating, it almost seems alive, like the Lamp, and he has the strangest feeling that it is trying to communicate with him.

Its eyes roll whenever he thinks about making his way back to the Tower, and he gets the distinct feeling that this thing started off as something a lot more than a siren.

Should look away from that. Now.

But he can't. His mind is gradually filling with the hiss of sibilants that he cannot quite link together, murmured information he cannot quite structure into meaning. He watches it, waiting for it all to fall into place.

"Maybe it can tell me how I got here?" He'd like to know that.

You already know that, between you.

Nothing useful. More hissing that blends into the seascape as the water slides across the far-receded beach. He turns away from the goat shaking away dark flakes of snow. This will have to be a mystery that remains unsolved. A step…

Something disagrees.

The goat's eyes high up above him roll back in its head, and its brick-toothed mouth brays out a pulse of deafening noise that echoes off the cliff looming over this sad little development. He staggers at the force, crouching, covering his ears, but the noise is in his head, and he cannot block it out.

"A-I-A-I-A-I-A."

It's real enough. Not morse code, not some weird nonsense that's a figment of his imagination. A siren shaped like a goat's head, or a goat's head moonlighting as a siren, is talking to him.

Done it now, haven't you, dull chap. I mean you were throwing a hundred corpses into the sea a moment ago. You really cannot see the disconnect?

"And all you are saying is vowels," he shouts over the din, turning his face to the furious caprine. "I can't understand what you're saying. Quit it!"

"A-I-A A-I-A A-I-A…"

A little more structure, the sound still meaningless. Whatever its function had been it is now clearly broken. And the medium through which it is broadcasting is giving him a headache, no, that didn't cover it. Not close. It feels like someone is taking an ice pick to his brain with every letter, cutting him into pieces with long deep incisions, one after the other, with each vowel raising the pick high and then burying it deep into his forebrain,

Memories of things that never happened begin to dance across his mind's eye and the goat's eyes continue to roll like pinballs whether in triumph or fury he cannot tell.

Froth drips impossibly down from its stone mouth hissing in the broken ice below the entrance, the message coalesces further.

"A-I-A A-G-E-N-T…"

I'd shoot it.

"Bollocks to this." He pulls his hands away from his ears and slots a pair of shells into his shotgun. Then rolling on to his back he blasts the damn thing with a cleansing enema of metal and propellant fumes. The noise of the shot echoes across the dead town, across the marina and down into the tunnels.

Silence once more, bar the sea and the sounds of wrecks creaking.

"Better."

Or is it?

He feels discombobulated. He rubs his eyes with his fingerless gloves. When did he tattoo his fingers? Why would he have tattooed his fingers? The etched patterns across his fingers are beautiful but he cannot remember when he found the time to engage in such intricate needle work and the friends he had who did tattoos were more at the 'shaky mother' stage.

His memory is shot, worse than before, there's too little in some places and too much in others and the screeching goat has triggered something. Whatever matrix forms human existence is struggling to keep it all in place. A game of musical chairs set up by someone who doesn't understand the concept and invited too many people, and the chairs keep splitting like amoebas.

Shit. Is this what it feels like to go insane? Six months of post-apocalypse and banjaxed by a bloody goat head?

...

He arranges the local facts into some kind of sense. He can do that. The siren was the warning the door was opening. He doesn't know why it opened, only that it did and whatever the point of storing a bunch of civilians down there had once been, it seemed to have played out its course.

And he's never felt great since things went to hell. That's what the end of the world can do to you. Keeping it together this long has been an achievement. Nothing's changed.

He tests out his logic. Most of it sticks. A little rattle around the edges where some of the pieces have come loose but that can be remedied with a good meal and some… wrecking.

An hour passes unnoticed as he works through his issues.

And then with a grin under his face mask he straightens and starts to move once more.

Close the door.

"Ah well. Best get this sorted."

He goes to the tunnel entrance and applies a little basic engineering to reverse the process that had let the things out. Anything left down there can stay there until the Union turns up or the ice build-up blocks the entrance for good. He's got other things to worry about, like finding a new lens for the lamp.

The Radio will have something to say about that.

He hopes that the Channel stays quiet tonight as today the door to the Union is open and outside the rats are swarming.

8

On the Radio

Back at the black flint Tower once more he waits out the remnants of the night listening for instructions from the Radio. He sits in an utter fugue, the absence of the Lamp is ache in his chest, he shells monkey nuts between his fingers and throws the discards into a makeshift bin with mechanical underarm tosses.

The Radio sits there. Inert. Unhelpful. Whoever is at the other end of the device had better be racking their brains over what he should do next or he might just have to move on to the Brazil nuts and that could get messy.

He waits for the lights to fire up, for some indication that the Union is actually watching as it always claims, huddled in his corner by the trapdoor to the lower floors with its trick latch and grenade bouquet. He constructs a hill of duvets and blankets, still shivering from his excursion to destroy the tunnel dwellers and trying to recover the heat he lost knocking down them down.

Worry gnaws at him as the minutes turn to hours, and night turns into dull blood covered morning, with nary a word from the Radio as to recover from this shit show. His head is full of half-heard voices muttering useless suggestions, though the one at the back is refreshingly silent.

The Lamp sits on its runners, nodding downwards like a depressed donkey.

He decides to sleep. His limbs ache from his earlier efforts and given how things are going he doubts that he'll be able to do more than doze. The chances of of sleeping through the Radio turning itself on are minimal.

With the windows closed one after the other and the faint glow of the occluded sun pushing its way up, the cold finally abates and the runes finally heat up his lair. He sinks down into the pillows and blankets and the chaos subsides, the echoes of the howling siren pass into memory, and he dreams of boats and the rumble of jet engines when sleep takes him at last.

———————-

He awakes to the harsh caw-caw of gulls, screeching their dislike of a world without unwary tourists holding unguarded ice cream and the empty 'gull proof' bins buried in ice along the streets. He can hear their claws skittering across the slate roof above. The Watcher shakes sleep away and stretches his aching limbs, starting the day by clearing away the inert glass shards that shimmer across the floor of his tower in the roseate light of dawn.

"We'll get you up and running, lad. You wait and see."

He pulls the trapdoor up and slides down the set of ladders to his workshop/storage unit. In the absence of instructions, and given his previous disobedience, he'll have to come up with something himself to get the gateway to England nicely trapped once more, and for that he needs fuel. Bodies don't run on air and water, as a lot of people had found out recently.

His workshop/storage area had once been a Shrine to

one of the more popular medieval Baptist Saints. He has an ache at the back of his head that suggests this wasn't always the case, and that something has changed, but he lets that one drift away.

It is dedicated to one of those missionaries who had sold the concept of the coming Messiah to a people more interested in reading, writing and record keeping but who'd accept a religion provided someone was willing to keep track of what the King was owed by his recalcitrant churls.

Maybe the King in question had grown to regret his bargain, religion had a way of wheedling its way into everything if left unchecked. He definitely looked grim enough in the third panel of the Triptych set above the shrine itself. The Baptists back then had been a harsh lot once they'd got their claws hooked deep. Handing out unbending rules to the minimally devout, they earnestly believed would speed the arrival of the Messiah, and enforced with delicate psychological torture and less delicate holocausts.

Yet no matter what strictures they imposed, the promised one never arrived and eventually rules had been relaxed and new churches had splintered providing royalty with an easier route to salvation.

It was the way of things. Sic transit etc.

"I bet that Aethel-whatever up there wished he'd got the updated rules."

Whatever its origins, the place suits him and his purpose, and he's never felt any urge to move to something more 'modern'. The black flint of the walls retains warmth, the tower is tall with a fine view over the channel, and the storage space, once he'd removed the excess leaflets, pews, and former parishioners, is ample.

There is also something about taking shelter in a former shrine in an apocalypse that appeals to him. Even if the hidden God had abandoned the rest of the world, it seemed unlikely he'd give up entirely on his own house. Even if he/she/whatever did insist on withholding any signs of his/her/their existence from the people down below who'd frozen to death before he'd arrived.

"And if anyone were using magic before we got a handle on it, it would have been our church friends…"

He whistles a happy tune as his bones warm cooking himself a mess of porridge on the rune-stove. The oats and rehydrated milk bubble and pop filling the air with a delicious smell. He drizzles on lines of golden syrup from a tin and settles down on a salvaged chair to admire his refuge as his meal takes flight.

Shape. Not flight.

He examines the maps and venerated objects of faith sat in their glass display cases as he eats, tracing the paths of each holy item across time. What must it have been like to up sticks from the eternal city and make your way to some hell hole on the edge of civilisation back in those days? Not too different from today, and if some Roman Vampire tried to land he'd sink the bastard.

Usually. When circumstances allowed. He needs to get the Lamp working. Those fangy bastards are supposed to be a handful if they get near.

Finishing his breakfast he shifts through a few of the boxes stacked around the walls, moving the contents around in a half-hearted search for the oil skin wrapped lens that he'll need to repair the Lamp. It's a forlorn hope, he's pretty sure the last time he'd needed a part it had been…

The Lido. He grins. Obvious if he thinks about it. The Lido is the place for a replacement lens. It's where he keeps all the important stuff. And at worst he can get some extra batteries and stretch his legs while the Radio gets its act together and tells him how to do the needful.

He makes coffee. Adds condensed milk. Warms his hands against the tin cup and ignores the sparks of blue energy in the darkness of the shrine.

Or he could wait for instructions?

He weighs up the alternatives. Waiting here and hoping, not great. The war is hotting up on the Continent. That meant runners and the thrum of motors getting closer and closer, the scratching shift of hulls being drawn up on the beaches, the pitter-patter of approaching fanged doom, likely followed by their Eastern Alliance pursuers, armed to the teeth.

He leans back in the chair, legs beetled up to his chest. Letting the possibilities play out.

His eyes lock on the door to the graveyard with its burden of bones and ash. He has an aversion to dying.

"Fuck it, let's go."

Mind made up, he drinks the last of his instant coffee. He sets down the cup, wraps himself up in his heavy outdoor gear and grabs his despised shotgun as he makes his way out into the shadowy scarlet of morning in the Ice Age in Scarlet.

The red light of morning plays across the sharp cut flint walls that line the road outside the Shrine and reveal the runes cut deep in the stone.

9

Are there people close at hand?

He passes through the graveyard, dodging the deepest snow banks in all their boot-pulling glory.

The Lido's a long way out from the Shrine, and his knees ache in protest at the thought of the trek.

It's two miles down the coast towards the bay that indents the southern coast of the Isle, where the slow moving Stour meets the sea and pushes outwards, or as it did before both river and bay iced over becoming a huge ice-rink studded with broken hulls.

He'd been collecting some pretty pictures of the view, as was, from the buildings he's scavenged. The past was a beautiful place. When the golden light of late afternoon played across the bay it had been spectacular.

Little boats bobbing, the hazy green hills rising off to the west sliding down into the Channel ports at the opposite tip of the peninsula tipped in chalk-white, with jetties pushing out into the Channel and liners laid up awaiting their cargo of excited tourists and booze cruisers.

Lovely.

He's stopped collecting the pictures now. There's only so many times you can pick at a scab.

Now the view down the coast is scarlet and shadow, broken ship hulls lining the coast. Not his work. By the time he'd entered the wrecking business the sort of pre-Catastrophe mariner manning those behemoths had all either made port or met their doom. Bereft of their navigation data the big old container ships had been blind monsters wallowing in brine, and the seas had been storm-force murder after the earthquakes that had taken out the Pacific Rim. Ship.

Cable TV reports showed spectral silhouettes of ship after ship breaking their backs against the coasts in dust storms so thick you wouldn't have seen your hand waved in front of your face and all the navigation electronics fried or screaming.

Poor bastards. Never stood a chance.

He pulls his mask tight as the snow patters against the back of his head like an over-caffeinated jazz player. The glow of the runes lining the flint walls light his route up the coast. He'd cut a good number into the stone over the months to stop the passage becoming impassible and there is a constant trickle of meltwater sloshing its way through the fresh snow and old ice at the edges of the lane, down to the Marina and thence to the briny receding sea.

He splashes his feet in the stream to clear off mud from his last trip outside and ponders getting a bit of polish on them before the leather gets stiff.

There's a rumble from up above as something big flies across, darkening the sky under its bulk.

Moments like this, the lane reminds him a little too much of the third panel of the Triptych with the King on his way down the dark valley to Hell to serve out his time for a youth filled with unsanctioned concubines, traitor beheadings and the occasional missionary boiling. Man hadn't known any better. Pretty harsh if you asked the Watcher. The walls are high, and oppressive, funnelling him along a path which he's not sure he's chosen and the jagged runes give the whole thing a devilish look.

Out of the lanes, beyond the constricting walls, it's better. Snowfall and ice build up a little less concentrated and the feeling of being trapped in a tunnel, less. As he leaves the flint lanes with their hint of hymns and hellfire he lets out a breath he wasn't aware he'd been holding.

The world opens up at the roundabout with its big house and frozen mound where a couple lie forever hidden by ice and a green backpack poking out the snow. He tips his hat and shakes his shoulders to get the tension out.

To the right the road off to the art-deco Station. Collapsed houses, some shops. The trodden-down path from one of his Tuesday patrol routes. That kebab shop with the bad voodoo and the sign half off its hinges.

Off to his left, his path for the day. Much nicer. No buildings, just the promenade where the town's folk had walked away the coast town blues or admired the views over the Channel. Baroque shelters line the route, a place to take a breather and catch some rays, or to huddle from the chill sea breezes in autumn, mature trees either side of a central path for shade and grass to touch if you were that way inclined.

Nothing special really. The way the world had been when the skies were blue and the clouds were friendly puffs of white and grey, not sullen slabs of clotted blood full of skittering things.

A good strong fence guards the drop down to the beaches a hundred feet down sheer cliffs, vines creeping along the metal from the new plant life. Those funny old fifty-pence rangefinders you could use to get a blurry look at the Continent where someone would be looking back at you from the Euro equivalent stand out of the berms at angles. The faint hiss of seawaves as they play across the sand and gravel and ice.

He spits and heads left. It's where the Lido is, always has been.

He passes dead trees, each being strangled by the cold and an aggressive strain of thistle with black veins that bites into the ground and claws its way up exposed brick-work wherever it can get a grip. As he walks, he avoids the puddles of gloopy dark liquid that leak down their trunks staining the snow, stinking of coppery blood.

A little further he notices motion from the cliff's edge and his ears catch the faint sound of an animal whim-pering in pain.

Those bloody plants…

He shakes his head and hefts the cold iron of his shot-gun. He knows what he'll find before he gets there but he still has a soft spot for the few surviving animals. Away from the flint lanes the fence that guards the drop is lined with clumps of what look at first glance like an aggressively fast growing type of blackberry.

They're not, they're something new and unpleasant imported from somewhere else. The giveaway is the way the branches sway like hooded cobras.

These plants can move and they've found something better than sunshine to grow.

He edges closer to the source of the whimpering. It's a big one and a line of branches edged in sharp hook-thorns rises up from the culprit perched at the tumble-edge of the cliffs. It is trying to hide a solid mass within its centre, protecting its prey with its outer vines waving menacingly in opposition to the wind's direction and his approach.

The first time he'd seen these damned things he'd tried to harvest some of the heavy and delicious looking fruit that sits at the edge of the mass, as he'd had a sudden jonesing for something that didn't come from a can.

He'd barely avoided the swipe of the vines as they tried to grab him. To be fair it had been a half-hearted attempt by the plant as if it hadn't been quite sure what to make of him and he'd ended up safe and sound and sitting down hard in a pile of snow, dignity lost but nothing more.

For other living things, birds, animals, whatever, those vines would slice out at remarkable speed, tangling around their prey and drawing it into the centre mass where it would curled in on itself like a barbed constrictor to feed.

He had a plan involving petrol and a lighter for the spiky bastards when he'd found some that hadn't evaporated, but for now….

He's close enough to see the fox now. Pulling itself in shivering agony against the the barbs that reach hungrily for its most vulnerable skin like sentient barbed wire, and the tiny bones, picked clean that surround the purported plant from earlier victims.

He finishes the fox off with his shotgun. Both barrels. The animal shudders, dies, and the pellet spray cuts at the centre of the monstrous plant slicing through thick vines that leak the same blood red gunk as the rest of them.

The thing curls itself into a protective ball and he steps backwards.

"I'll be back for you later."

That earns him a sneer of derision from the voice at the back of his head.

"Should have seen what it did next. How are we ever going to learn anything with you around?"

"Will you just shut up?"

Back to the cleared path with its occasional patches of

blade grass that'll go through a boot. The whole ecosystem seemed to be in flux and he crushes the new growth as he goes along. Part dislike of the newcomers, part prudence. Given time to grow the blade grass stalks developed a hard ridge with razor sharp edges that would pass for a katana edge.

And they were opportunistic. All it took was a gap in the snow cover and before you knew it there was a field of razor-sharp green leaves jutting up towards the cloud haunted sky, the tips near black.

The Radio said that if you left a stalk for a week or so then the upper section would twist in on itself and blossom into a passable facsimile of maize, even down to a propensity to pop into cascades of popcorn in the presence of heat. Good eating or so it claimed.

He'd leave that to someone with less tinned food and less need to go on long dark walks to discover.

"Something to remove anything that survives the cold, something for the kine to eat and something to guard dangerous cliff edges or the edge of guarded camps from those who might choose another ending to being a Master's snack. Quite clever if you think about it. I'd say our friends have planned this for some time. Brooker was right for once. Seems almost unbelievable."

A mean laugh tries to push its way through his lips. He chokes it back and lets the lurking thing at the back of his mind subside back to insignificance.

He passes the great manses of the rich as he reaches the half way point of his odyssey. Big old four-five and six bedroom detached houses with imposing garages. Each made to its own plan. Cookie cutters and econohomes were for the plebs, not the sort who commuted or had home offices serving the remnants of the global elites.

Some of them are truly impressive, views across the Channel and big gardens out the back. They should be good scavenging but most are locked up tight, boarded in solid wood, and with the tell-tale bleep and flash of alarms running off battery packs or the dribble of power from solar panel across roofs keeping the home fires smouldering.

Some of the roofs were even intact if you had a yen for climbing. Always amazes him…

He stops dead, a stalk of blade grass the size of a bastard sword has slid out all innocuous from the wall of snow to his left. It is roughly at neck height, edge presented and two steps ahead of him.

"Nice try," he uses the barrel of his shotgun to carefully press it back down into the snow till it snaps with a satisfying crack.

His gardening and botanical musings are interrupted by an unwelcome sound.

"Crunch..."

What was that?

"Crunch."

He recognises that sound, and it's unwelcome. A blast from the past, like the siren that's set him on this unwelcome journey.

It's the sound of someone walking across a field of old snow that remains uncleared by his patrols or by his runes. The crunch is distinctive, early Catastrophe snow was laden with the dust of broken continents and the occasional fist sized lump of rock that had dropped more than a few unwary scavengers and smashed more than a few roofs.

You could see it like tree rings along the paths he's cleared at the lowest levels, a frangible almost-concrete. And when you walked through a thin layer of it it made that very familiar crunch.

"Oh bollocks." People. Or something worse.

More crunches follow. Playing out the rhythmic swing of boots in motion, not tired or dying. Steady. Moving with a minimum of effort and with purpose towards some clear goal. Whoever it was wasn't some staggering last man on his last erg of energy. This person, people actually, there were too many footfalls for a single intruder, knew where they were going.

Intention implies threat.

He drops on to his haunches, hoping the snow fields and razor grass clumps will hide him from the intruders. If they hadn't seen him already. Sound was treacherous and if it were funnelling just right they could still be miles away.

Possibly. Not likely though.

Then there was the steady clump of their advance, that didn't bode well. If you saw another human in the current circumstances, his experience was that you either ran at them or ran away from them following the oldest playbook in the human canon.

Unless you were supremely confident. Or well armed. Oh he did not like that thought.

Indecision. The chorus begins.

"Make a run for it. Shift for yourself lad."

"Get the shotgun, give them a blast of that. That should see them off. Show you've got teeth."

"Hide in a house. I knew a good one just off the road."

"Jump off the cliff. I'm done with this shit. Why…"

"How about we ask them if they can help us? They could be friendly?"

"The boat. Get to the boat. We can still get away… The masters promised…"

He swears under his breath, and then swears again as the puffs of condensation rise upwards. Hide. That's the best of a bad lot. He has to hide. Give him time to assess risk. Let them get closer if they have better guns than him. Gods above he hated the shotgun.

"Crunch, crunch, crunch."

"Fuck my life." He's got a fix on them now. They're coming down the side roads. Only positive is that it gives him time to get to the Bimmer.

A plaintive whine. *"The boat… are we going to the boat? Don't hide, they'll find us. They found us. I can't see…"*

He can feel butterflies gathering in his stomach as he slips and slides his way towards his bolt-hole, ignoring the cacophony playing out across his forebrain. He keeps as low as he can. The hairs on his arms are twitching like spiders as he passes the ice-covered bowling green where before the Catastrophe all were welcome to engage in a game or two with the elders of town.

The further he walks the more convinced he is that his attempt to avoid detection has failed.

A glance behind confirms his fears. Shadows move amid the snow, negative space bobbing up and down as they march, heading in the same direction, clumping along at a regular pace, melting the ice as they walk with hand held staves that glow blue in the red of the morning.

"Should have just jumped. What's the fucking point?"

"Mouth shut, lad. Always worth a try to live."

"Live?"

A torch flashes out, the white light blinding and unnatural in this world of reds and shadow. It slides past him as he ducks, and over the cliffs, it gives him an idea of where they're looking and that in turn gives him a chance to get to where he needs to be.

The car.

He ducks down behind its protective bulk, keeping the body between him and the intruders. They're close enough he can hear their voices. They're bickering. At least they're arguing in English, the cadences obvious even if he can't pick out the words, no panic, no anger, almost good natured. Then silence.

The torch flicks off.

He risks a look, peeking over the bonnet. Nothing where his estimates would have put them. The snow swirls on the wind and a gentle cloud fall of sigils slip down from the clouds in streams over the sea obscuring his view. The voices are gone as is the sound of footsteps. The storm wraps up around him like a coat of cotton wool, snug and warm.

"Anyone else find this a bit weird?"

"Go with it…"

Maybe he was wrong, it could have been pure chance that they were moving along the same route as him. The were paths down the cliffs nearby and plenty of people felt the call of the sea even if it were just to see if there might be somewhere warmer further south.

That's where the torchlight had gone.

And taken from the standpoint of a scavenger this area would have appeared unpromising, bar the big old houses with their vestigial alarm systems all too likely to attract attention from above.

There's an entire town down the other way, and it's barely touched, he's managed to clear maybe a couple of dozen houses and a shop or two. All that's this way is the Lido and the old park with the swings hanging off rusted chains and a large plastic elephant slide with little practical use for a connoisseur of post-apocalyptic survival.

Wouldn't it be his luck if the intruders were connoisseurs of ironic artefacts?

"Might have gotten away with it, lad."

Head of the Baptist, but the exertion of running

through the snow has nearly killed him. His muscles burn from the unexpected exertion and the back of his throat stings from the cold air he's forcing down into his lungs. He adjusts his mask and carefully slides the shotgun round so it's ready if needed.

Warning shots first. Only if needed. The weight of it. He feels a visceral dislike of the gun, holding it makes him feel like someone is clawing his stomach from the inside out. His face stings… he breaks open the joint of the gun.

A light catches his eye as he loads a pair of shells into the breach. Radio? Blue light flickering from an LED display inside the car and the burble of screams and a string quartet on the air.

Sudden relief. The tension melts away. It'll be okay.

The back door is still open swinging on perfectly engineered hinges, and he slips inside, settles on the soft leather, and keeps his head low. It's warm on the backseat, the seats heated, the leather luxurious. This is where he needs to be. Wait out the problems and maybe, just maybe…

There's a click as the Radio in the vehicle settles on a signal. The information panel flickering out patterns of sigils before transforming into a sine wave that matches the clipped cadences of the Union presenter.

"This is a special program addressed to those of good-cheer at the gateway to the Union. Remember, in moments of danger that it is a fool who rushes in. A cautious man, one of sensible nature, who may survive to protect his country, avoids risks. The Union requires that you conserve yourself for the important business of the day. Errors have been made. Errors will be corrected. They are not your concern."

"The quiet of the day requires reflection. The night will be full of dangers. ***Stay where you are and do not stir****. The Union will provide the means to* ***guard your post****."*

"We hear from certain reliable sources that the corpse-things mass across the Channel. They are preparing some foul gambit directed

towards the coast from their collapsing lines at the expense of their failing defence of Paris. Although we cannot identify a logical basis for this vexatious gambit, its existence appears to be a fact which must be addressed. Were our friends who watch to drop their guard whilst this threat looms then all would be lost."

"Together we must deny them. Together we must repair our defences and watch the sea. Tools will be provided. A minute lost is nothing, a hasty action-action-action could be the end of you, will be the end of you."

"Eyes forward soldier."

He feels the cacophony of voices in his head with their endless awful advice fade away as the calming voice of the Radio sets out the facts. Almost. There is one exception pushing back to get one last comment in before being erased for a time.

"You're not even real, idiot."

He shakes his head and relaxes. Sets the shotgun across his lap. Feels the voice subside back. It likes the gun less than him. Keeps his eyes locked forward through the icy covered shimmer of the car's windscreen.

"Thought that would shut you up."

A muffled *crunch* from behind him, then another. Not close but approaching at a steady pace.

"Feeling's mutual. Guess I'll leave this one to you, moron."

The parting words are sharp, leaving a paper cut that itches across the surface of his calm.

He waits. He can feel eyes on the back of his skull staring from every half-ruined building in the cemetery landscape. The itching from the parting comment spreads into his spine and through his nervous system. His back prickles and every nerve in his body is screaming that he should run like the devil is chasing him, or find some way to burrow deep into the iron-hard snow-covered earth and stay there, buried until the world reverts to the bygone days of supermarkets and tax codes, yachting lessons and navigation tickets.

"He's coming apart. Get someone up there."

The music becomes louder, flutes and violins and all things soothing.

A female voice joins the mood music, emitting from the speakers in the car. The heater switches itself on bathing him in warm air and pine scents from garage bought fresheners dangling on frayed string.

"There is no one behind you. You are panicking. ***That is perfectly normal****, the world is a scary place right now, but if you* ***just let it go*** *the fear will melt away like the snowflakes on your shoulders.* ***Don't go looking*** *for troubles. Look to the world inside you, even the clouds above you are transitory. Things will get better."*

He looks through the sunroof, watches the flakes slash across the sky towards the grey-red slag pit of the sea. Each flake settles on the vehicle's bright yellow chassis and melts into droplets that slide across glass and steel in a perfectly timed ballet as the heat in the car reduces them to their constituent elements. He wonders if they retain some memory of their former existence or if everything is transformed to its next state as it transforms from crystal to liquid and loses itself in the earth below.

The clouds are busy today. Dark shapes move above, some serpentine, some insectoid, some purely geometric, all dance as if celebrating the fall of mankind. Each different in shape and size and motion. A fine distraction indeed.

Crunch-crunch-crunch.

He smiles. He's comfortable in his little cocoon. Evening is on its way, earlier than he remembers from previous sun soaked Autumns, the dust in the clouds must diffract the last light of the far sun bringing forward the day's end.

A shiver. A shard of something, cuts.

Last light. There's something about those words. Makes him think of sacrifices on stone tables with sharp flint knives. Sometimes he thinks there's too much in his head. Sometimes too little.

He's spooking himself out. He should just let it go.

Movement at the edge of his vision. The figures are blurred into nothing, a dead spot in his vision. Office migraines from instant coffee and the flicker of fluorescent lights, the flash of geometric figures dancing on the graveyard of objective reality. A faint hint of music he half recognises from the Radio broadcasts in the counterpoint.

His arms burn, the feeling pushing upwards past his elbows and up through his shoulders where they are met by the comfortable warmth in which his mind seems to bath. The pain is trying to pull him back to the now and he doesn't want to be here right now. The traitor voice at the back of his head is stirring again.

The Radio crackles, the music as counterpoint.

*"**Stay still.**"*

They've arrived. They're stood outside. Voices growl and buzz, the sounds senseless and unknowable, wrapped in the same blanket of confusion as the one blurring his vision and dulling his hearing. The snow crunches under heavy shod-tread as strangers walk around the car, investigating it.

A voice whispers to him, as close as if the speaker had been standing by his shoulder, outside the passenger side window which is now inexplicably wound down.

*"Poor lost thing, **you're too early**. You should have waited for instructions. You can **go home**, rest, **come back tomorrow**, everything will be so much less confusing."*

"Leave him, Coral. Places to be, people to see and I'm damned if

I'm staying here. Lensing is horrific if you haven't noticed, maybe half hour before things get weird. And I'm still dubious about the bindings on him. Seem frayed to me."

"We'd know if they were."

"Yeah, quickly too. You never met who's under there, kiddo. I did and I know I don't want to be here if things don't… hold. Do your job. Okay? Keep him here and Arnie can do the drop off. Saves us a walk. Then we're gone. Calais awaits."

"Okay." A sigh. "It's weird, I don't feel any one there. There's something there, definitely, but it's not him, feels a kinder than I'd expect, maybe."

A snort of derision, a sing-song voice, and tapping on the window in a tattoo that leaves him in a painless dream.

"… No choice in the matter, Calais says they're moving a VIP up, half a corp sacrificed to make it to the ports. Think what that might be? We need him working and the idiots at the 'Castle dropped the ball…"

"I know. It's tough."

"Enough. Everything's tough. Stand around in this much longer and we'll be staying for good. There's a team incoming."

"I might mention it in my report. The gaps. Could be important?"

"Knock yourself out. No one reads them anyway. We make our deliveries, they file it in a box. World's gone to shit, whatever Brooker and that coterie of weirdos might think."

"Cynic."

An electric motor buzzes and there is a voice close to his ear, he can feel the warm breath.

*"**Go home, D. Get some sleep.**"*

"Finished?"

"Yeah. Do you see what I see?"

"Oh for fucks sake. Arnie? What are you doing? Get the box up there now, tide's turning and they'll need the designator quick-quick. And stop whining. No one made you step on the fucking grass…"

"It lashed out at me like a fucking whip…"

"Get a bandage on it. You're spilling red everywhere, last thing we need is a cloud incursion. I want…"

The voices drift away, down towards the beach maybe. There's a set of stairs near the Lido that zigzag down to the beach with its covering of flotsam and jetsam from a world's worth of shipwrecks and the boats he keeps ready for his trips out to the banks.

Time passes.

When it has passed the warmth and accompanying torpor drop away from his muscles and he feels the cold and cracked leather against his skin. His arms are tingling and the day has slipped away from him. The glow of the dust-occluded sun dips over the landward horizon faster than he can believe, a time-lapse stream on double speed, dropping below the line of the Downs, outlining the skeletons of trees and a broken tower block. Passing into blood-red darkness.

He can see lights in the sky as the first fisher flies start to prepare for their night's work landward and hear the groan of larger monsters ready to feed.

It is night, and the lures bob up and down in the gathering wind as a storm comes in from the north.

He yawns and stretches the tension out of his shoulders. He can hardly stay here; the car is ice cold and the Radio is silent. He should get back before the death cold falls. That means no chance of making it all the way to the Lido and still repairing the Lamp for the night's work.

He'll have to keep an eye on the coast and take notes.

He has the oddest feeling that just for tonight the Channel will be safe. The storm is lashing everything to hell out there. Waves foaming and crashing against the cliffs all along the coast bar a channel of calm leading off through the gap in the orange barrier towards Calais.

There are no footprints in the snow behind him when he gets out of the car's husk.

Best thing would be to get a good night's sleep and head out fresh and early tomorrow.

Down at the seafront an outboard motor does not start up.

If he does see something the Union can take care of it. They're there to help him do his job, a mutual dependence. He smiles at the thought. The idea of being one of the lost, wandering around this nightmare without a purpose, that would be a real hell.

A boat does not pull out of the harbour and make its way across to the continent along the unnaturally calm sea road.

He is calm. He is alone.

"Never quite alone."

He heads home using his patrol paths, past the frozen humps that jut out of the snow where the bodies couldn't be burnt before the old Government moved out, and when he arrives, gratefully bars the door from the graveyard behind him as the fisher fly lures snatch up their first catch and unwary wildlife falls deep into thorny pain bushes in the pitch blackness of a starless, moonless night.

When he reaches his nest his dreams are disturbed and disturbing.

10

Or are they all trapped down below?

Nothing has been simple since the skies closed. He glares upwards at the shifting nightmare of dust and ruin, then turns to look at the real source of his issues.

People. Awful, stupid, slow lumpen people.

After a decade of elective solo missions and equally solitary research he's experiencing a reminder of why he hates working with them. He's not a natural loner. It's just that everyone around him seems to run at about half the speed they should and he spends so much time explaining exactly what they need to do he may as well have done it himself.

Exemplar?

A snatch mission that has turned into a veritable Odyssey, with dull stone companions and Ithaca notable by its absence.

Exit, Archibald. Stage left. Holding Q box. Pursued by hobbled bears.

Instead, detritus of life and cautious back-steppers blocking his mission and wasting his time. Mere bagatelles impeding his natural inclination to explore this new world with the light of science without having to chase around after traitors with a yen for the Vampire Family.

He comforts himself with the thought that if he's having trouble getting anywhere his targets will be moving even more slowly.

Less distance to travel though. A grimace and back to the present.

He leans against warm ceramic side of an armoured car, crouched slightly to avoid the turret traverse as the optics fitted coaxially to the cannon, track the barricade and its guards blocking the road south. The optics feed through on a short line of wire duct taped to a tablet held by the Captain who the Military have 'kindly' assigned to support him in catching their pair of coast-bound traitors with their unfortunately active link to 'Tony'.

Navy says no ships to cut them off at source. The few they have all in refit to run in the new conditions.

He suspects that he and the military are not on the same page when it comes to the end point of this mission. The Captain and most of his subordinates seem to be caught in the rules of the world as was like bugs in amber. Catch and keep? Stupid when there's not enough food for even the essential staff.

Knock Vamp sympathisers on the head and save it for the good guys. He smiles in memory of a cleansing he'd conducted immediately before everything fell apart. Sword providing mightier than the pen even without the cloud's power boost.

At the moment the Captain is deep in thought, assessing the armaments of the figures flitting between the barricade and the reinforced buildings these renegades have made their base.

The man is taking his pretty time about it too.

"Any way round?" His voice mellifluous and deep. It's not the voice he remembers using but it seems fit to purpose. If he'd been on his own, he'd simply have walked around the problem, but a convoy needs a road, and it is arguable he needs the convoy given the endless bands of marauders and scavengers cluttering every suburb. Evidence supports hypothesis?

Yes.

If he'd been on his own that sniper might have taken him out at the last roadblock rather than the Captain's batman. He needs to work on his wards. Ironic if he were to be taken out by a slug thrower when there's finally all the power in the world to shape.

"No." The Officer's tone is sour even over the circumscribed crackle of his tight beam radio. Conditions and masks preclude most direct communication, even with the subject stood next to you. "Snow's metres deep either side and the buildings are impassible without lifting gear."

A drone buzzes above them, a companion to the lenses slotting into place in sequence over the vehicle's single bright eye. And there he was mourning the absence of a Cyclops in his own personal Odyssey!

"Something funny, Agent?"

"No."

The drone's operating from a slide-ramp shackled with chains to an antiquated relic of an APC bringing up the rear of the convoy. Men in green-grey are perched atop the mechanical dinosaur, operating console controllers, trying to keep the civilian drone in the air long enough to complete a Tri-D view. The drone sweeps overhead, for another sweep. The smooth whir of its engine interrupted periodically as it chokes on clumps of thick volcanic dust which turn the every lungful of air into a taste of hellfire.

He's the only out of salvaged Noddy Suits. Clumsy NBC protection from the same era as the APC with updated filters scavenged from mining gear. Given time he could have provided them with more effective protection, but he doesn't really want to get down to that level of granularity.

Another smile.

A trick grudgingly accepted from Thespian and involving static lets him wear his favoured long coat and Ushanka combination. He's got an earpiece to tap into their comms-net though he doesn't need it to guess what they're thinking.

It's not that he feels he is any way superior to the soldiers. Feeling has nothing to do with this. He is superior. One day they might get the training to step up to his level, but that day is not today.

And they'll need to know whether they're goats or sheep.

The grin extends. People have said that his smile resembles that of a shark. Ridiculous. Sharks lack the mental capacity to emote in that way.

The Captain misses it, intent as he is on the icons popping up on the grainy screen, eye pieces reflecting green and matte. "Burnt out ruins either side, scattered piercing and drop traps, some makeshift explosives. No way we can get the vehicle through without a JCB and a month.

"We don't have a month, Captain."

"I know, I know." The officer spritzes his mask from a water bottle and turns, redundantly, towards the drone operators. "Let's try southern quadrant again, looked like there might be a…"

There's a pop from the drone's engine as its engine intake ingests a larger piece of pumice, and the buzzing from above is terminated in a spit of flames. Suddenly powerless, the drone spins down like a broken bug with the gyros struggling to balance its descent. For a moment it looks like it'll make a soft landing near enough for repair and recovery, but then it is caught by a gust of the endless storm, and it's smashed to flinders against the blackened walls of an office building, gutted by fire.

There's some jocular booing on the comms net.

"Fuck these conditions." The Captain freezes the feed with a clumsy tap, and holds out the tablet to him, voice crackling. "I'm out of ideas. You see what you can do with this fucking disaster." He acknowledges receipt with a tap on the man's pointed head covering, the limited tactile inputs from the Noddy suit making it quite the chore to avoid dropping an expensive and most likely irreplaceable bit of kit.

A couple of the squaddies slouch off to retrieve the crashed drone, covered by the rest of their squad. Maybe they can salvage some of the parts and stick something new together. They stay low and keep to cover. The insurgents haven't got much in the way of long-range weapons but it's best not to take a chance as they found out breaking through the renegade territorial unit outside High Barnet.

He scans the tablet, he's kept up to date with mil-tac terms, back in his active service days there had still been the occasional joint operation. Renegade Kappa setting up a research node in the cliffs outside Salcombe, Alfar incursions on secondments, the usual. There's been no meaningful change in the symbology, or technology, and he's got a sharp mind.

Hmm.

The Captain's right, it's either straight up the middle or a twenty-mile detour and they don't have the fuel nor the time. Those traitors would have to do some ducking and diving on the way to the Coast but he didn't rate the stay-behinds watching the road highly. You didn't get to be a stay-behind without being a Brooker rating of 'expendable' and that man knew sheep at a glance.

"Going to send up another?"

"No point." The Captain shakes his head emphatically. "That's our lot for situational awareness and the designators aren't working so even if we got the armed drone up we can't use it to hit any of these anarchist bastards." He seems to be chewing on wasps. "Plus, we're down to two drones and they both needing repairs. Damn this dust."

"Tablet?."

"Of course." He returns the tablet to the officer and kicks up clods of dead earth pondering arcane solutions.

As he does, the recovery team come back at a jog with the old drone in a hemp bag. The movement attracts attention from the makeshift fortress. One of the anarchists, a grubby looking woman in a bandanna wearing a surgical mask sticks her head out of a window and shouts something unintelligible at them. Maybe calling them monsters.

Water off a duck's back. The Captain, who usually takes these things a lot harder, doesn't even notice as he seems to have had a brainwave.

Surprising.

"Fucking amateurs. They've not strengthened the struts holding up the barricade at the right hand side. AT missile blasts it out, barricade weakened, lots of covering fire from the squad supports, armoured

cars through the gates, lads out the back… won't take long. Andrews…" The Captain's pen works quickly across the touch sensitive screen directing his teams to positions and time frames. That was new. Quite clever.

Plan? Overstating it a little.. Straight lines. Fire arcs burning through scarce ammunition. High chance of friendly fire. Hey diddle diddle, straight up the middle. The cold and the endless tour holding things together was getting into the soldiers' brains, even the tough ones. There are limits to human endurance and the military was approaching them. You needed to be cold to survive this.

Plans might need to be moved up.

In fact, this sort of 'hussars' charge' was how they'd lost their only other personnel carrier and the proper armed drones. The anarchists did love their petrol bombs and slowed reflexes when you're in a big metal box mean you're not much more than a ready meal in a big old oven.

Ah heat. He'd almost welcome a fire or two to keep the battlefield toasty whilst they removed this obstruction. The cold is merciless.

The Captain finishes his work and holds out the tablet. "Good enough?"

He looks over the squiggles, dismissing them with a shrug. "Well, if you think this will work. My only issue is we have an appointment to keep. Mr. Archibald cannot be allowed to make his channel hop given what he knows."

"Nothing you want to add?" He imagines the man's eyebrows raising hopefully. The Army may not like Agents but they did like the tricks they could bring to the table.

"Contextual support. I'll try and 'fit in'." He can feel the stirrings of power running through the clouds. Last Light was paying off but there was no way he was going to waste power doing something a military unit could do… practically.

Soon, maybe. Foundations being laid, the house would come later. For now, they were digging in the dirt. "I'll follow, maybe I can pull a trick or two. Doubt any of these former citizens have seen even even the flashy tricks from before, and morale is flaky at the best of times when you're starving."

"Shame we can't save them all." The Captain growls to himself. The man knows him well enough by now to know that'll initiate a response. Stupid needs to be stamped out.

"Incorrect assumption, Captain." He gestures at the barricades as the two-man anti-tank missile team line up their shot and the hail of rocks and glass bottles is suppressed by the rapid-fire pops from the squad fire support teams. "I'm rather of the opinion that this so called Catastrophe has been quite the useful world view shake up. You may not like it now, but when it's all over the good will have risen to the surface and this…"

The armoured cars engines rev, and turrets begin to rotate into place ready for the charge.

"Will be remembered as something of a colonic cleanse of the worst elements of society. Survival of the fittest isn't something you can opt out of."

"Ease!" The missile team loose and the wire guided relic speeds to its rendezvous with the barricade.

The explosion is disappointing, concentrated on its function rather than being visually impressive, the force however, is sufficient to shatter the makeshift barricade and the men and women around it in storm of fragments, metal rebar, concrete, blood and bone.

The Captain is watching him closely as his vehicles and troopers push forward to take out the survivors. "You live up to your name."

"It's not my name."

It isn't. What is he doing here?

Confusion. His face stings and there is black-blood dripping from his fingers when he touches it. He…

11

From the footsteps it would appear

The storms of the night before had been something else, and the day dawns dark with the barest hint of sunlight making it through the shroud, more dust in the air than he's seen for months forming spectral shadows of men and women in grey uniforms who approach him from the corner of his eye whenever he turns his head from looking out over the Channel.

Some seem to clamber up the cliffs to peek at him over the gravestones outside as he empties a bedpan out the window of the Tower, hollow eyes flitting from window to window, muttering comments he cannot quite catch about his cleanliness or lack thereof.

He ignores them. The Radio has confirmed there is neither an afterlife nor dwellers beyond and that he can believe. Whatever's left after death, seems to be nothing more than words and shadows.

Plus they had nothing to complain about. The snow would bury his leavings soon enough just like it buried everything else, and even if a miracle happened and the whole ice age ended in a whimper and a warm breeze, the only person who would have to worry about what was be uncovered was him.

So the not-ghosts could suck it up.

There is a cold easterly blowing across the Channel, a remnant of the night's festivities, frothing up lines of scarlet-topped waves, bringing with it the stench of Europe's wreck. He's moved on from shadow watching to something of greater interest, the war playing out across the Channel leaning against the silent, sulking Lamp.

By his reckoning the war's seen quite the resurgence in the last couple of weeks. A slow river finally breaking through a dam and flooding the whole damn plain into a muddy morass fit only for pig-wallowing. This morning something's pushing back and it's quite the fireworks display.

One of the sides has a point to prove and they are using a lot of ordnance to make it. The sharp tang of explosives, the barbecue pit of smoke and burnt flesh, the copper of the blood drifts across the Channel, though the blood might have been pure imagination.

There can't be that much blood being spilt? Surely?

Not just foot slogging either. There's the pop-boom of jets and the bright-slow fall of screeds of flares behind them as they make low level attack runs below cloud level. That means things are deadly serious. No one flies if they can avoid it.

The clouds are busy too, unnaturally so, and it's not an occasional swipe at an infringing jet. The Radio says the Vamps are using the damn things as weapons, shaping and pulling and pushing and *dropping*. Over on the frontline whole Eastern battalions are getting swallowed and chewed up. And it still wasn't stopping the Alliance.

Maybe the Vamps would try something more drastic as the Easterners continued their drive. Maybe it wouldn't work. The Radio said the Easterners had brought witches with them to counter it though.

For now whatever they were conjuring up between them, he was bloody glad to be sitting this side of the cold salt waters.

He watches the uproar from his vantage point and wishes both sides well in their mutual destruction.

A series of explosions like firecrackers make him flinch. More debris as an upwell from the ground of some indescribable force smashes into a downdraft from the clouds of swirling sigils and monsters. Tentacles and claws scattering all over the ports recessed into the opposing cliffs, many of the parts still moving.

"That'll be some fun for somebody."

A sonic boom and a fireball. Calais? The dark shape of one of the attack jets is caught by a chasing line of flash-tracers as it scoots its way back south. It staggers in the air, pirouetting helplessly upwards, missing some vital control surface to keep it level, before disappearing into roiling chaos of the clouds.

A bright explosion, an engine emerges a moment later flaming out as it speeds towards old England and into the orange barrier to the north of the Tower where it fizzes out of existence with a zap.

"Big ole fight, indeed."

He plans out his day in his head as he sips at sweet tea. No issues of conscience here. With the runners it's tougher. He can understand the urge to escape what's going on over in old Europe, even the dead things, though he'd never tell the Radio.

The various militaries? Doing their job, he supposes. Same as him. Can't feel overly sorry for them or indeed, himself. Nary a tear would be shed if one of those plane bits and pieces or half a rocket smashed his roost and turned him into mulch.

No one would even know.

A rogue pang of loneliness, that's been a pattern this morning. He winces and sips an overly hot mouthful of tea that should have broiled the inside of his mouth.

He woke this morning feeling disorientated, lethargic and lonely. A drunk waking up after chugging a bottle of turps, the day before a hazy dream of grasping thorn bushes, soothing music and a woman's voice telling him it'll all be fine.

Even now his brain feels coated in a thick haze of funk that makes everything feel edged in a nightmare from which he cannot quite awaken. It happened now and then. Generally too much time to himself was the culprit. He feels like he's trapped in a team chat with people he doesn't like.

Know thyself? He's not sure he really wants to.

He tries distract himself by estimating which side was winning in the clashes. Who was pushing and who was falling. It might seem voyeuristic, but direction mattered to his job. Vamps heading north would be more of a problem for him than Russians heading south. Up till today it's been clearly all one way, North pushing south triggering bursts of refugees and boats bobbing their way out of ports with the flow staunched as the Easterners took control in the pop-pop-pop of mass executions.

The Vamps had seemed on their last legs but today there had been a switcheroo. And that meant trouble for him. He can feel it in his bones. If they took back the ports they could swamp him and his Light in a deluge of boats and there were warships still lurking. They might even try an invasion or something and his shotgun isn't going to stop that.

That's if he even has his Light.

The Lamp still stands, down at heel, awaiting repair. Without the lens it resembles a blinded eye and he feels a little sick looking at it, its absence is part of what's making him feel lonely. Even if it were an inanimate lump of magical oddity, it is about the only company he has and it feels like every minute he leaves it there, maimed by his own stupidity and curiosity, he's betraying the friendship they have.

Man and Lamp. Human and lighting accessory. Pile of gunk in a toughened-skin and pile of parts in a beat-up case.

He stops.

"Or I could have gone completely doolally overnight." A snort of derision that's not really him but that suits the mood of the day. He glances over at the Radio which is flashing blue lights in a rhythmic pattern. "At least some-one's happy."

The Radio is indeed in a good mood. All morning it's been playing a light music seasoned with a background murmur of news and rumours about the war he's watch-ing, a Greek chorus of snidely. After what he's seen today he suspects he knows more about what's happening out there than the Radio itself. At least for the bit he can see.

A crackle and more rumours.

"We understand that the City of Munich has been swallowed by the Clouds in a devilish attack orchestrated by the Vampire Masters holed up in the ruins of Paris. Initial reports from friendly sources indicate that the death rate is one hundred percent with no survivors possible."

"The Masters can be assured that they will pay for this atrocity at the hands of the brave Eastern armies advancing across the Rhine and pushing through former Belgium at this very moment, despite their pointless offensive towards the Channel enclaves where the best of

their forces over extend themselves as a tortoise extending its neck too far beyond its shell."

"Our countermeasures for any attempt to cross the Channel from these bastions are prepared. ***Our vigilant watchers stand ready****."*

A shiver up his spine. He glances around. The blind eye of the Lamp damns him as it stands worthless and defeated.

Today for the lens.

No, he can watch the battle a little longer. Finish off this tea…

"***There is no time like the present, brave gentlefolk****."*

Now. It's time to get moving and he's sliding down the ladder before he's even clear what he's decided.

Once in the shrine he suits up, he can hear the Radio playing out happy tunes and war reports along with martial music. Step, step, step. FAST!. Long coat, shotgun (damn it), fedora and backpack, before half-falling out into the blizzard to the martial accompaniment of gunfire on the wind.

The seagulls perched on the Tower don't like that. They soar and squawk and screech out their hatred of this cold world.

His journey up to the Lido passes quickly, his focus is razor sharp. Step, step, step.

Right up to the point he notices the shadows of footprints in the snow about halfway up the promenade.

"You really don't remember?"

"What the hell do we have here."

"There's still time to make it to the boat you know. We don't have to be here."

"Hush."

There are three, maybe four sets of footsteps of various

size that head up to one of his favoured hiding places, a broken-down luxury sedan with smashed windows rusting into the ice. There's nothing special about the car, it just happens to be about halfway up to the Lido and parked outside a house for which he has a bit of a soft spot. The mildew smell of the rotting upholstery and the chill of the wind through the empty windscreen has left it good only for hopping atop and a quick look-see up and down the Promenade.

Ice Ages are no respecters of German engineering.

A swift investigation reveals the terminus for the footprints. Two head down to the cliffs, cutting down to the beach using the long stairs. Those he can safely ignore. Anyone wanting out of his little slice of heaven is good with him.

Another reaches the car and doubles back to town. He squints in the direction of retreat and tries to follow the pattern but his vision greys out.

"Familiar? No? Not even a little?"

"Leave the lad alone."

He discounts those. Plenty of scavenging in… a bitter taste of deja vu. He shakes his head and brushes away the snow on his shoulders, an exercise in pointlessness given the ongoing storm.

That just leaves…

The problematic set head further down his patrol path to the Lido. There are drips of black blood running parallel to the man's route along the easiest path, kept clear of snow by the berm walls and chance.

There's not much, but he has an eye for such things, a nose too. Source? He traces them back to a patch of blade grass whose tops are already heavy with the corn-like fruiting buds.

Someone had provided quite the feast for the edgy

plants, and they barely acknowledge his existence as he passes.

"What an idiot."

The gulls, hardened survivors and better scavengers than he, screech out their agreement from the streetlights that lead up to the main road out of town. He gets the feeling they're following him.

One of the gulls extends its wings and pecks away at a loose feather, before letting out a good loud warning yell.

"Yeah." He nods to his avian allies. "This is a potential shit sandwich, isn't it? Shall we go find out how big it is?"

The gull cocks its head at the mention of a sandwich, potentially large, and flaps off towards the Lido. Its knowledge of English is impressive as is its opportunism. The local seagulls have benefited from their willingness to eat just about anything and their ability to switch to a seafood diet at a pinch but this is something special even for the half-carnivorous giants.

He pulls the shotgun round to wince of pain from the back of his head, and picks out a couple of shells but is surprised to find it already loaded.

"Okay, let's take a big bite."

He follows the footsteps along the Promenade and hopes he won't have to use the damned gun. Though given the amount of gunfire going on across the sea, he doubts anyone would notice.

———-

12

That they're stalking through the snow

His hopes that the tracks would veer away from his store house at the last minute are forlorn. They head straight that way with brutal precision coupled with the spots of blood here and there, under which shoots of blade grass are already emerging.

He crushes them under the steel of his boots as he tracks the intruder's path to the Lido.

The Lido is a strange place, it always reminds him of an eastern-bloc workers retreat, the sort of place Soviet Man would have headed for a week or two of sun, sea and lectures on the nature of socialism to break the monotony of the meeting work quotas at the tractor factory. It has an uncomfortable combination of utilitarian design blended with out-of-place artistic flourishes, as if the designers couldn't stop kicking against the limitations of their budget and constraints of council planning permissions to sneak a set of Corinthian columns either side of the work-a-day main entrance into the blueprints, or adding a mosaic of crabs, dancing with coral men against a wall.

These flourishes do little but add confused purpose to

the overall pattern. The Lido consists of three flat roofed buildings in a 'U' shape, the open side seaward and a boating lake plopped down in the middle.

To add to the East German feel, there's even an atom-inspired sculpture set between the buildings and the cliffs on a plinth raising from the ice covered paths that he has to pass on the way. It's a detail that would have done Honecker proud. He supposes it was intended to celebrate atomic power before the concept became linked with power stations going pop and scattering radiation around themselves like the world's least festive Piñata.

The sculpture seems to have attracted the attention of his unwanted guest as the footsteps pause from their single minded pursuit of Lido attendance to veer towards the monument. He raises his eyebrows under his hood, trying to determine meaning.

The footsteps stop, dither, at the sculpture as if the intruder had taken a moment to read the inscription, some homily about the advance of humanity through struggle from memory, set in stone below the rusting metal frame orbits and take a breather before continuing onwards.

Waste of time.

"No one wastes time."

"Bar you."

Or maybe something there was something more. He runs his fingers over the metal and stone and stops when he gets to the base.

The inscription has been changed. He frowns as he traces the gap between the new plate screwed in place over the original and its predecessor.

"Don't get too attached to this place, there's change afoot."

Who'd waste the… never mind.

He walks the last stretch to the Lido over the frozen

boating lake. Plastic pedalos cracked in an icy grip along the edges mirroring the sea beyond in miniature. The complex with its playground and park benches, boating lake and dodgem cars, had never thrived. Even during the short boom in local tourism caused by the collapse of some of the cheaper foreign alternatives it had been gasping for air. The world before the Catastrophe had been an afternoon tea with the sun going down, and either heat or cold was going to come and end it, one way or another.

In those circumstances people clung to their homes. This was a place of wistful regret and scrabbled moments of happiness amidst confusion and change pressing in.

For all its kitsch, the Lido had been a blast from a happier past when things had made sense. It was also a lesson that things change and you either adapt or die.

He likes to think he's helping with that. Part of that utilitarian nature is a sturdy roof held up by those partially load bearing colonnades, which he has repurposed to store a little of the old world for future generations.

Early on in his career he'd set to work on the place. He'd blocked off the windows, set up a hidden entrance behind some loose boards and cleared the roof with a few practice heat-runes to stop it collapsing. After some issues with damp he'd even added a bit of scavenged guttering from the houses up the coast to give the meltwater somewhere to go.

Now it formed a hidden slip-slide that could catch the unwary a one way trip into the blackberry patch, or over the cliffs entirely.

The runes had been the work of a hard scrabble week with paint and a thimble of his own dark blood. Their faint glow is visible even from down here.

Might have been a bit too obvious, looking back on it. This fella seemed to have found the place easy enough.

"Can't change the past," he mutters in a gust of condensation.

He's insulted that the footsteps make their way from the monument to the front door. He'd left that padlocked and with a nasty surprise for any interlopers. It appears his efforts have gone to waste. The lock is carefully placed on a perspex table by one of those Corinthian columns and there is a trace of blood.

On the positive side he can see matching footprints leading out too.

Artillery rattles from across the sea, doppler-popping as the sound arrives after the shells explode.

"Bastard could have at least locked up," he mutters to the warlike accompaniment over the Channel. "What have you taken, something specific or a bit of pot-luck take your fancy?"

Whatever it was, the interloper had either found what they wanted, or given up. The outbound footprints lead off beside the ice run, back towards the treacherous steps down to the sea. There's even a collapsed section of the berm where his likely larcenous quarry had clearly slipped on the ice and ended up on his arse along with a good splash of blood.

He follows the trail up to the steps and then picks out his binoculars to follow them to termination. They head off in the direction of the broken freighter blocking the entrance to the new port. A ruined cathedral of metal and giant icicles tipping slowly down at the bow.

"Okay." He turns back to the Lido and the line of seagulls watching from the roof, drying their wings and watching, like little feathered muggers. "That's that. Time to check…"

"Optimism. That's that is never that."

The voice inside him sneers at the mere concept of things being easy. As if there's something wrong with hoping for the best rather than planning for the worst.

"Walk through that door without checking and you'll get a face full of shotgun pellets. Believe me. After all, you left a little surprise for visitors, even if it was half-witted and you don't know your visitor hasn't done the same. It's easier to die than you think. I'd like to see a little more before you take us over the edge."

Deep breathe, let it out, grip the shotgun and let the voice pull away as it always does.

Maybe it has a point? Something big moves overhead.

He checks the time. Hours before he needs to be ready for whatever's coming over the horizon and if the lens isn't there now, nothing he's going to do now is going to change that.

He backs away from the Lido to one of the ornate shelters that line the promenade beyond the slip, towards the end where the walkway finally terminates in a brick wall and a footpath off to a children's playground. Setting his pack down, he lays the hated weight of the shotgun across his lap and settles in to watch and wait as he listens to the pop-pop-pop of automatic weapons and mortars exploding.

Definitely passing by. It's a northwards drive and a fast one. That hopeless offensive the Radio mentioned. He wonders what they could be doing.

He sits dead still, eyes fixed and without blinking. The wind blows across his rags making the ends swirl. He's another ice mummy set forever into place by the darkness and blood red clouds.

An hour passes, that's as long as he's willing to wait, voice or no voice. There have been no signs of people, no signs of movement and the explosions of artillery and grumble of massed tracks are pushing closer and closer.

"No objections?"

Silence from within.

He feels a little silly going in through the hidden entrance when the front door's wide open, figuratively, but it's the way he's always done it and he's a creature of habit. Routine can be difficult to break when you rely on it to keep sane.

He'll sort out the front door on the way out along with any nasty little surprises left by his monument amending pal.

The hatch slaps back into place behind him. An extreme example of the cat-flap principle, hell on squeaky hinges.

The Lido is cold inside, not a huge surprise. Everything is cold now, but it isn't the same cold as outside. That cold is alive, it tears at him and everything around it with poisonous talons actively pushing death. Without protection you could freeze in an hour, and the very sea is clogging up with drift ice with every passing moment bringing closer its triumph in a great frozen unity.

This is the dead cold of disused buildings. The cold that gets into the fabric of the walls and covers everything with parthenogenetic black creeping mould. The sort of cold that crumbles plaster and makes the damp metal of the building's skeleton sweat red rust.

It waits and it is patient and it will kill you without fuss or triumph leaving you sitting in a tomb all alone forever.

He's not staying in this tomb. He just needs…

He sniffs the air for intruders. People stink, if his intruder had stayed any length of time, he will smell them.

No sweat, no smoke, no shit , no gassy hint of puffed-up gangrenous death from untreated wounds.

The blood on the path had been fresh. Day old at most. His visitor had come in, done his business and left.

Time to find out what he took. Find anything he left.

He chuckles. Hopefully not 'literally done his business'. The ghosts wouldn't stand for that.

He crouches, fumbling at the side of his belt before settling on the cold rubber of his torch. He unclips it, and flicks the switch, completing a cursory check of the rooms inside, not quite trusting his instincts or that finely honed sense of smell.

The clean white-blue beam of the torch beam feels like something from science fiction after the endless red of the outside, and the sigil haze of the Lamp beam, and he resolves to turn on the lights in the Shrine tonight when he gets in.

Too much red is bad for the soul.

Sharp etched shadows dance in jerking motion as the beam plays across the detritus of the former café, the tables bracketed to the floor, the upturned chairs in sad stacks, the decaying mounds of cardboard into which the kitchenware had been piled before the end, as if the owners had intended on coming back in happier times.

All clear.

He picks himself up, and scoots handily over the linoleum floor to the counter where he keeps the storeroom cupboard keys on a hook by the till, one of the old type with pop up numbers on a ribbon. Trying to keep track of all the locks at his various storerooms back at the Tower had proven awkward and he's accepted that you keep the keys nearest the place you need them rather than getting all the way here and finding you've picked up the wrong set when digging through the boxes of crap he keeps at the Shrine.

"Moment of truth."

He opens the door to the storeroom, torch raised.

Nothing moves.

He can see the dust on the floor is disturbed, the cobwebs across the door snapped. His spider friends will be busy repairing their snares tonight. Someone got a face full of spider webs when they made their unwelcome entrance.

"Sorry fellas," he apologises to the spiders. "None of us are very happy about this."

He runs inventory. He can remember every box he's hauled up here.

The only thing that's visibly missing is one of the big round tubs of instant coffee and a plastic container of creamer. He does a double take. Snorts in derision. Really? That's what they took? All they had to do was ask and he'd have handed the stuff over. He's got enough instant coffee to last a dozen apocalypses and he's always been more of a tea person anyway.

No. Wait. Is there something new?

And there we are. Over in the corner, exactly where he'd expect it, a cardboard box, one with a handwritten note stating the contents to be:

"Lenses (special edition, drowning lamps only), for use at the Thanet egress. Did you read the plaque?"

He strides across with a huge grin on his face. The cardboard is dry to the touch and inside, carefully wrapped in greaseproof paper and bubblewrap, are four lenses of exactly the type he needs.

What a surprise. They're not even trying.

Really, he had nothing to worry about. Difficult to keep track of everything. Why did he forget about this?

No matter.

He takes one, slides it into a carry bag and picks up a couple of car batteries, some fuses and a plug adaptor or two to save having to collect anything for a while if he's going to run the lights at the Tower for a bit. No more unexpected detours no more fucked-up days he can't remember. Head back in the game.

No more screaming goats. Definitely no more of those. And the sirens can fuck right off along with those dead office wankers.

He locks up the supply room with a spring in his step and heads out front. He resets the lock and piles up a little trash to discourage any more visitors. Then he does the same for the back, smashing nails back in with iron-hard fists to reattach the boards. Stepping back, he admires his literal handiwork.

Efficiently secured.

It takes him a moment to notice that the weather has cleared whilst he's been inside. Maybe all that cloud-work going on over the Channel will warm things up for a while?

He leaves.

The tracks from earlier are gone and the sun has a hint of warmth to it as he makes his way back home with his treasures swinging at his back. He tips his hat to the corpse pile next to the Bimmer and the backpack couple at the roundabout, makes his way down the confines of Flint Lane to the Tower. The hammer of war and the warmth in his heart adding impetus to his step.

Wouldn't want to be late to the party now.

13

What is it they want?

Home sweet home. Through the broken teeth of the graveyard where age and erosion obscure the epitaphs of the formerly great and good, back into the shrine.

A gust of warm air welcomes him back to the best place in town.

That thick stone build, flint and concrete, and the heat runes he learnt from the Radio, keep it toasty to the core, for all the discomfort of the Tower level with its enforced freezer dynamics. The glow from the runes is warm too, waves of burnt sienna, though always associated with the smell of brimstone, shifting the Shrine's ambience from Christmas at a department store to borderlands of hell given the religious iconography that lines the walls.

The King stares down in the final panel of the Triptych at his inevitable route from his royal state, for all are worms in the inferno.

Still, there's something really comforting in setting up shop in a holy place when the skies are filled with monsters and magic appears to have turned from the subject of novels and old wive's tales to something that could bite you on the ass anytime you drop your guard.

After twisting the locks in place with a snap, snap and slotting across the DIY bolts, he rolls a pallet of heavy wooden crates across the door to the graveyard and grins. They are filled with a variety of junk he's scavenged, and which he suspects he may have a use for at some point. More importantly they're heavy.

It's a bit of a compulsion, this impulse to collect. The ruins of the early 21st century have so much you can pretend might prove useful one day that no matter how much storage you may have, it's always going to run low. After all, there was a point to these items back in the past and if you want that back some day, well. Why risk losing something you'll need?

The Radio encourages it. Future proofing, it calls it.

His fingers sting at the change of temperature, from the freeze of outside to the warm embrace of the Shrine's lower levels. He gingerly pulls off his fingerless gloves and rubs the cold from his hands with a little motor oil, mixed with chili powder, then unwraps himself from his various layers, coats, jackets, jumpers and scarves.

He stands opposite a mirror, in a pair of grubby black khakis and a grey polo neck and peers blankly at the grey smear in the dirty glass checking for stray cloud fall .

Finally, he cleans the shotgun with an oiled rag and slots it back in its box by the door giving it a wry look. "Hope I won't be seeing you for a while."

His kingdom is a mess, cramped and shadowy, littered with boxes in six vaguely arranged piles and in the corner is the battery stack that powers the electrical lights, currently empty with a pile of discards scattered around below it. He's promised himself a break from the red, and he'll take that break.

After a little fight with the serial leads he flicks on the lights and lets out a breath.

"Lovely."

Over to the little nursery of plants he's raising in a trough from seeds scavenged from a garden centre. He absent-mindedly waters the little fellas and adds a dash of plant food to the grow pots flicking on the UV lamps he's set up after a check on the batteries here. The plants come first when it comes to electricity, one day that dust will be down and the sun will be back and something will need to compete with those bastard blood sucking horrors.

The sight of old-world, non-carnivorous plants in all their green and immobile glory adds to his feelings of joy. A little of the old world saved and the tomatoes are fattening up nicely so that's beginnings of a salad some day.

A crackle from upstairs.

His eyes stray back to the backpack containing the lens and thinks on the battle raging across the water.

Best to get that sorted now, the company would be nice.

He collects the bag, a selection of watching snacks and a little light reading from Magazine corner. A ragbag collection of journals he picked up from the thrift shop. He's made a point of trying to read them in the order they're stacked as variety is the spice of life and acid-pulp paper decays like you would not believe in the cold.

He looks at the title of the top-most magazine. "Modern Bride. January 2031 edition." Heaps of mobile taffeta, barely mobile. That had been a strange time.

You did get the occasional dud. He flips to the magazine behind. A 2028 edition of Bitcoin Entrepreneur from the 'real person' collection phase. Another grunt. Definitely something for another day.

Behind that a copy of May 2032's Military Review, with the title 'Who are the Benefactors?' and articles on the rapid build up of armaments following the Taiwan Straits conflict with its smorgasbord of sunken Carriers.

"Well, we know who they are now." He takes that one with him.

He switches into his upstairs clothes with a little regret. The tattoos that run along his arms itch when he's fully togged up without the cloth-wind bindings, but the cold up there will be murderous tonight without the opportunity to walk it off.

He ducks the grenade bouquet that guards the entrance to the second floor. Another little bit of scavenging luck. He'd found the explosives on a dead soldier down by the cliffs. The man had clearly toppled over the edge at some point prior and landed on his head, based on the absence of rat and seagull action. There had been a couple of crows, they were the quickest…

Poor bloke had been wearing Russian looking camouflage, blotchy brown and green like you saw in the brushfire wars over in the East before the big event. Would have stood out like a sore thumb on the modern battlefield, he could remember that the UK's troops had switched right after…

Maybe the army had run out of the good stuff and were running down stocks of what they had. And that had been months back when the Russians had been fighting their way across Poland and the Vamps were discovering that they'd spent a lot of money on weapons that weren't going to work in a world of clouds and cold.

Up flips the last trap door and he pulls himself into the chill of the tower and the faint tang of spilt chicken broth once more. The Lamp looks forlorn, head down and blind.

"Don't worry lad, got a nice new one for you. Be right as rain soon as."

He carefully slides out the jagged remnants of the old lens still held in their copper brackets and slots the new element in place with a click.

"See how that went."

"It'll work. It would be a special day for even those idiots on the Radio if they messed up something as simple as a lens."

He pulls up the windows and watches the flashes on the horizon as the war between Vampires and Russians continues into the greedy, bitter night. They seen a bit north of where they'd been that morning.

"A new challenger arises," he chuckles as he pats the Lamp then taps in the activation patterns. There's a moment of horror as it remains inert, but then it flickers on and shivers into life, awaiting instructions.

It seems happy.

14

No one really knows

Things are going well.

He lets the Lamp find its footing after the trauma of the past two days, try out its new eyes. It takes the opportunity to throw beams across the sea in a cascade of sigil-tinged light, chasing icebergs drifting south and sizing up wrecks. Whilst it flexes he eats a little dinner, noodles, jerky and a meal in a can that might once have been beans and sausages. He'd left it on the rune cooker a little too long so its individual constituents were dubious, reduced to a paste of grey nothing.

The blandness of the food drives him to other pursuits and a hunger to understand what is happening in the war from a point of view other than his friends in the Union.

He works the ratchet on his back-up clockwork radio. A cheap plastic thing with a lever to power the battery and a tinny speaker. If he tunes it just right using the clumsy twist knob, he can pick up a digital bleed from the comms across the Channel.

He remembers the day he found it, sat forlorn on a supermarket shelf on the remaindered aisle. That had been back when the transmissions from the Family had been news reports in French emoted by cheerful young vampires explaining the new rules and how they would be 'stepping in for a while to help out the Continentals until the sun came back but not to worry as the Family was humanity's friend'.

That and light jazz. Vampires were coo-coo for light jazz.

Those had disappeared around the same time the Union's own broadcasts had begun and the cheerful Vamps with their bad French had been replaced by local transmitters begging for help, seeking lost relatives, confirming deaths, until the screaming had blotted them out.

Now it was military traffic, everyday and all the time, high powered and in plain to burn through that never ending screaming.

He spoons up the last of the mulch and tries to catch a human voice or two. With the battles going on directly across the water he hopes he'll be able to get a fair picture of what's what. He might not be able to understand much Eastern Slavic, and Vampire battle cant has had some changes since he last…

You could get a lot from voice pitch and the tone.

Sure enough, the frequencies are crowded with activity popping and farting through the cheap speaker. Tonight's messages are all about unexpected advances and hideous magical death.

"The Vamps are really pushing," he comments to the Lamp which is too busy chasing shadows to pay attention.

Sometimes he wishes he had a little human company.

Night draws in, and tonight is hotting up. Figuratively.

He doesn't know why the Vampires always make the

Channel run at night. The sad ghost of the sun that pulls itself wearily up every morning to glow weakly above the clouds seems to cause them minimal difficulty. Even if it did, most of the boats they use for their Channel scurries have decks under which they could lurk whilst their thralls direct them to their destinations.

The worst any sun-sensitive blood drinker risked was a splinter or two from badly made deck sheeting or the humiliation of smelling faintly of fish.

The Radio had confirmed that the older ones didn't care a jot for the sun, only the concentrated light from the Lamp, but that they had an antagonistic relationship with flowing water which explained precisely nothing about the night-runs even if it were true. The Radio did seem to know a lot about Vampires and had been known to drift off to more esoteric matters with an air of knowledge clearly lacking around its explanations of the new plant life for example.

Yet as with much that it offered up, what it said was strangely uninformative. It was if whosoever was in charge of the broadcasts was unable to break from a lifetime of keeping things to themselves.

"About tonight's broadcast, Carruthers. Any chance we could cut back on the need to know? You're aware this information is highly classified and it's not like he's the only thing guarding the Channel from a Vampire invasion. There are tolerance levels I am happy to live with. And I stress, tolerance. Basics only or we'll need to have a conversation."

"Sure thing Mr. Brooker."

How do you even get into an antagonistic relationship with water? And what would happen if the Channel froze?

Ice skating Vampires, glissading across the sea in battalions.

Whatever the truth, the Vamps and their followers

always set sail and fought during the darkest hours. For all the spooky stuff he suspects the real reasons are far more mundane. Avoiding the Easterners with their low flying missiles or the occasional hunter-killer craft or drone swarm that ruled the thin layer where human-directed flight was still possible without being swatted by the monsters above.

That made for a duality to the war on the Continent. During the day the Russians pushed forward, during the night they hunkered down and waited for what passed for dawn while the Vamps crept forward to eat them in their trenches.

The glow of the sun drips its last beams behind the tower and the shadow of the Watcher's adopted home reaches out across the graveyard where ghostly grey figures huddle in the cold.

The shadow pushes out, down the red-stained cliffs, across the beaches and out to restless sea, somewhat like an accusing finger pointed at the sinners of the Continent or a knife tip ready to stab at approaching enemies. Either side of it the orange-glow that burns all it touches provides framing to the purpose of the Watcher and his Lamp.

On the opposing shore Family soldiers consolidate their gains amongst the wreckage of Russian tanks and soldiers, and set up defensive positions to hold their enemies back long enough to complete their mission.

He checks his watch. Quarter to seven. Nearly Radio time. Instructions for the night. The gabble of fighting words emitting from the wind-up radio has a feverish intensity to it. Something important is happening and the word 'Magisterin' keeps cropping up in the Eastern broadcasts.

He gets the feeling that's not a good thing but he's got about as much as he's going to get from the gabbling and he turns the wind-up off for the main event.

The clock ticks to seven and the Lamp ceases its roaming and quietens. It knows what comes next.

The LED on the Radio (the real one) flashes on, in the usual barrage of gibberish symbols and hissing background noises drawn from the past. Today's background seems to have been taken from the final broadcasts of the BBC.

Music of dead bands, out of sequence lines from theatrical productions, a hint of the theme tune of an old farming drama. A surprisingly complete report dating back to the earliest days of the Catastrophe when the old Government's evacuation planes disappearing over Ireland.

(Hadn't that been a nasty surprise?)

"...Initial reports from observers indicate that it is not just the evacuation planes which have disappeared. Ireland is gone. Reports from amateur drone operators indicating that it is as if the entire island has been scooped up by a giant hand."

"Attempts to contact Belfast and Dublin via regular and 'technical' channels have proven ineffective, with Government officials providing no assistance or theories other than to suggest that 'atmospheric conditions may be to blame'... indicate... that they expect to be able to re-establish... within the week... bullshit"

"How this addresses the disappearance... For those with relatives..."

A pop and the report fades, replaced by the calmly insane voice of the Radio.

It's oddly formal today.

"Ladies and gentlemen of the former United Kingdom, this is your emergency broadcast system transmitting on short wave frequencies from Union Headquarters currently situated in the vicinity of Newcastle on the Tyne.

We trust **you have had a productive day** and send you **greetings**."

"Productive day." That makes him smile. "Could say that."

"This is the News, at Seven. Greetings."

He frowns. There is something even more 'off' than usual about the way the presenter is speaking. The words are too clipped, syllables cut short as if by a guillotine. Time's up for that one, move to the next and the next and the next. Someone forcing out the words in blurts as if every expression is an effort, or using a program to counterfeit a the real thing.

"What you thinking Lampy?"

The Lamp remains silent, sometimes he thinks it likes the Radio more than him.

"Reliable sources on the Continent inform us. The Eastern army approaches Paris from the Rhine. With rapidity and optimal single-mindedness. As our listeners will be aware. Paris is the de jure capital of the Vampire Families. A hive of monstrous insects eating away at the heart of Europe."

"Although we do not entirely approve of their ongoing ingress. Into the territorial boundaries of the former European Union. We believe. This Russian. Eastern Alliance. Activity. Can be the subject of general agreement. It is indisputably in every true man's veritable interests. To excise the vampire canker. From the heart of the Continent. By whatever means necessary. And no matter the short term cost. In human lives."

"We therefore offer our fraternal best wishes. To the sadly deceased Marshal Alexei. And his decimated legions. In their advance. We warn them not to expect this battle to be easy. And note the Family. Has plans to the North."

"In cognate news for those gentlemen. Of good cheer.

Our sojourners along the southeast coast. We would remind you. **Be alert.** As to the **risk of refugees.** Using the seaways to escape. Their tragic fate. A short-lived offensive. By units of the Family's collaborationist army. From the Family's last redoubts. Around Paris. To certain of the Channel ports. Making effective use of our friend's concentration to the North and East. And abominable sorcery.

To push an armoured column out towards the Ports."

Ports. Right. That's an instruction. He pushes the Lamp over to the optimal position to catch anything coming from the North.

"...and it seems highly likely. Despite their dolorous outward appearance. Any such groups of foreign citizens. Making use of this breakthrough. Will include among them a far more dangerous strain. Which could incorporate the menace of the Masters of the blood sucking kin. **Remain vigilant**."

"They are dangerous. We will not have them infest our green and pleasant land. Their filth is being cleansed from the Continent. We do not wish to suffer the fate of the former nations of the Orient."

"Back into the depths they must go."

"If you observe any boats wending their way here; voyagers on the wine dark sea; where possible plunge their bodies deep; into the eternal saline moat that guards our land; let them freeze in the dark and the deep. **Better that a thousand die than that one vampire escapes their fate**."

"The Union will understand. The Union will applaud. We are here for you. We know **you are there for us**."

He takes a moment to digest. It's not that he doesn't understand why he does what he does, but put so bluntly it leaves an unpleasant taste in his mouth. A traitor voice whispers to him, asking if there were any alternative to what he is doing, would he take it? If you could save the humans and keep the Vampires at bay?

If. If wishes were fishes then we'd all eat chips.

Best not to think about it. No one's coming out of this one clean. He'll have to settle for 'alive' and get on with what needs doing.

The whispering fades away, seeming to ebb like a tide towards the lights on the opposite shore and the voice on the Radio acquires something of its old fluency.

"Closer to home we remind our compatriots that they should take care when approached by **strangers**. Although our plans **are** successful across. The majority of these fallen lands, and we have registered **a** two and a half degree increase in temperatures across Union territories though the operation of. Our new Union Science, there have been some unforeseen complications. Although we are moving to address these failings with some speed, there is still **residual risk** that people are not **truly** people, but instead **murderous simulacra**."

"Where possible dead bodies should be **destroy**ed and covered or buried to reduce risks of bo**th** infection spr**e**ading in this ti**m**e of plague, and unnecessary infractions against the laws of nature."

"Infractions." That Radio really needed to take some time to digest that thesaurus it had eaten. Murderous Simulacra? Plain English seems to have died in the cold along with most of the world's population.

"Friends on the outside can rest assured that the relevant officials guilty of. The egregious dereliction of duty that has led; to these unfortunate incidents have been most severely. Chastised."

The Lamp seems eager to start the nights work and has lost interest in the nonsense the Radio is spouting. It likes the new lens and dislikes words. He can feel the gratitude flowing from it. It reminds him of a loyal old hound. It's almost like having someone around.

The Radio concludes. "That is the end of tonight's broadcasts. Additional calibration methods will be implemented to address the earlier technical difficulties. *Do your job, D, we're sending help, couple of issues to sort here first.*"

"Ready to get to work mate?" He asks the Lamp.

The arc light stabs out, full power, blinding and focussed and beautiful. Electric blue and hissing with rune power, casting harsh shadows all around. He feels a sense of elation as it begins its elegant quadrant searches all sense of doubt removed.

"Beautiful."

He settles back into his chair to watch and make any adjustments required to his boon companion's workload. He's done a good job today. He could probably make another lamp at this point, wouldn't need the help of...

Who had helped him in the first place? He frowns. Time slips.

15

Change will be here soon

Deliveries

A van pulls itself to a halt on the road outside the tower, a delivery vehicle pushed along by a noisy old diesel engine with the original operator painted out in military green but still visible through the thin paint. A line of nonsense is scratched along its bumpers that pulse with scarlet light that matches the sky above and melts the snow as the van pulls up in a hiss of steam.

The army's gone, along with the last of the Organization. The Town is empty, except for him and whoever it is in the van. The leavings of their visit remain. The two bodies by the roundabout at the top of the road are already covered by a layer of ash snow.

The man's green backpack sticks out like a hillock from an ice rink. He had mattered to someone, and recently. Who had that been?

He feels bereft, his mind overfilled with junk, without function as he stands in the cold, in familiar but forgotten grey coveralls and a greatcoat without insignia. He remembers having a function relating to the ribbons and bars, but then there had been a searing pain that felt like a hail of red-hot stones against his face. A rumble in his chest he couldn't shake. Icy cold creeping up his arms as infection spread and an older man with bad teeth looking down at him with a mix of compassion and contempt.

Awful.

A hefty gent in grey coveralls and an Ushanka with a Union Jack pin and a goat's head overlay on the front, steps out of the van's cabin. Two more similar sorts lower themselves gingerly from the back and look at him with caprine indifference. Each of them has a cross belt with a pistol and a torch hanging from it.

He looks down, he has the belt but no pistol, no torch.

And there's another figure up in the Tower. Watching him. He can feel its stare. It is not a good feeling.

"Well well well Mr. D., looks like you've had quite the knock and no mistake. Seen yourself in the mirror lately?" He has a face like a bull. Little eyes, large nose, flat teeth and meaty with it, there's an undercurrent of pensiveness to the man's voice as if he's not as sure of himself as he seems and his two companions are hanging back, hands near those pistols. "Bit of a mess my old mate."

"Do I know you?"

"Don't think so my old china, you were a bit above my grade before the accident. The top brass have a bit of gear for you though. Makes things all better."

"Why are you talking like that?"

"That's rude, didn't your mother teach you no manners? And me with this lovely lamp for you." His two companions amble to the back to the van and pull out a large box. They gently lower it to the ground, stepping away sharply, as if it were either a present for the world's most difficult to please billionaire or a phial of something nasty and gene spliced ready to multiply in the veins of unsuspecting idiots and they want as little to do with it as possible.

Or it could be both. Billionaires could be funny like that.

"Yeah. This is a pretty nice little Lamp. You're going to love it, gonna set you up in that Tower..."

A lamp? He looks behind him at the tower. "Looks heavy, don't think I can get it all the way up there by myself."

"It is heavy, my son. That's why I've got these eager lads here who'll set it up for you." The other two men mutter mutinously.

"Oi. Quit it. You fancy staying here? You heard about the lensing."

"Didn't rightly follow that."

"You get to join the funny division with this messed-up wreck if you stay here. Capisce?"

"Right. Yeah. Don't want that."

He is about to ask if they know about the gaunt figure staring down at him from the top of the Tower but decides against it. He doesn't want to appear insane.

The bull-man turns back to face him. "You know what you've got to do, don't you Mr. D.?"

"Who's that?" It's familiar in the same way as a lot of the junk floating around his brain at the moment. He likes yachts. He hates long shifts. He loves his family though he's not married. He needs to get information to Paris, or stop it. One or the other or neither.

The bull snorts. "Right. Yeah. You do 'you'. Lads if you wouldn't mind, I think our friend would like the lamp up in that bloody great tower and I would like to be the fuck away from here, pronto. Those military buggers aren't going to hang around."

A final whine of protest. "Can't he heft it himself, it's fucking heavy and he's plenty strong enough to…"

"I'm not speaking English here, Mikey? You do as you're told and then we get to go home or you could keep flapping your gums and stay. Your choice, mate."

The other one, not Mikey tilts a head at him. "What about him?"

"He's got the lamp. He'll do fine. Seriously, shift it, you want two heads? This bloke is going to guard the Channel for us so he's doing us a solid."

"Thoughtful of him."

"Yeah. Guess so." Then a snort. "Oh. Mr. D. Nearly forgot,

Thesp wanted you to have this. Thought it could turn out useful. Or maybe he was just being a shit. You know him."

The bull hands him a shotgun and a box of shells. "Have fun."

He hates shotguns, he finds this one positively malignant.

"Chop, chop lads."

His back aches, and he's got a lot to do if he's going to make this place homely in time for his first shift. The men pick up the lamp and pick their way past the lions guarding the door as if the things could bite. After a little load shifting the box is up the stairs and they are back in the vehicle. Bull man joins them slipping back into the driving seat with a relieved sigh.

He knocks on the window. Bull man lowers the window and pulls a face.

"Ah, will you be coming back?

"Shouldn't think so. Got a few of these places to set up though none with quite as illustrious a janitor. Brooker's a fucking wanker when it comes to work assignments."

Another familiar name, and a muttered, "Fucking slave driver," from the back of the van.

"Shut it, Steve. Fucker's probably listening." The man gives the car radio a meaningful stare.

The words come out without conscious thought pushing past everything he is like a hot knife through butter. "Brooker? Officious idiot. Plans with layers in layers without the will to do what's necessary."

They stare at him, 'Steve' shifting back in his seat as if he's some poisonous snake flaring upwards unbidden from a box.

A beat, whatever it was pulls back and hides in the recesses of his mind.

"Who's Brooker?"

Bull man laughs heartily, and the tension disappears. "That's our lad. All ready, lads?" Mikey and the other one bang the side of the van and Bull man waves. "See you in the funny pages, D."

The van pulls away, low gear, creeping and swerving across the half-cleared snow and he's left on the side with a rattle and a cough. Time to do whatever it is he does now.

The figure in the Tower watches them go and when he looks up to see what it is doing, it teeters for a moment before leaping down at him, it's doing something that might be called smiling if you didn't know what a real smile looked like.

He raises his arms but his last memory is the thing crashing wordlessly through him. All spider legs and staring eyes with its face peppered with bloody holes.

16

And our Watcher has to go

He's feeling sharp tonight. His mind is a razor. He scans the narrow seas, following the track of the light sliding across the wave tops.

The Lamp's beam covers the dark horizon in figures of eight eager for the promised by the Radio. They're a team, cats ready to pounce on a hapless rodent, injured bird.

He watches for the tell-tale disturbed water trails of a ship's wake or the glint of the metalwork on deck. The snow may as well not be there.

Every so often, he lets the Lamp rest for a minute or two in an attempt to lure out potential targets who might be thinking of running but who see the beam combing the Channel and are discouraged. He likes to think of it like fly fishing until he remembers the buzzing from the clouds.

Five, ten minutes off and then back on, full power. Go get 'em boy.

A boat's not going to get far in that time, and it gives him a chance to rest his eyes.

Eyes closed, he can hear muttering from the continent. Blood suckers planning to hop the Channel and continue their reign of terror, lackeys bleating in the darkness. Plotting some treachery against humanity on behalf of their deathly masters.

There are real people here too even if you don't like us. And we're not all that bad... Maybe if we met...

Shouldn't he be thinking about what he's doing. Those are humans drowning in then brine...

He feels a moment of disconnection, a record jumping its track. He can see a pale hand with long delicate fingers delicately snapping him to the wrong place, and the wrong time.

His fingers burn, pins and needles play across the joints and up his arms.

Someone's trying to distract you.

That's ominous.

Focus. Work to do. He's protecting his country, the Union *(is that a Country? None of us have heard of it)*, against the Vampire threat *(Come, come, we've no interest in your little island)*. Maybe a little against the Russian threat too. Marshal Alexei's men and women might be avenging their homeland *(they attacked us first, we wanted detente)* but he gets the feeling that for all its warm words, the Union would rather they did their avenging on their side of the Channel *(keep it away from them, just like they're doing with you)* and didn't get any funny ideas about what is on the other side.

What is on the other side? Your friends seem to like to hide...

With the death counts, there will going to be plenty of land to go round on the Continent soon as this nightmare is over *(so why would we want to hurt you humans?)*. Labour will be what's needed and it's looking a bit sparse Kent ways right now *(and who did that?)*. The Easterners didn't know that...

Maybe you should...

He pushes down the whisper insinuating itself across

his mind. The voice helps him push it back, helping for a change.

It never has liked Vampires.

The Lamp catches a little as it swings with, a plaintive whine. He pulls himself up and oils a joint. The Lamp seems to sniff something out, the beam focussing on a momentary shimmer in the water just where he'd expect a boat to be coming from, cutting power to disguise its intent so that the light is a ghostly shadow shifting across the wave tops.

"Good boy!"

He picks up his binoculars, letting the Lamp do its thing. Definitely something there. The beam hovers in place, the halo of light barely visible in the snow storm that whistles across the Channel.

He zooms in close with his binoculars, eyes cutting through the interference like gimlets.

"What do we have here, boy?"

A large fishing boat, hundred-footer at least, crawling out from the breakwater of a port along the Belgian coast. He draws an imaginary line between the signs of fighting earlier and his estimate of the ports which the Vamps may have recaptured with a little leeway for safety.

"Yep."

Vampire spearhead could easily have made it there, for all the ground-hugging Easterner rockets. He looks further North and notes that the bursts of flame and fire from the night's fighting are directed outwards rather than inwards as earlier. Defending the port to get someone out?

The boat is moving slow, crawling across the sea, engine at minimum power, the crew obviously nervous, the course twitchy. They could be worried about attracting the attention of the Russians or they might know that someone is watching them.

"Tricksy."

There's a couple of men on the bridge, no one else visible. Military types in grey-green. They seem jumpier than the boat, uncomfortable in the snowstorm.

He whistles slowly.

"Something odd about this one, lad. Let's give it a bit of a head. Remember the fly fishing?"

The Lamp's beam cuts away from potential target. His attention doesn't waver.

God of the Baptists but it's moving slow. Patience is a virtue.

Thirty minutes in and the Lamp is getting irritable. Broad beaming across the cliffs opposite. Daring something to come out and challenge it and hinting at its interest in the target he's following with occasional darts back to the wallowing target, nibbling at it.

It's getting to him too. He's always known he's not overburdened with virtue.

The bloody thing is acting like it's on an honest to Gods' *fishing trip*. Sliding up North then turning on a dime to chug a mile or two south back to the waters outside the port. Keeping good distance from the orange barriers and never getting anywhere.

Clumsy as hell too. It's barely avoided a couple of ice floes.

Fishing. That might be it. Food's scarce and there's still fish in the sea. *Can't blame a man for trying to get a meal?* Whispers.

Ridiculous. He needs some clarity.

"Hey, lad. You okay to have a quick jab at the stupid old ship? We need to give it a scare at least. Kick it back to port?"

The Lamp shivers its assent, and the beam brightens, moving in a bee-line towards the boat, not as fast as it could go, the Lamp is emitting menace. The boss wants to scare it, it'll scare it.

"That's got some attention."

There's a flicker from shore. A searchlight flashing out what looks like morse code directed at the target. Its engines rumble into life, echoing off the cliffs, the screws frothing up the sea behind it and shaking loose the settling snow from its masts.

It runs for port.

The Lamp's chase instincts engage. The beam brightens once more, clutching at its target with magical power, though a lot less than it could be using. It's showing restraint, it knows what he wants even if it's having difficulty suppressing its mechanical enthusiasm.

The stronger beam clips the vessel and something strange happens. Red flames erupt from the vessel's hull at the beam's faintest touch. Ethereal and hissing. He takes a step back, surprised and concerned, what if it's a lens buster like the damned dead things from the tunnel?

"Careful lad, no… wait."

No, they're not actual flames, the hull is undamaged, the crew standing tall and no wave incoming.

"It's a shield." A lift of the eyebrows. Surprise. "Well that's new."

He peers at the boat's hull through the snowfall and shadows. Sure enough, he can see lines of complex arcane symbols scratched into the hull that light up with power as the beam plays across them. He can't read them, they're not cloud sigils, though there is a hint of understanding from the thing at the back of his head. A hint of admiration, like a connoisseur enjoying the aroma of a fine wine.

Impressive in a childish way.

Whatever they are, the crew does not cease from their high speed skedaddle into port and the Lamp's motors growl at the realisation.

"Sneaky bastards. They're *fishing* all right. They're trying out protections for a proper attack."

Why not let it go, it's not hurting anyone.

He checks the power level on the Lamp's output. Ten-percent of the maximum. As he does there's a flash from the shore further south and he jumps at a sonic boom that rattles across the tower. A missile slams into the boat, a blur launched from the Russian positions up the coast, the stern disintegrating in a burst of real flames and sharp wood splinters.

The wreck slides sideways, the engines driving the splintered hull in unexpected directions, and slams the wreck into the Port's breakwater. The crew jump into the icy water, and he leaves them to their fate.

Nothing doing he…

Shut up.

A test. Something big is coming.

Not tonight though. The explosion seems to have woken the Easterners up from their torpor and fighting flares up along the coast in a hail of tracer and drone swarms rising like fireflies from the opposing forces. The clouds surge above them and the lights of the Port are bright as the Vampires move to rescue their crew.

Everyone seems to be busy tonight.

"Keep an eye out, lad. Things are about to get interesting."

The Lamp growls out its irritation at having to wait once again and he consoles it by oiling the runners and letting it do whatever it wants.

It spends the rest of the night chasing random objects,

working out its frustration through beam-based aggression. That includes an attack on an unfortunate line of birds from the continent disturbed by the fighting. White wings flare bright in the glare as the Lamp pursues them across the waters, driving them towards their doom.

It eventually corners them, pushing them into the orange glow outside of Dover and they disappear in puffs of ash.

He dozes, catching some sleep while he can. His focus is slipping and he can feel the long nights begin to catch him up.

Rest.

17

...

He's awoken that morning by seagulls squawking and scrabbling over the roof of the Tower.

They're angry and they've been busy.

Their rage has manifested in an attempt to defeat their light-emitting opponent, the cause of multiple avian fatalities, by shitting all over the Tower's windows. Strings of gloopy bird shit drip down the glass falling in globs along the flint-walls down to the cemetery as he gingerly taps the glass.

He groans. Seagull shit is sticky and he's going to spend hours clearing it. Plus there's the practicalities of the thing. Dragging out the ladder, cleaning supplies from wherever he's got them stored.

"Damn it!"

And this was a serious attack in bird terms. They must have been shitting for hours to create this level of sticky repulsive, dripping, vaguely nitrogenous screen.

The Lamp looks glum. It has limited traverse up close and would have been helpless against the avian assault.

Oh well.

He switches on his wind-up radio. Usual gabble of orders. With daybreak the fighting across the Channel seems to have turned in the Russian's favour. There's a professional curtness to the orders he can hear, whilst the few gabbles of battle cant from the Vampire side tend to cut off suddenly in static or have an edge of hysteria you only get when the speaker can feel things falling apart. The dam's leaking and the leak's getting bigger…

Unless the Vampires get a move on the Russians are going to be in the ports before they've launched whatever escape plan they're working on.

Interesting that they're working on a shield against the Lamp. Doubly interesting that they might think they've succeeded in creating one.

He starts the day as he means to go on by settling the Lamp back in place and cleaning the windows. Sometimes the sheer variety of stuff he's accumulated comes in useful. A scrabble through boxes downstairs, heavy duty glass cleaner first smears and then clears the gull's revenge and subject to a second attack he's ready for the evening's hunt by lunchtime.

Not even seagulls would be that petty. The crows? Maybe. They've gone inland though. Something interesting up north that's attracted their attention.

He closes-up the now thoroughly sanitised windows and drops down through the trap doors to the shrine to change his sodden and icy outer layer of rags.

His eyes wander to the kitchen and then bounce off, hard. His appetite is gone after the morning's work. Seagull shit has a smell and a texture that makes porridge, his go to breakfast, sound just terrible.

Weekend's off to a bad start.

Schedule says that Saturday is a sweep day. A brisk trot

along the old residential roads that loop their way around the Town in a hopeless attempt to avoid reaching the cliffs and the end of the line. It's good exercise and he decides to work up an appetite and forget the morning's cleaning by taking it at a jog.

A good long run would do you the world of good, friend. Get out all that nervous energy. You'll feel better for it.

He's feeling devil-may-care today. The world feels like it's opening up a little, the end of the war on the Continent seems near and tonight he's sure something big will be coming. He checks the atlas hidden in his pile of novels and confirms that the port from which the fishing boat had come had been a base for some smaller units of the French national navy. He's beginning to understand what the Vamps are up to.

Patrol boats, long range. Perfect escape vessels if you had a bit of fuel and armed too. Dangerous too. They could be sallying forth with malice aforethought, and the only thing between them and the coast of the Union was him and his faithful and fully operational Lamp.

The responsibility would usually weigh on him like a lead coat. Today he feels like this is a chance to give it his best shot. Show what he can do.

What is up with you? The Vamps aren't stupid. Don't underestimate them. They'll use everything they have to make sure one of them escapes and that includes operation at a distance. You need to concentrate, fool.

Don't let that old stick in the mud run you down, things are looking up!

The only thing wrong with today was the endless back and forth between the spectral voices. It's much worse than usual and some of the usual participants aren't involved. He finds it easiest if he tries to ignore all of them and gets on with something physical.

"Or don't. It doesn't matter to me."

See? Let's have some fun!

He begins his patrol with a spring in his step, locking up the Tower and fantasising about leaving the place for good.

He heads down Flint lane towards the town centre. What there is of it.

The small terrace homes down this way are in poor repair, flat roofs collapsed under the snow, barely recognisable as dwellings, and the cars outside are mostly burnt out heaps of snow. The fire spread from a petrol station whose only identifying feature is that it is a large hole in the ground with a bent sign at the level of a third-story window declaring that battery charging spots are available.

Pre-booking necessary though. Visit our website.

The town centre had been a zone of boarded-up shops, rusty seating proximately situated to overflowing bins and a general malaise of absolute decay, even before the big C had hit. The whole retains elements of its original layout, even in the post-apocalypse. A letter C cut out around the harbour with its harvest of cracked hulls and wonky masts poking out above the snow banks.

He takes a breather at the main bus stop, sheltering from the weather and watching the snow settle on the ruins of a marina-side bar. The place feels even more bereft of life than usual and he wonders why he's stayed here so long.

Isn't there more to life than sinking ships?

He walks up past the supermarket that marks the point where the town centre turns back to wasteland and housing.There had been quite the melee around that place for the brief period between the the security guards disappearing and the last of the loot joining them.

Hadn't there? He remembers something along those

lines. Getting some supplies for the ladies and gents at the home…

Up along the crest of the hill that looms over the entrance to the tourist tunnels. Now closed for good, and their makeshift caprine guardian smashed. He wonders for a moment who had put the head there, and what purpose it had served other than to give him a royal headache. Then a moment to wonder again about who the hell had been living and dying there.

Good question! You should find someone to ask.

Then up past the rows of grand three-and-four-story town houses with names like 'Dundrinkin' and 'Salamanca' glowering down in patrician disgust at their derelict modern counterparts. With their heavy-built, peaked roofs, they'd survived the conditions pretty well but were just as abandoned as the rest of the place which almost made it worse, doors hanging off hinges, broken windows staring out blankly at the icy sea.

This area of the town had a Napoleonic war theme running through its street naming conventions. He guessed it had been a pleasant time to be alive when the worst you could expect was a touch of starvation or getting hanged for stealing a pocket watch. Or getting a cannonball bounce through you.

He jogs on. Away from the Napoleonics. Cursing as he slips and catches himself on section of fence sticking out of the ice.

Faster. See how far you can get!

He's past the usual stop point on this leg, but presses on. Making his way along the winding roads around the edge of town at a limping canter. Past roads named for Kentish Kings and Queens through Wessex types, that judder with a crunch into the Normans and then a gear shift to modern Generals and Admirals.

A historical lacuna catching everything from Longshanks to the third George in its pall of oblivion.

He looks up pondering the choices he's made in life. He looks up and ponders whether anything is looking down at him.

He looks up and notes that the clouds look heavier than usual. He's due a serious cloud dump. The whole gathering from all directions as if directed.

Time to speed up.

Round the crescent that mirrors the shape of the town centre. Through its open communal spaces now head height snow fields, hiding the dodgy playgrounds.

"They'd been the sort of place where young 'uns never had a chance to use any of the play equipment as they had teenagers lounging around on them. Half of 'em with knives. I hated that sort. Should bring back national service. Put a bit of backbone into them. They want to act like big men they can take it out on Jonny Foreigner. Not their fault thinking about it. Can't blame the kids for getting bored…"

Now for the last leg of his sweep.

There is never anyone there.

Why are you wasting your time here? Press on.

No. Home time.

He hates the last leg, viscerally. It leads along a road that used to head up to the Station before that was blown up by the Army, then back to the Roundabout at the top of the Flint Lane.

There's something about this part of the patrol. An aversion to one of the buildings up along the right-hand side as it heads back to Flint Lane. A kebab shop of all things. It's in a parade of shops that have weathered the conditions rather too well for his liking. Better if they'd collapsed and taken their contents with them.

It makes him feel physically ill every time he passes it.

It's not in his head. Not like the occasional aberrant voices or the twinges of imagined arthritis in his joints. Actually sick. Cramps in his stomach. Echoes of something he must have experienced enough for it to burrow into his psyche and stick.

Why? He's not sure. There's enough gaps and contradictions in his memories of the time before the Lamp that he's given up digging.

The place has a biohazard sign next to the door with the old Government's quarantine regulations fading to nothing and awnings with dead plants hanging from icy dripping pots.

And there's a door he refuses to open no matter what could be inside. There are places that are better left unchecked.

From his vantage point as he catches his breath next to the station ruins he can see the sign for the place, swinging outwards into the road, half on, half off.

He doesn't have to do this. He doesn't have to do anything specific. There are alternatives. A half smile. That doesn't sound much like him.

"No. It doesn't. Think about why that might be, idiot."

"Or don't, you could just take a chance?"

He looks left. Alternative route. Uncleared. *Looks interesting*. It'll slow him particularly with that knock from earlier, but?

Sod it. Got to switch it up sometimes. He whistles as he walks, pushing through the thigh high snow like some steam powered colossus. *Somewhere new*. And it's Kentish Kings again in the naming stakes. Who'd have thought there were so many?

He pushes his way past roads named for Ethelred and

Ine, Oswine and Bertha with the insouciant ease of a man walking through water.

I am sure that Bertha was a Queen. She had a lovely chapel, quite the break from dark age misery. Oh. Ignore me. Wool gathering!

He blinks. Where did that come from?

The new route is a definite improvement. Why he didn't do this before is beyond him. *Too much routine*. There's change in the air and the further he goes the easier the going gets. There's joy in this work, he's an ice-breaker in miniature clearing new roads and avoiding… that place.

Where the hell are you going? This is nowhere! The clouds…

Ah… That might be a point. There are some vicious crops of full grown blade grass along the verge nodding their heads at him.

Go take a look! They might be interesting.

For all that it makes him happy, the problem with this new route is becoming more evident with every step. He's out of his comfort zone and he's not entirely sure how the layout of this area works. It's all circles and crescents. Roads that loop back on themselves and his legs are beginning to tire, the knock aching.

The town planners here seem to have been incapable of drawing a straight line if you paid them.

Still, he can get a general idea of his location by looking off towards the fake castle that tops the hill, seaward, some sort of light industrial place with crenelations that had been switched into overpriced flats.

"Everything's too expensive nowadays, lad. You'd think they'd painted the walls in gold, the prices they charge for a rabbit hutch. Back in my day the houses were houses and the Corporation would see you right even if everything were a little damp in the winter."

He shakes his head, trying to clear it and wincing at the ache in his thighs. Time to get back on course.

"At least it has stopped snowing." And the air is still. TV shows about the calm before the storm…

He turns right. *Then right again.* For a moment he thinks he's on the *right path* to get back to the Tower, but then the road curves back on itself dumping him back at the start of his detour. That's insulting.

Don't let them beat you. You're your own person. Make your own decisions.

He's made a decision and he'll be damned if some urban planner's going to force him past the bloody kebab place. He's been bossed around for too long.

That's when the sleet starts. It has a warmth to it that makes his skin tingle, he even loosens his scarf a little. It's the first thing other than snow he's seen since the early days of the Catastrophe when the weather was a shit show of storms, blasts of heat and dust with the odd tornado thrown in for luck.

He pulls away his mask and lifts his face up to the sky, lets the slushy water play over this face, removing layers of grime that have built up due to his lax personal hygiene and the twinges of pain that come with rubbing at his left eye with anything more than a wet wipe.

A deep heart felt sigh. Things are changing.

Change is good. Maybe take a night off from the routine?

But then he feels a stinging on his skin and he touches his cheek. It comes away red with an oily feel he recognises all too well.

"Oh, you absolute bastard." He feels betrayed. He is betrayed. "Damn you clouds!"

They're not to blame.

He picks out his knife and looks at his reflection in the tip where the blacking has worn away. A grey swirl, but sure enough his skin is crawling with sigils of meaning, red and squirming. Cloud-fall, not sleet. He watches as a flurry of the things plop down in the hissing snow around him, wriggling and trying to catch at each other to spell out words of disaster.

"Damn damn damn." Mask back up, hood pulled over. Do what he can to protect himself from the raw magic. Get out of it.

He needs to get under cover, quickly. Where's the nearest house with a decent roof on it? At least this area didn't have the flat roofs that were the end of most of the cheaper homes. The old age home is.. he dismisses it. Houses.

Still, the Ice Age hasn't been kind to them and his options are limited.

"Nope, nope, nope." His legs are fire, the burn matching the feel of the sigils trying to change him.

He identifies a likely candidate and sprints across the ice field, slamming through the locks and ice blocking the door with impressive brute force and collapsing into a heap against the opposite wall from sheer momentum.

Once righted he props the door back in place and heaps wrecked furniture against it, the doormat with its incongruous invitation to 'abide a while' jammed against the bottom to block the ingress of the red squirming tide.

He takes his bearings. Nose twitching. The place has the same fungus smell as the Lido, though there's something else too. An undercurrent of sweet rot. He doesn't have time to investigate, yet.

Clean them away.

He drops his backpack on the rotten carpet to root around for a packet of wet wipes. "Not good. Not good at all." If the sigils crawling across him settle, link, spell out forms of change, they could do untold damage to him and his equipment. He remembers the dead things from the tunnels and the way they'd been distorted by the power of the runes.

His search gathers pace, gloved hands clumsily fumbling with the contents of his backpack, pausing to wipe away runes trying to creep on to his arms and face.

"Bandages, first aid box, spare shells, where the hell are the damn wet wipes?"

An electronic crackle from deeper within the former home. A flash of blue light from somewhere below that lights up the ceiling revealing veins of the same black mould as the Lido. Something natural. His heart jumps, there's a Radio somewhere down there.

He'd welcome the guidance once he's found some wipes. More of the contents of his pack are strewn across the slanting floor, higgledy piggledy, before his fingers grasp the sealed plastic container with its bounty of slightly moist baby wipes.

"There we are."

The radio is an old model with a dual cassette recorder and built in CD whose release spring has long since broken forever jammed somewhere between loading and closing.

It sits forlorn on a walnut coffee table, its three-pin plug set next to it along with a flat charging pad with a crack running down its centre, as if the owner had been pondering a change of power priorities, when the Catastrophe hit. In the time before it was both obsolete and without the hipster cachet of a record player.

Couldn't give those away.

The eerie glow of the blue report panel lights up the room as the radio crackles into full-life. He finishes wiping his face and hands, and slides off his coat to shake it clear as he listens to his instructions.

The old familiar, slightly condescending voice begins.

"This is the Union Radiographical Service broadcasting to our friends on the South Coast. Interruptions expected. We're busy. We're still ***look****ing* ***out*** *for you. A reminder to all those of good cheer that the sigils of meaning are a* ***danger*** *where not applied to a surface in one of the prescribed manners set out in previous instructions or as approved by one of the illuminated experts of the MDR… experimentation is highly deprecated. Is the door locked?"*

The sigils shrivel as they reach the dampened ground, threadworms cut into sections with a razor.

"Failing to comply with these simple instructions. Get the Minister. Can result in an irrecoverable disaster on both a spiritual and artistic level as the sigils are capable of the most interesting ***side effects****. Rumours spread by our enemies that new abilities can be attained and new states of being achieved through their application directly on skin are entirely false. Where's Lawrence? We need him. The sigils will attempt to impose meaning on their environments…"*

He can feel burning starting across his scalp, and the same in his fingers. It reminds him of something. Being in a car, the whispers? He grimaces as the pain grows, checking his face against the mirror set on the wall, wiping away condensation and filth to catch any errant little monsters. He can't see any more of them, though the greyish planes of his face are unfamiliar and hazy.

What he can see is that he's taken quite a beating since… the last time he saw himself. There's a reddish raw look to his left eye and the socket around it.

The more he looks the less he can see himself.

"But the problem with order is that it is often not necessarily a form of ***order*** *that one would choose. Fucking goats have taken thirteen. For an excellent example a recent termination was achieved through failure of one of our friends to address a light fall of meaning from the Clouds triumphant. No, no. We need them now. And the order that was achieved was one more resembling a spider's cephalothorax than his own mundane human form."*

The burning begins to ease as the last of the sigils drop away. Sink into the floor, the pain reducing down to a prickle like a man who finally releases his hand from a rat trap and winces as he explores the damage.

To be sure he finishes off the packet of wipes, cleaning every inch of his coat and jeans, rags and mask.

"So remember, if you find yourself in a cloud fall ***stay calm*** *and make your way to shelter in an orderly manner. Make use of any absorbent material such as a towel to* ***wipe*** *away any lingering* ***sigils*** *and where possible wash thoroughly after. Soap and water are a sure-fire cure if you should be lucky enough to possess such luxuries. Those protected by minor wards may expect some residual effects similar to burning though engraining is unlikely."*

"In the event of engraining it is possible to counteract the effects through tattooing and we will address this issue in the next recording from your friends in the Union. To avoid any future risk ***return to your usual patrol routes without delay.*** *For gods sake get more of Them out to the Ministry, we've got maybe an hour…"*

The Radio crackles, the background music being eaten away by a whispering voice that sounds familiar. The Voice accelerates, words tumbling out at speed.

"Stay safe, stay alert and beware of the unknown dear listener. This is the voice of the Union signing off, it is nine thirty-seven on the sixty fourth day of September, two thousand and thirty-nine. Light and Darkness will now oscillate on these channels until our regularly scheduled programming resumes in one hundred and sixty-four days' time. Cut the feed. Cut it…"

A moment of sweet silence, and the light expands outwards and then is gone, leaving him in shadow. He takes a deep breath of the damp air and looks around.

No one has been down here for a while. There's still time to get home.

Or you could scavenge for bit? Oh. What's that? I could work with that…

His scavenger instincts kick in urging him to pack up some of the wood and electronics for later use.

He pushes back the thought. It's getting late and he's still not sure how he can get back to the Tower without getting back via the parade. He doesn't want to be stumbling around in the dark with all that blade grass around and there are going to be runners tonight.

The Watcher sighs and starts to leave, noting the house and its companions for later investigation if he ever comes back down this way.

Not bloody likely. Neighbour here was an absolute arsehole. Wasn't even willing to trade.

But then a burst of static and the bulb in the centre of the ceiling flares bright, then pops.

A high-pitched whining voice like a buzz saw cutting through metal howls from the speakers of the radio and then fades away into a high pitched buzz that bites into his forebrain like a hungry demon.

"Remember to check the basement. Remember. Remember. Remember."

The cassette heads rotate wildly and the CD loader bounces open and closed as the LED display flashes before the whole of the antiquated music system flares up and burns out in a burst of electrical fire. There's a hint of smoke in the air and suddenly he's aware that there's something below him.

"Place has a basement. Of course, the place has a basement. What else would it be falling into?"

Thumping from below him. Something trying to get out of the prison in which it finds itself, awoken by his activity. He has a fair idea what's waiting down there.

"Not again," he groans and takes out out his tyre iron, the cold feeling good against the imagined burns lining his fingers.

The stairs down to the basement are rickety, the whole projecting out some distance into the back garden as becomes obvious due to the fact the basement's low ceiling is cracked, water seeping in from above in a trickle of warmth from the cloud fall. He steps gingerly into the soup, boots disappearing up to his ankle in the freezing liquid.

It is also crawling with disintegrating sigils.

He turns on the torch to illuminate the source of the thrashing.

Sure enough there's one of them, like the things that had emerged from the tunnels. It's half buried in the rubble from the cracked vaulting, splashing and howling silently in the water, arms thrashing and teeth gnawing at brick. The sigils are swarming around the body trying to attach before the water destroys them, detecting raw material to work and urging action.

There is an oddly human look to its eyes, a mix of horror and disbelief and it reaches out to him with a hand made of bone and oily slime that drips like wax on a fire.

He takes a step back. Light fixed the thing in place. This is worse than the tunnel things. "What the hell is up with you?"

Come on. Get up. What's stopping you?

It is disconcerting. The previous ones have just mindlessly tried to grab him or had emanated the same mindless malice as the clouds above. This one seems to have marinated in a sort of sigil soup and the result is something that's a lot more human. Something with echoes of whoever it had been, locked in a rotting, altered corpse.

The thought disturbs him.

"Interesting, isn't it? Someone could work with that concept."

"Shut up." He hefts his tyre iron. "Least said, soonest mended."

Splashing his way across to the dead thing, he raises the weapon above his head and prepares to finish it off. No reason to leave it suffering.

"I'm stuck help me I'm stuck help me, help me help me, help me."

"Fuck me."

It's not exactly a voice. More like the sound from the Radio at its worst, distorted and out of synch, a recording being played through broken speakers. A simulacra of speech from something that lacks the capacity to speak but is desperate to convey meaning.

The thing's lips move as it tries to pull itself towards him. He steps back, maintaining an arms-length distance as he absorbs the fact it can talk.

"That's. Erm…"

The voice drones out its pleas. Unchanging and stuck in a loop of intention without any capacity to change.

"New."

It looks up at him with red flecked sunken-eyes, sigils are swimming a ballet in those grey orbs. He wonders how they get into the eyes, maybe they sink in if you didn't manage to clean them out fast enough? He wonders what that would feel like. He wonders what you would see.

"*Pain.*"

"Finish it off, lad. Be kind."

"Give it a hug? Oh this is ridiculous. New plan, friends."

He has a mad moment. What would happen if he released the thing, let it go to find its place in the world above?

"Or, hear me out, we could smash it. Does it look like it would be good company?"

The madness subsides. Whatever it is now, whether there is something of the person still trapped in that melting sigil-ridden form, still dressed in fragments of leisurewear and the remains of a rotten woollen coat, it wouldn't last long up there. He doubts its legs still work and all he can pick up from its madly rolling eyes is fear and horror.

A trapped animal. If he lets it go it'd go for him, try to take a chunk of him with it.

Even if it did run, it would do nothing else. Run forever on a programmed loop from the last thoughts in its broken head until it tripped into blade grass or those fucking blackberries along the cliff's edge.

He takes a moment to mutter to whatever gods there were up there, raises his tyre iron, and stepping forward, smashes its skull in. Three strikes and the thing is down and twitching, even though the voice still protests and the eyes still roll.

It's going nowhere but it's still mobile. He's pretty horrified. Anything should be down for the count with that little skull left.

"Nope."

He gives it a couple more good thumps, putting all his strength into the blows. Then a couple more and more and more and more, letting out a level of frustration he hadn't been aware he held at the world and the sorts of tricks it played.

"Couple more for the road, sport? This is fun in a sort of Neanderthal way. Suits you."

Eventually its struggles tail off. A couple of arm splashes and a sigh and the thing is done.

He takes a deep breath. The water coming from above is clear now. The cloud-fall over. Snow again.

He gives it a suspicious look. "Had enough yet?"

No reply, and silence. Acceptable result. The sigils across the practically beaten flat corpse begin to slide away as their purpose disappears. Dissolve into cleansing water.

On the way out he gives the Radio a salute for its warning, before heading back to the Tower, following his route back up to the main road and abandoning his foray into freedom. It just wasn't worth it.

He pays his tribute of stomach acid passing the damned Kebab shop with its dead plant garnish and window staring down at him accusingly with good grace, before slipping past the dead bodies next to the Roundabout and the biggest house in town, and making his way to the Tower.

He sleeps away the fatigue from the day's exertions in the comfortable warmth and musty odour of the Shrine.

What had possessed him to use up so much energy on stupid diversions?

He vows to do better. The damned King looks down disapprovingly from the Triptych.

18

... ?

Have we tried dear Serah's idea? They can't have covered all approaches?

. . .

He wakes around six]to a throbbing ache in his shoulder muscles. When he reaches to massage the ache away they are knotted into iron hard rigidity and his arms are burning.

He doesn't remember smashing that dead guy being that much effort. The tunnel hoard hare barely warranted a stretched ligament.

His eyes catch something lurking in the graveyard outside through the frosted glass of the visor-like windows lining the area nearest the old kitchenette with its packets of porridge.

That was wrong. He'd climbed up to the Tower to sleep, as he always did.

He nearly jumps out of his skin when he sees the pale figures silently watching him from the graveyard. It takes him long enough to grab his shotgun in a facsimile of panic before he notices that they're not moving.

"Umm."

Someone has been busy, and they've been busy making snowmen.

"Fuck me."

The ridiculousness of this nearly knocks him over. What kind of a lunatic makes snowmen in the middle of a bloody apocalypse? The weather's not bad by the standards of the post-apocalypse, but still.

How is this helping, exactly? I don't think you understood the instructions? I said to keep him busy… only one navigator? In the whole port? If you say so, Camelle.

He goes out to find out what the hell is going on.

The encroaching evening is cool, the snow eaten away a little by the earlier cloudfall and he stands, bemused, in the graveyard. Running his fingers over the new arrivals and pondering their meaning.

If any.

Some talent's gone into their manufacture. The sculptor hadn't lacked for raw material, even after the earlier warm patch. In fact, had the urge taken him, the Watcher suspects that he could have rebuilt the entire town as life-sized ice replicas from cut-ice gathered about the place, if you didn't mind the lower levels being thick with old dust.

As to the snowmen? There are five of the…

Well. Snowmen doesn't cover it. The more he looks the more impressive they become and the more ridiculous the idea of building them under a sky full of monsters and a world filled with vampires becomes.

These are not simple balls of snow rolled up and piled one on the other, a couple of branches sticking out of the top and a button or two passing for eyes. They're ice sculptures, cut and sliced into a simulacrum of life with verve.

He has visions of people working with sharp scythes, slicing quick and close, sprays of ice flying away from their master work. There'd been those whose entire jobs had revolved around that before the Catastrophe.

"We had some at an office do, before it all…

"Shh. He doesn't want to hear about us."

"We can still get away. Need to go. Need to go."

Didn't answer a thing. He sincerely doubted that any of them had survived this long. And even if they had, why would they have set up shop in a graveyard.

"And even more so, why would they be doing this for free. Blew through half the departmental budget, and that was before the cuts."

"Shh!"

The first four sculptures are pleasant on the eye, a man at rest on what passes for a bed, its features softening under the new fall. There is a hint of a twist of pain in the man's posture as if he is in some discomfort and there are echoes of plants in bowls around him.

The second is a taller figure, a military air to his clothing hinted at by lapels and the ghosts of medals at his breast, a hint of age to his stance though it is a proud one. There is a hump that might be another recumbent body to the sculpture's left though it is impressionistic in its simplicity, maybe a hint of an arm over its face, a feminine curve to the back. The figure raises a hand towards something that approaches him and he is using the other to reach into an interior pocket. There is a crater just above where the sculpture's heart would have been

Were it not made of ice.

The third is a young woman sat heavily on the ground with her head in her hands. She's dressed lightly, and there is ice that may be part of the sculpture forming around her face and upper torso. It is someone who has sat down to rest and passed from sleep into something deeper without realising what has happened, dreams fading into endless night.

Not a bad way to go.

The fourth is a man in a suit leaning against a wall, head slightly dipped and arm extended. There is something in his hand though his grip has failed him and whatever it is, maybe a weapon, is falling away in a nest of icicles.

The four are well sculpted and roughly in a line with each other, maybe a little variation. They are wrapped up in their own worlds and barely impinge on his.

The fifth figure who crouches in pieces by the cemetery wall makes him shiver, and not from the first hint of cold breezes coming in off the sea as night descends and the pop-pop-pop of drone fight across the Channel. The parts of the being that watch seem to watch intently. That attention is focussed on him from whatever angle he views it, and it is also observing the other figures.

The major part of it, a torso, is sat squatting on its haunches just before the flint wall that protects the fall down to the cliffs. Its feet are elsewhere, maybe the other side of the wall where the figure's head is embedded.

A hand reaches out impossibly from one of the gravestones, pointing out to sea. The other clutches at the sky, its fist clenching in fury.

Were he to put the parts together and stand it to, the sculpture would have been tall, wiry, though broad at the shoulders. A rower's physique. it wears a featureless costume that resembles a jumpsuit under a trenchcoat, and its individual features are distorted.

He gets the impression that it is trying to pull itself together, but that the other figures are somehow in its way.

As is he. And it hates that.

The face in the wall is missing around a quarter of its

substance. It has a single eye that surveys all it sees and there is a cruel grin playing around its mouth as if it knows that one day it will succeed in reattaching its appendages.

He can't help but notice the sharp nails projecting from the hand.

Was it meant to be figurative? It lacks subtlety.

"Bollocks to this. It's a fucking snowman. See how you like this."

He picks up a spade and knocks it down, portion by portion, before he heads back in to deal with the approaching monsters, leaving the other four to cheer up the graveyard. If the worst the world offers up tonight is snowmen, he can live with that.

19

Interference

A late-night shift at the shop.

The red-eye. The drunk arsehole sauntering in at two-in-the-morning and demanding fucking cod and fresh-fried chips and then starting up when you don't have it just farmed-pollock like everywhere else.

Eat a kebab, you dreary faced cunt.

No customers right now, the pub kicking out time rush is long over and the bar crowd came and went without incident for a change. He spends the wee hours of the night turning spits, spraying meat, and watching the dumb reality show playing out silently on the tiny television suspended on a swing over the counter, dubbing his own dialogue on to the lives of strangers to keep sane.

Night's lonely and he's skint till pay day. Two days to go. He'll have to live off the freebies till then. Fucking council tax. Don't even collect the bins now and they want a couple of hundred a month for that.

Some silly bugger has locked the door to the shop. Might have been that old geezer from the home down the road buying a party box for his geezer mates. Stay safe, he'd said.

Well. Absent customers, he's got no incentive to open it.

Not with the dark shadow that's lurking out there opposite the shop. He hopes it'll go away soon, but he's got the security camera feed fixed directly on it and every time he looks, there it is.

Guy in a long coat. Missing half his face. Seriously messed up.

They should lock people like that up. Stop them scaring people.

He shakes a fist. "Fuck off, Billy no-mates."

He considers a quick trip upstairs to his flat to water the plants but decides against it. The thing across the road might kick the door down whilst he was away. He chuckles. Might even nick the cans of drink set out in the fridge. All flat of course. Been there for months. His plant darlings would have to wait a couple more hours. After all, over watering is as bad as under and he's sure they'd want him alive.

A month or two passes. Or it feels that way. The TV's dead.

The security camera glitches. He turns his attention that way and swears.

The shadow has started to move towards the door, one foot after the other, coming closer to the pool of light from the street lamp outside, suppurating head tilted to one side and raising a fist to push at the lock.

He reaches for the baseball bat behind the counter and winces at the thought of his plants being left alone.

Is it patience if you have no real choice in the matter?

He cooks up a mess of porridge with a whole tin of peaches and a tin of condensed milk dumped into the pot for energy.

He's in *that* sort of a mood after the corpse in the basement and the bizarre mistakes he's been making all day. At least the rest has done him some good. He's finding the focus he's been lacking and the plan is for the sweet sludgy mess of food to provide the fuel to put that focus into action.

Snowmen. Seriously. The bowls go into the sink and he leaves them soaking in greasy water.

The Radio's uncharacteristically restrained tonight, the Voice lacking its usual vim as if it has other things on its mind. The Voice doing that 'almost automated' thing. Maybe the Union's running out of air filters or the water chip's broken in their bunker way up north and the presenter is wondering who'll be volunteered for a run to the nearest bulk goods store?

The news at seven is a simple litany of unfamiliar names and an imprecation to be particularly careful about arcane contamination. There's nothing about the continental war, or the nascent fall of Paris or the Russians capturing anything much.

The Radio can barely spare him the time of day.

The eyes of the world are somewhere else tonight and he's just going to have to get on with it. He leaves the music on after the presenters distracted sign off for a bit more company and because the Lamp seems to like it.

It scans the seas on low power, sneaking around in the hope of catching something tasty and sinkable.

More fighting on the horizon when he glances that way, and it looks to be much closer to the Port than yesterday. The wreck of his attempted visitor's fishing boat visible now only as a few bits of wreckage iced up against the breakwater.

Lots of small arms popping. The Russians must nearly be in town by now, grinding down the trapped Vampire forces as they screen whatever big VIP they plan to get out of the town.

Now or never fangies. He chews on that thought for a moment and on a hunch, switches off the Lamp.

"Give it a minute, lad. Bit of fishing might catch us something good. A little line, a little patience."

The faint luminescence on the waves disappears and the Lamp drops to standby, understanding his words.

He picks up his binoculars. Maybe they can tell when he's using the Lamp and it's discouraging them. The Vamps aren't stupid, and they'll have seen what happened yesterday. Hell, what's happened to every sad ship that's passed the coast since he set up residence.

That's not good. He'd rather they made their play and he made his and the world got to decide who won.

A win or a loss would be fine by him.

A minute passes. Then another.

Then…

He is almost knocked over by the sudden expansion of fire coming out of the Port, artillery, mortars, the lot. All directed North and East. The shells and bombs fired near as possible to flat, outwards at the approaching enemy. The sound is joined by a cacophony of automatic fire and the pops of cloud lightning arching down to tickle at the Russian positions. The whole screams of a diversion, but it's one hell of a diversion.

He whistles. Maximum effort, indeed.

A smile creeps over the Watcher's face. "Any moment now, Lampy. This is a breakout for sure."

And sure enough a grey, shark-like patrol boat bursts outwards from Port in a plume of foam and ice crystals, out from the breakwaters from a hiding place hidden from his point of view. Engines at full power and covered in the same lines of arcane protection along its sleek flanks as had 'protected' the fishing ship from his attentions yesterday.

"There, we, go."

It's quite the sight. The vessel's a good five-hundred tonnes, one of the Marine National's newer ships and according to his copy of Jane's, is heavily armed for its size. More importantly it's fast and it is already making good progress out of the Port and down the Channel, heading South at thirty, maybe forty knots, to pass Dover, aiming for the Bay of Biscay, undoubtedly and then to all points South.

"Helm control's a bit shonky though, lad. Drunk at the wheel. Or some ground-pounder with inshore navigator's license."

Whoever is using the craft does know how to run the engines and has a basic idea of the controls, but the way they work the boat lacks finesse, and their sea keeping is atrocious. They're pushing it around like it's a four-by-four on a field with no concept of the importance of the currents or winds.

Or huge bastard great ice lumps that rule this Channel.

"If they keep this up they're going to reenact the Titanic."

As if on cue, the bow dips into a heavy wave and pulls up again in a plume of ice and water, nodding like a donkey as it tries to push its way through. Whoever is on there seems to be in one hell of a hurry.

"Amateurs."

The port is lit up by fires as the Eastern return-fire starts to match and overpower the defenders' last throw. Frantic soldiers pulling at triggers of overheating machine guns, dropping bombs into mortars, lining up sights on approaching Russian tanks before being crushed under the tracks or torn apart in showers of fletchettes. The full awful experience that only ends in bayonets and clubbings and screams and the fall of the last redoubt...

It's an impressive last stand. They'll get their time.

Another patrol boat starts to slide out of the Port, as badly piloted as the last, wallowing sideways in the swell and turning using powerful water jets to avoid the dead end of the breakwater.

Then the noise of battle stops. Dead. In the surprise he almost loses track of the patrol boat's progress and that of its twin, as his attention is drawn to the suddenly silent former warzone.

"What the hell is happening over there?" The room does not reply, and the Radio's music plays on obliviously.

An answer comes quickly enough. Something slides across the port, low and fast. A big attack bomber accompanied by a swarm of decoys and hunting drones. Staying below the clouds and zeroing in on centre of its target. Popping the smaller drone defences of the Port as it goes.

Then it's gone, raising south and twisting as the tentacles and lures start to drop from above. He loses sight of the bomber as the core of the Port explodes in a sun-like pillar of fire accompanied by low reverberations that shake the floor on which he stands.

He twists away from the sight as the bright flames burn away his night vision and the defenders and attackers, both. When his vision clears of the red spots conducting an unwanted jaunt across his retinas, he opens his eyes to the sight of flocks of birds erupting from the cliffs.

"Looks like the Russians aren't taking any more chances. Neither should I." He switches the Lamp on to full power and starts to look for the first Patrol boat, the second visibly on fire and wrecked, its back broken against the ruins of the breakwater.

The beam cuts along the water as he traces the last known course of his target. It's been mere minutes since he last had eyes on it and the Lamp knows its work, but the patrol boat is fast and is nearly out of his engagement zone and behind the southern curtain of orange light before he catches it once more.

He's got a minute, two at most. And the Lamp is misaligned. The Vampire's last gamble might just succeed. The Watcher plots out the vessel's track. It'll pass well away from Union territory.

"You could let us go. We won't bother any one. You don't need to do this."

A sneer from the back of his head.

"If you let what's on that Boat go then you're condemning whole continents to the status of kine. Do your job."

The Radio says…

He pushes the Lamp laboriously to the southern extreme of its range, the remnants of the day's over-exertions slowing him down. The target is right at the edge of his engagement zone by the time it's in place.

It shivers in anticipation. He loosens the gimbal and just before the Patrol Boat can make it through the arc of danger he directs the Lamp towards its target, a little ahead of the vessel with the edge of the beam playing on its wallowing prow.

"Oh so close," the Voice gloats.

Said prow is wreathed in magical flame as the makeshift wards try, and fail, to repel the Lamp's arcane attractive force and he can see the the guiding eyes painted on to the very tip of the hull like some bronze age galley peeling away from the power being directed at them by the somewhat smug Lamp.

The boat's course shifts, a dope on a rope, back towards the shifting sands where its compatriots have previously broken their backs and where the ice mummies wait for company.

"This is too easy," he mutters to himself. "I'm forgetting something. Oh. The weapons. I forgot the weapons."

He can see the crew now, haloed in white-blue, running across the deck towards the mounted weapons. There's what looks to be a well-dressed woman in business casual attire directing them, moving with preternatural grace towards the front of the vessel. Likely the target? There's something immovable about her, whereas the military types are being thrown around by the rapid manoeuvres as the patrol boat struggles against the pull, she remains uptight, floating along on elegant pins as if sitting on a cloud.

They're manning the weapons.

"This could get nasty." He mutters. The patrol boat has a lot of weaponry, and the Tower isn't that far away from the mouths of their barrels. Not in ranging terms.

The turret gun, a long smoothbore that Jane's informs him is capable of firing both conventional and rocket-assisted ordnance, is slowly shaking itself into life, ranging mechanisms lighting up in a kaleidoscope of targeting prowess. The soldiers in Vampire grey-green are racking magazines into the flank mounted automatic weaponry in a sea sick dance on the shifting deck.

It's a conundrum he's never faced before. What do you do if you're luring in a target that can shoot back?

How far away is the damn ship?

He must make one hell of a target what with a bright light to aim along, he prays to the gods of the lost that they're as bad at using their weapons as they are at handling the ship. Boat. Whatever.

"Patrol boat. It's literally in front of you in that… book."

The Lamp has similar concerns. It's shifting in his hands, pulling away from his aim point and whining its motors. Given their shared potential doom, expiring in a hail of explosive shells, and his absence of any form of counter to that particular potentiality, he decides to let it have it its head.

The beam shifts to play along the hull of the boat and the crew working the guns.

"Ahh. I see."

Or don't. The light's blinding. He smiles the smile of a man who's missed something so obvious that it's a delight when it happens anyway and he can take credit. The boat's already on the right course and the crew will now be either blinded or taking urgent cover.

He's struck by the unwanted concern that Vampires might be able to fly. Bats wasn't it?

"Then they'd have flown here months ago, idiot. They don't fly and they don't turn into bats. Not that we know of anyway. Lawrence did a fine set of stress experiments on that point last year."

"So you say." The Watcher's face pulls into a taut expression that's halfway between disgust and irritation. "Any chance we could check things are going according to plan? I really can't see," he asks the Lamp, which gladly obliges, moderating the beam to something that allows him a near-perfect view of the spotlighted vessel.

He can see the crew locked in position around the wheelhouse or crawling around rubbing their eyes. One of them, a man in officer's braid, staggers towards the back of the target on stiff legs, and topples off the stern, falling into icy sea to be buffeted by the water jets emitting from the rear of the boat flailing and then dropping into the deeps as the waves engulf him.

"No!"

"Poor bugger."

Although the crew seem to be stupefied by their encounter with the Lamp and its powers, there are other powers at work aboard the patrol boat. Some mechanical avatar attempts to comply with its last orders and the quadruple targeting array on the turret fires up into a lock that plays across the Tower.

"Ah…"

"Wait. The Watcher…"

The turret judders as it fails to turn to match its targeting mechanism and stops in place.

"Iced?" He chuckles.

Movement still. The small figure of his presumed target who has made her way to the control room and is pushing madly at controls, then moving to the pilot's position, shoving the frozen man out of the way to twist the control yoke. Crackles of red power flicker their way across the metal.

He blinks quickly in disbelief. In the normal course of a catch anyone still touching the controls would be thrown back but she appears to be made of sterner stuff, her problem is that the Lamp's attraction has long since overridden the physical controls and her strength is apparently prodigious enough that he can see the exact moment the control yoke comes away in her hands, to be thrown with an assumed burst of swearing through the side of the control room.

The metal yoke plops down into the sea a good half mile past her.

"If she'd thrown that at us, we'd have been in trouble," he notes in passing to the Lamp, but his comrade is entirely fixated on its catch and ignores him.

She steps away from the broken control. The patrol boat is rapidly approaching its magically-directed doom as evidenced by the flames flowing like water around its hull.

She moves to another station, pressing at a push bar, the sole effect of which is to increase the power to the engines and speed up the terminal event. He hears an irritated screech of, well, not desperation, more annoyance.

There's usually a lot more drama when someone's about to die. He shrugs. This was always going to be an odd one and she must have quite the lungs on her for him to hear her from here.

The Watcher cannot see how anything is going to interrupt this one. After a few unexpected twists and turns the usual will be taking place and he'll be out for salvage tomorrow just like always.

The Patrol Boat is fast. The distance to the banks is small. He watches the inevitable occur with a twinge of regret over the deaths of the makeshift crew crammed on the decks of the boat, helpless in the Lamplight.

A visible wave of force ripples its way along the vessels hull as it impacts at full speed on to the banks and the broken wreckage of the Lamp's earlier victims. Given the size of the vessel and the powerful engines that still propel it as its prow bites into the sand and rock, it cuts someway in before the sound reaches him. A crack, a snap and then the hungry sands have it.

A blur appears around the impact point and the front of the vessel begins to shake.

It's as if the banks are grasping at the boat and its cargo, hungry to bury it in the darkness, streams of rock and sand clutching the hull and abrading the paint from it, finding gaps and tearing. The crew disappear into the blur as the patrol boat is torn apart around them.

"Hasn't done that before." He remarks to the Lamp. It's still watching events unfold with the intensity and focus only a lamp can bring to the table, and does not respond.

It takes less than a minute for the boat's lights to go out, and the catch of the day is in.

He locks down the Lamp and checks the Port quickly with his binoculars. It wouldn't be beyond the wit of his enemies across the sea to use this boat as yet another diversion whilst another escaped as unlikely as that might seem. However, the Port is clearly in ruins, the fires burning their way through anything flammable whether animal, vegetable or mineral.

Nothing more will be coming from there anytime soon. It's a melancholy thought. Triumph and sadness mix.

Still. Credit where credit is due.

"Well done, lad." He pats the Lamp. It's been a night. He toasts the remnants of the snowmen below "Here's to another successful night, gentlemen. More friends for you."

They appear unamused.

"Keep an eye out for me, would you Lad? I need a pick me up. It's soup time."

He heads down the ladders and to the makeshift kitchen. The Triptych looks down on him as he heats up a tin of tomato soup. Its rich mouth-feel is just the ticket after this big win with its hint of sadness.

He luxuriates in the creamy taste and wonders how many more ships there will be before his position is obsolete.

"That felt… final."

"Can we go then? I want to leave. The boat's leaving…"

"Shh, you."

Once done he heads back up to wait out the night huddled in the blanket nest with his cup of thick red soup.

Though what is waiting for him isn't what he expects. The Lamp has switched itself back on and is flashing weakly towards the banks.

"What is it, boy?"

Initially he can't work out what the Lamp is trying to show him, the greasy blur around the banks has persisted and most of what he can see is a smear of colour, like a candle viewed through melted glass, the elements split into a glowing rainbow without meaningful information content.

The pulses from the Lamp gradually burn away the distortion and as he sips at his supper he begins to see what it is that's causing the Lamp concern. A closer look is necessary.

He picks up his binoculars, peers down them.

What he sees forces a grunt of surprise from his lips.

The woman from the boat is standing on the sands, next to the twisted and chewed remains of the patrol boat. Every so often she shifts position to avoid burped up cargo containers rejected by the organic and metal-loving sands.

Even though the Channel is choppy with white caps bobbing along the southbound current among the ice floes and bergs, the sea around her is calm and she stands in maybe a foot of water, tapping her foot impatiently and gesturing to him.

He lets the binoculars drop down beside him and rubs his eyes.

Then he looks back through the be-lensed contraption she's still there. "You're not supposed to be doing that!" he shouts. "You're supposed to sink and go away!"

She really is.

To add to the disquieting effect, she is looking directly up towards the Tower, limed in a pale white light. He can see every element of her old-fashioned business casual wear, and he can physically feel the gaze of her huge hazel brown eyes as they stare straight at him. He also gets the distinct impression from the set of her mouth that she has very sharp, clean teeth as there are a couple of incisors poking over her thin lower lips as she mouths something towards him.

He narrows his eyes. He can almost make out the words.

"I see you."

He looks up to the heavens where the Fisher Flies play out their lures and everything is surely much simpler.

"Been that sort of day hasn't it."

He reaches for the Lamp to see if it can melt away this turd in the punchbowl. Her gaze flicks across to the faithful mechanical contraption with a distinct look of irritation. As he fumbles for the controls to flick the power back on the woman tilts her head back with a snap, and he is nearly blinded by an eruption of multicoloured light.

Apparently two can play at that game.

He manages to avoid the majority of the effect, whatever it might have been, by ducking below the rim of the window and lifts up a trembling hand to close the windows, for whatever good that will do. For a time the room is like a crazed circus, colours and shapes playing across the black flint and giving it a psychedelic feel. A 60s mescaline trip from some floppy-haired band's film project.

It makes him feel nauseous and a little untethered. The Radio is silent, even the mood music gone.

He covers his eyes and waits for the effect to dissipate, both on walls and the shadows across his vision.

Eventually his desires align with reality and he picks himself up. The whole situation is so ridiculous. He has a feeling that the woman on the sand bank, still standing there, knee deep in freezing water and likely still tapping her foot unseen, is expecting him to come and collect her.

He's not sure that's a good idea but at this point he's at a loss as to what he's supposed to do about her. This is the first person who has managed to survive being wrecked and he can hardly do his job if she's standing there watching him all the time, waiting to ambush him with whatever those magical pyrotechnics were intended to be.

He steadies himself against the Lamp, moving it in an implied threat so that the lens is pointing at her.

Then he shouts at her. He hopes her hearing is as good as the lungs on her.

"You should jump in the water and float off or something. You're dead, you don't breathe. You'd eventually wash up somewhere."

No deal.

"GO AWAY!"

She gives him the finger. Just a flicker. It could have been his imagination.

His eyes flick over to the Radio. Nothing doing. Usually, it has a good idea of what's happening down at the Tower and instructions would follow. Maybe it's taking instructions. Even the lights are off.

Maybe it has other concerns.

He suspects any orders would be to go over and bash the Vampire on the head, or keep the Lamp focussed on her in full force in the hope she'd either disintegrate or decide to jump into the Channel to avoid the unpleasant effects of the beam.

He isn't feeling that either. He doubts either course of action would be effective and he's got that on good authority. The Radio's always made it clear that the Masters and their top servants, of which this woman is clearly one or the other, are massively powerful creatures who could, if they could ever get their act together, most likely turn him inside out with a glance. Similarly, the older the Vampire the tougher, so keeping the Lamp focussed on the woman could just as likely result in a hail of fire from her servants when she gets her ducks in a row. Surely she can speak to her friends ashore, what's left of them?

He waits for the inevitable bout of sarcasm or stupidity from the voices. This seems like prime territory for the one at the back of his head to make a comment about his stupidity or claim to know more about Vampires than anyone in the world.

There's nothing.

He's missing the usual hubbub of competing nonsense bouncing around his head. Instead, silence, absolute and deafening. Someone's turned off a constant hiss that he's barely even been aware of up till now except when an individual element pushed its way to the surface.

He stands. He does nothing. Time passes.

Eventually his mind clicks back into something more active.

Maybe her servants would pick her up overnight and get her back to the continent. That would solve a whole heap of problems. Or the Russians would handle it for him, take her out from a distance in one of those hissing clouds of hypervelocity darts. Or maybe she'd disappear as she is really a figment of his imagination?

"Wait, and see. That sounds like the way to go."

Nothing from the voices. Holy shit.

He opens the window and speaks to the wind confirming his interim decision. He's sure she can hear him despite the distance.

"I tell you what, weird lady with big eyes, if you're still there tomorrow I will come out and see if you're real. If you're real, then I'll decide how best to handle you and you better not try anything. For now, I'm writing you down as my imagination or some side effect from having to deal with the wide variety of shit I've had to deal with lately."

She's giving him a 'look'. It's disappointment.

"For now I'm going to get some sleep and reconsider some of my life choices because honestly they're looking pretty shitty right now."

Her mouth opens. She does have the most remarkable teeth.

He chuckles to himself and shuts the window before she can speak, pulling down the slat blinds for good measure leaving the room lit by the rune wall and odd little flashes of light that linger at the edges of his vision like fireflies dancing in the forest.

"Night, Lamp."

Silence from the Lamp.

Sleep comes slowly and the darkness welcomes him. Just as he is drifting towards sleep for the first time, he is jolted to full wakefulness by a moment of terror.

A vision of that damned impossible woman gliding over the seas towards him, long fingered hands outstretched and dark hair flowing as she traverses the ice floes towards the Tower, intent on providing him with a clear indication of her disappointment that he didn't leap in a boat and bring her ashore.

"After all, William, you did sink my boat. You owe me…"

He growls to himself and buries himself deeper in the blankets.

After that the inevitable dreams of other people's lives are almost a comfort.

20

...!

Roads

The lights of a roadblock.

Of course there's a roadblock on the main A road-to the coast. To the survival hub under the port where the old Gov had a listening post to keep an eye on the stay-behinds and escape. The MDR arseholes may not have known about the nodes but they haven't entirely abandoned the outer zones yet. They've got business hereabouts, draining every bit of life for their Project Last Light before they scuttle back to the core zones to wait out the horrors they've sanctioned.

"Shit. I thought they'd pulled everything back," she says. There's no fear in her voice, exasperation. It's been that kind of journey.

"Well we've been wrong before. Keep your head up. We've got clearances and the way things are there's no way they'll have got the burn order out yet."

She flicks through the local map they'd brought. It was a decade out of date but there hadn't been much road building in that time. All the road budget going on automation and electrification, neither of which was working in the death-cold of the approaching ice age. They had been lucky the Ministry had maintained a couple of old gas-guzzlers and kept them fuelled.

"No way round either. Sweet books of longing these old paper maps are garbage, Steve. Ordnance Survey must been on drugs when they made these. And the clearances are from the Government. You know, the one that disappeared a week ago. Who do you think these fuckers are working for?"

He knows exactly who they'll be working for. "Find out soon enough." He says as non-committal as he could manage. Goat, Square or Union Jack is the question.

Factions. He sneers. They're splitting apart even before they've taken over. He hopes they kill each other and have done with it.

He slows the car to a crawl and moves across to the side of the road in accordance with the signs painted on the ground and the legal authority that the old Government had left the stay-behinds of the MDR.

Did they not realise the sort of people they would be leaving in charge? Maybe they didn't care. Brooker could put on airs when he wanted, unlike some of his lackeys. He honestly seemed to believe he was right. He was a better actor than Thespian.

A searchlight plays over the car, its beam cutting through the dust.

"Didn't realise this car was actually red."

"Hush." A figure looms out of the dust-fog, the man appears unarmed, but he'd give good money that there were a dozen automatics levelled at them. Maybe even something a bit heavier if the roadblock's handled by the military.

"Only one of them. That's odd. Why is there only one of them, Steve? That's not procedure…" Disconcerting. She sounds confused.

"True," the tall man moves with sure steps towards the car. A raised hand gestures for them to drop a window.

The hand strongly resembles a claw and there are glowing tattoos along his skin.

He grits his teeth. "Goat."

"What?" She sees. "Shit."

The figure tilts its head and walks across the beams of their fog lights which are barely making a dent in the dust and snow. There's something wrong with him. Something about his face. It's the fact most of it is missing and he's still grinning as he walks to the driver's side.

She screams. The men who had wiped out the safe sites had looked like this. They'd both seen the videos feeds. That had been what made them jump. Run. Even Vampire couldn't be worse than this.

He reaches for the stolen pistol but he's moving ever so slowly and the figure is moving in a blur as it approaches. The broken face always towards them.

She turns in slow motion. Lips moving. "Drive you idiot. Get the fuck out of here…"

But now the man is no longer approaching the window. It's in the back seat of the car, the grave smell of damp earth and formaldehyde filing the cabin. And the woman is gone.

The pistol is still there. He grabs at it.

"Too late," comes the hissed termination.

21

Lady on the Banks

The weather the next day is atrocious, a storm blowing hard with more snow than he's seen in months. At least it's relatively clean, the sigils seeming to have exhausted themselves in the nightmare of the day before. The snow that falls is almost beautiful.

If you corrected for colour it could be from a Christmas movie, though hadn't that been fat or tinsel?

And of course, when he looks, she's still there, standing on the sand banks. Still knee deep in Channel water, surrounded by an unnatural calm, the digested remains of her ship and scattered supply crates that he assumes must have formed part of the cargo of the defunct vessel.

He feels like she's not taken her eyes off the Tower the whole night and he can see her by the faint glow that surrounds her even without the binoculars. She's persistent, he'll give her that.

It's almost a relief. It means he's not going mad, seeing people where there are none. He discounts the snowman incident from yesterday, somnambulism being a real thing and the remnants of the figures now nothing more than featureless lumps protruding from fresh snowfall.

He risks a look down the binoculars. She stares back. Disappointment and reproach in her eyes.

What are you waiting for?

The look reminds him of a gestalt of every teacher he had ever known when he'd done something wrong. He shifts his view away from her, out of a misplaced feeling of embarrassment, and directs his glance across the Channel to see if anything interesting is happening on the Continent, but the snowstorm has cut everything beyond the sand bank out of view.

There are no sounds other than the howl of the northerly wind and the crack of ice on the near shore. His mind is empty.

He doesn't want to go too near a Vampire, but what else can he do?

He looks hopefully at the Radio. At first he thinks there is nothing doing, but when he passes it on the way to cook some 'thinking time' breakfast he catches glimmers of colour around the edges.

Intrigued he taps the plastic casing half expecting his fingers to be burnt but willing something to happen.

An ache behind his eyes is his only reward. Even the Lamp seems downhearted today, lacking any spark. A mechanical lump to join the snow-mounds in the graveyard.

The Tower is as silent as his mind seems to be. It's disturbing.

"Sod this."

He clambers downstairs, switches on the lights and chalks up a couple of extra heat runes as he's feeling cold, numb around the forehead and his fingers are tingling.

Breakfast is some slowly reheated porridge, and even

the freshly brewed coffee tastes stale as he washes down the stodge and considers his options, logically.

Killing the monster on the sands would be difficult. He doubts he'd get close enough to bash her on the head even if he had the urge so to do. She's just too damn human looking, not some undead monster clambering up to kill him, a woman who could have stepped out of a college commercial.

With teeth.

Distance would help. The shotgun might be an option? With a solid slug, maybe. But he'd be firing from the boat and that means he'd most likely miss, and he doubts she'd give him more than one attempt. Plus, why would a shotgun kill a dead thing?

The few magical tricks he's memorised lack any effective offensive potential, unless she were willing to stand still long enough for him to set her on fire somehow.

That might work. He could make a molotov. There's a magazine in the pile downstairs on how to do that 'urban commando' or some such shite, and he's got some bottles of alcohol in the piles around the Shrine.

Then he hears the wind whistling through the stones of the Tower and he is consumed with reasonable doubt. In this weather, the fire would never burn long enough to do anything more than singe a vampire even if he could hit her with the bloody things, and she'd be damp from the precipitation.

He'd always been a lousy projector of projectiles. His arms might as well belong to someone else for the throwing skills they brought to the table.

He swills the last of the coffee around his mouth, the grounds swishing around with the lukewarm liquid.

Nothing. Useless. He returns upstairs. Technically he should be conducting a patrol of the beaches around the

Isle, finishing off up at the headland all the way to the North where you could see the old Saxon church tower squatting in the ancient Roman fort across the bay which if you followed far enough would have led to London in all its frozen deathly majesty.

The headland is the limit of his world. Even though the world is empty.

Why? Why doesn't he take a walk in that direction? See what's in the coastal towns. Maybe even make it all the way to the Capital and see the sights.

Maybe even keep walking north from there, find those cowering bunker dwellers and ask them what was what. Why was he here doing this stupid job when every boat he'd ever sunk had been heading *away* from the British Isles. Why aren't they talking to him anymore?

What did they think was here?

"Never been told to." He mutters, the Lamp's just a lump of metal today and without purpose what is he? A man with a problem that's standing in the Channel waiting for him to do something and all the time in the world.

He sits himself down in high dudgeon besides the Radio. "What now gents? Any ideas?"

It is silent. No comforting military bands or clipped tones directing him to do anything. Not even the doomer version of 80s hits he heard in the old days. He taps it with a finger. It remains sullenly inert and the pain in his head returns.

"Come on, you bloody lump. I've been following your instructions this whole time. I need you to come up with something. This is exactly what you wanted me to do and now I have a vampire staring at me from the bloody sand bank and no way to get rid of her."

The storm grumbles outside. After fifteen wasted

minutes tapping away at the Radio's controls he decides to use his initiative.

The only reason he'd not tried the Lamp before had been the risk that one of the woman's servants might use a large gun to blow up the Tower. Given the weather that risk is, practically speaking, zero. Or the risk of a kaleidoscopic counter. Honestly that had done nothing.

He therefore makes that play.

It's tough to focus the beam on her. Either The Lamp does not want to illuminate the monster on the sandbank or its rails need oiling.

"Come on. She might disintegrate or something. You're powerful, old fella, lets give it a try?"

After a further struggle and a little oil the Lamp relents and allows him to direct its beam at the vampire woman.

"Nope," He spits out.

She raises her hand to her face to block the light, much as you would do if you had a faulty lightbulb in your reading room that started flickering, and tilts her head to one side with a slight hint of mockery. He bets she's waving the finger of admonishment at him.

"It was worth a try."

Initiative, that's good! Carry on!

\-\-\-

He spends the rest of the morning putting off going out on patrol and wracking his brains for the various ways to kill a vampire in the movies.

Hypothesis, the things actually exist and have existed for some time.

Surely the movies must have some element of truth to them?

Worth a try. He scavenges around for some wood to carve himself stakes. Physical violence must do something. There's a whole war going on across the Channel that points in that direction, particularly as the vampires have been losing that war and losing it with aplomb.

It would involve getting dangerously close to her though and there seemed a fair likelihood she'd tear him to pieces, as strong as he seems to be. When the hell had that happened?

How about garlic? He's got some cloves of that. He rustles them up. He'd been saving them for a bolognaise sauce once he got hold of some meat… The cloves look delicious rather than some kind of vampire slaying magical weapon and what exactly was his plan again? Get her to eat them? Rub them in her eyes?

Rely on the strong aroma to drive her off the sand banks and into the sea?

A peel of thunder from overhead and some noisy hail stones the size of eggs rattling against the roof nearly distracts him from the Radio switching itself on.

"YES!" He rushes to squat in front of the heaven sent object. "Tell me what to do. I've got a fucking Vampire to kill. Come on, come on, come on…"

The blue lights play across the screen, there's interference, he can see it. The sigils that normally run down in perfect lines are mangled and sliding across the LED readouts like drunks on ice. Intersecting with runes like those from the ship's hull running in counter-clockwise swirls.

Still, it's the best thing he's seen in years. There's the usual hint of music and then some popping sounds.

A voice!

…

"+***URP***+"

…

And nothing. The lights slide down the screen and the Radio switches itself off.

"Fucks. Sake."

He's still holding the garlic. He puts it back but not before he realises he stinks of the stuff.

Then he goes out into the storm and kicks one of the lumps of disassembled snowman as hard as he can. The enormous snowball is punted off, over the wall at the end of the graveyard and into the sea.

It might be childish but it makes him feel better somehow.

When did he get so strong?

22

Lost the tune

When faced with the inability to complete its primary purpose a system with some degree of redundancy will often engage in an inappropriate pursuit of secondary objectives.

In this case, faced with an obvious lack of targets for wrecking and his inability to deal with the Vampire woman standing on the wrecking banks, the Watcher on the Water engages in an enhanced pursuit of his need to collect supplies.

Short form? It's a mixture of environmentally initiated distraction behaviour, what with a powerful predator lurking nearby, and diversionary busy work to avoid the need to make a final decision given the general (if you forgive the obscenity) 'shittiness' of the available options.

And the one source of supplies that he cannot get his displacement-activity-addled mind to stop rounding about to, are those sitting in the stowage boxes next to the vampire woman on the sand banks.

It also fits with a treacherous undercurrent of reason

running through his mind which has come to a possible conclusion to this problem of the lady on the banks.

If the Union can't tell him what he's supposed to do, then maybe he can force a decision. What would they do if, for example, he brings the Vampire ashore? That would surely trigger the need to send a team to deal with her, and relieve him of his burden.

Plus, box after box of supplies, and the sort not scavenged from a dead town with its best days behind it.

Decision made.

He picks up his pack, slides a couple of shells into his hated twelve bore, and heads down to his boat.

The boat is a Deep-V rigid he has stowed below the cliffs. Orange and black with a seeing eye painted on the front to help with navigation of much the same sort as the Patrol Boat had. Another of the uses of the sigils passed on by the ever helpful Radio, given the absence of other navigational aids and the omnipresent risk of the weather closing up.

In the normal course, he uses it for his beach patrols and collecting any interesting salvage from his collection of wrecks, or a quick shufty through the broken cargo carriers that line the coast. Sad sentinels of the past. Therefore, it's an easy win for him to take the stairs down the cliffs to his wooden shelter, ignoring the plump berries sat enticingly among the temporarily quiescent thorn bushes, and pull the boat along the sand down to the surging sea.

He checks the seeing eyes, cleaning away ice and sea mulch and clears away a little snow from the deck with a sweep of his arm. Then he starts up the outboards and heads out on to the jostling, jesting sea on a buzz of power.

The sea is rough. Less so than he might have expected from the gusts that pushed him around on the way down to the beach or what he had seen the previous night. It's as if the storms are concentrated along the European coast holding whoever controls it in in much the same way as the orange glow holds the former UK in its grip.

Down here on the water it's no worse than choppy all the way across to the sands and the closer he gets to them the better he feels about his choices.

Supplies are waiting there for collection, and he can hardly leave anyone down there, let alone someone as interesting as the woman seems. Whatever she might be, he is human and he needs to show compassion. His prolonged thoughts on the cinematic methodologies of vampire killing have also brought up some half-remembered stories about the way the monsters worked, mentally. Vampires keep their word in every story, as long as you were careful with the wording.

If he just asks the woman to behave until the Union team arrives to take her into custody then she'll stick to that. It would get her out of a bind and she could always negotiate with the Union team?

Even the Radio had been clear on that reliability. Thinking back. Hadn't it?

Doesn't matter. The Radio's abandoned him.

He can see her on the sandbank. She's watching him, moving not at all, she could almost be a statue, though one dressed in that snazzy business suit, the fabric is brittle with ice. He can see tiny blue flames burning in her hazel eyes and her hair is streaming out behind her like a flag in the wind.

The dark hulks of older victims form jagged teeth protruding at crazy angles from the sands. It gives her the air of a Queen sat in a madman's fortress of jutting teeth.

He's sunk a lot of ships since he's been here. Why did he do that?

As he gets closer, he notes that she's helpfully stacked

the supply boxes that had been scattered around the shipwrecks into neat piles. Even some of the ones from earlier victims.

He scans the area for a safe landing spot. It's a good job he's arrived at low tide.

She speaks.

"Hello. I don't suppose you could direct me to your superiors? I think we may have things to discuss. If you would be so kind."

The woman perches herself on the gunwale towards the stern of the boat amongst the salvage. It isn't the most comfortable place to sit but she seems comfortable enough, moving not a jot and watching him intently.

She seems interested in him. He finds this uncomfortable.

It makes him feel like a bug under a microscope and the only reason he's not reconsidering the use of the shotgun sat beside him is that that interest is accompanied by an air of good humour that plays a half smile across her thin blood-red lips.

Or he assumes they're blood red. Under the clouds everything is the same miserable blend of red, redder and black.

He'd played along with the woman's suggestion that there was some kind of base filled with armed soldiers hidden in the tunnels, and that he would take her to meet them. It isn't exactly a lie, he had every intention of handing her over to the Union, and she seemed to know more about them than him.

Still. She seemed awfully sure that there was a base right there in port, and he's having to play it cagey over exactly who it is he works for.

Time to leave. He twists the engine into lock and the

water froths out behind the RIB in a metaphorical blood spray, as they head back to the beach and safety.

He'd hoped that the storm would blow over by the time he was on his way back but if anything the weather is deteriorating, closing in on the safe passage, and he has to use most of his concentration maintaining the course to the shore, dodging the occasional ice floe and keeping them away from the orange glow that delineates the safe passage into Britain or the Union or whatever it was now.

After a rough quarter of an hour, bouncing in the spray, when he's nearer shore, and comfortable that the seeing eyes can deal with the rest of the journey, he turns back to look at his… whatever the hell she is.

Guest?

She notices his attention, opening her mouth and draws in a breath, releases it, then another. The whole effect is unnatural or at least unpractised. She reminds him of the first amphibians making their way on to land, reliant on primitively adapted swim bladders. Breathing isn't something she does without purpose.

He frowns. "What are you…"

"Thank you." Her voice is quiet, yet he can hear it perfectly over the wind.

"For what?" He returns his concentration to the sea ahead avoiding the blue-flamed stare. "I couldn't leave you out on those flats. It's… Cold out tonight."

The curiosity gives way to humour as if she were pushing a slider between two extremes with nothing else on the register. "Well it's morning, not night. And I'm dubious of how true that statement is, to be entirely honest. You sank my boat. And my friends. My honest belief is that my comfort is rather low on your list of priorities." She brightens. "And you must know I don't actually feel the cold."

"True." He shrugs. "Maybe I wanted to speak to someone. It's been a long time."

She points at the store boxes he's brought onboard. "You are also stealing my supplies. Some of our people went to a great deal of effort to obtain those items and pack them to my satisfaction."

"I'd say I'm salvaging them. For our uh, cause. We need to grab what we can. Higher ups say so. The future's going to need a whole lot of everything to get back on its feet. And I er, we can always use more supplies. Why can't this be a win-win for both of us. I get company until my friends arrive and supplies and you get to wait until we decide what needs to be done with you, somewhere that's not up to your knees in salt water?"

"Ankles. At most. Anyway. Water is quite unpleasant. The future, though. That's interesting. Is it something you get to decide? What weight do you views hold in the counsels of the Union? They must think a lot of you to leave you so… alone in a boat with a vampire." She gestures vaguely up towards the Tower. "Do you operate the lure from up there? I had thought you were based in the tunnels. So much we don't know. Babeuf was a real loss. So sad…"

He keeps his counsel and adjusts the course a little to avoid some floating wreckage. Some part of a plane, the Russian markings still visible. It's washed away by a wave out into the swirling snowstorm.

"Hmm. You are not good at conversation but your piloting is admirable." She stops breathing and twists to look over in the general direction of the storms blotting out the continent before commenting wistfully, "I wonder how my brothers and sisters are faring. I can still hear them, but I think they have other things on their mind than me, and I suspect I shall not see them again. Goodness. What a melancholy thought."

Her accent is faintly exotic, he'd assumed she would be French for some reason and his mind had conjured up an expectation of some kind of "Inspector Clouseau" accent, or the knights with the cow catapult from that old comedy show they showed on the retread station.

In fact her accent is closer to what he remembers of the Polish family living two doors down from the house he shared with his Mother. The ones who always cooked up a nice stew at the holidays and left it outside whilst she was sick.

Now where the hell did that come from. He frowns.

"Family is so important." She raises an eyebrow. "Do you have any friends or family? Or have they all been consumed in this nightmare? So much loss. Almost like being one of us, but concentrated into such a short time."

He shakes his head in irritation.

"Hmm. No reaction. I feel I would benefit from speaking to your support team. From what I remember there's a clade of Union officers based in the Town. I assume you're working with them? Maybe we can come to an arrangement for my onward travel? We are not at war, though I fear we have not been the best of friends."

He'd not shared a house with his mother, not since he was a child, he'd been in the merchant marine on tramp steamers before transferring to container ships then retiring to the home where he'd helped out best he could, and worked in an accounting office in the City and gone home to his daughter and his girlfriend every night late due to the damn trains and spent a fortune on that bloody car, and worked at the kebab shop in the evenings whilst finishing off the botany degree and… the Yacht. Kappa.

What's a Kappa?

Too much isolation, too many icy nights and too much stress. A psychotic break? This wasn't an easy situation. He should cut himself a little slack.

The voices are gone. That's a positive.

The boat jolts up and then settles back into the waves. The weather is approaching white out, though the lightning from the barely visible clouds makes the whole experience closer to being trapped in at the bottom of a pot whilst some sadist pours thick tomato soup on your head.

"Nothing?" She cajoles.

"I have no support team. It's just me," he blurts brushing the heavy flakes away with visible irritation, sweep, sweep and a cutting motion of his open hand back to the tiller. "I need to concentrate on getting us home. Visibility is awful."

"The eyes help, no? They look like ours." She notices his discomfort. "Right now you look like you are trying to digest a little too much for one human brain, poor thing. Alone you say? How terrible." And then continues right along with the source of his discomfort. "I hope my questions aren't confusing you as I have a few more if you're minded to listen? Like. What is your name. I should know the name of my saviour."

He ignores her. Don't tell Vamps your name. That was something he remembered from the early public information broadcasts before the TVs stopped working and the announcers still had that "what the hell am I saying," expression on their badly shaved faces. The effort it had taken to get those past the newly appointed censors. If he'd only known what they were planning then, he'd have been out of the country faster than…

"Thinking again?" She smiles, sharp little teeth and blue glow to her pupils. The water sloshes in the bilges. "You must do a lot of that if there's no one there with you up in that cold tower. Tell me your name, I might recognise it. The AIA only had a hundred or so agents and…"

"You don't need to know my name, I know what you are."

"Then why rescue me at all?" She does that head tilting thing again. It is unnerving how she simply does not breathe except to speak. There is a stillness to her that reminds him of a demonstration he had seen of a Japanese care robot back when the demographic crisis had really hit. Almost, but not quite right.

You never knew what you'd miss until it stopped.

Or maybe one of those early CGI actor films where they had plugged in a replacement for a dead actor using big old computers to fill some missing footage rather than just rewriting a wasted scene to remove them from continuity. The ones which were used for nightmare fuel uploads with the soundtracks swapped out.

Silly. No reason to remake the classics at all. Let the dead rest.

"Everything deserves a chance, kid."

Now that really did not sound like him. A northern gruffness to his voice he does not recognise.

"I'm a pretty positive sort of gent or so the grandkids say. Little scamps."

"Hmm," she murmurs, thumb poised over her chin. "That is surprising. You look too young to have grandchildren, though there is not much of you to see. So many bandages!"

"I don't have grandchildren." He replies peering myopically into the snow. Where is the beach, has he got turned around? Where's the barriers?

"I see." A hint of sarcasm. "Would you mind if I say some things while you drive…"

"Pilot."

"Yes. That. Not questions, I promise. Some words that I want to see if you recognise"

"No. Do as you want. Not like I can shut you up. Don't expect me to be too responsive though. Busy."

"Accepting reality. Very sensible. I think we're going to get along wonderfully."

And with that they're approaching the beach. It's a relief. It would have been his luck to find himself heading at twenty knots straight into the buzzing wall of orange light when he's finally found something interesting, or twirling helplessly in the North/South current out towards the Atlantic with only a blood sucking leech for company.

He knows this as he can hear the sea against the sand and pebbles despite the storm. He half listens as the woman tries out a variety of nonsense words. Well, not nonsense exactly. More meaningless. To him anyway. There's some official sounding stuff and some magical descriptors that he does recognise but which he gives no indication he does, no reason to give her anything. Then there's the Union and then there's something called the MDR and finally there's…

"The AIA."

"You said that earlier."

"Yes, I did, didn't I? It's an acronym for your country's former magical investigations branch. Run by a rather pleasant woman and an awful man named Brooker. Ring any bells?"

Oh there's something there and it takes the form of the mother of all migraines.

Welcome to the Organisation, you'll get a codename when the boss gets back from his holidays. You did biology as a first degree wasn't it?

True. Imperial and then Darwin College for postgrad. C.V's up on the system. You know that. Why are you wasting my time asking?

Oh. No reason. We like to pick a codename that's based on your interests. Some poor bastard got codenamed Sucker as he had a bit of an unhealthy interest in Vampire literature which got him the tap originally.

Okay.

He's gone though, turned out it really was unhealthy and most of the books were plants by the Vampires themselves.

Stupid shit. Who'd fall for that nonsense?

You're going to fit right in, D.

"Lost you for a moment there. I hope you don't mind that I helped?"

They're on the beach and he's pulling the RIB back into his makeshift shelter with no indication of how any of that happened. She's pulling the stowage boxes down from the boat onto the sand.

For a vampire she's extremely helpful. It's making him nervous.

By the time he's stowed the boat she's finished with the boxes and is raising her face upwards to sniff the air. "Ah, terra firma. Not that I am complaining. I was getting tired of sea air. Thalassa, Thalassa and all that."

He stops.

"Is there something wrong? You were telling me about this Union you work with. I can't say I'm too sure I've heard of it."

"I was?" Hadn't she been telling him about it?

"Yes. You had the most interesting things to say." She kicks one of the stowage boxes. It's marked in French, five years of the language and the best he can do is ask his aunt to open the window. "Do you want me to move these anywhere? I'm not sure what's in them. It's a bit below my pay grade as they used to say, back when we had pay grades." A snort. "That's something that's gone for good I suppose. Good riddance. A stupid invention for our kind. Neatness is the only thing that matters."

"No. It's fine." The snow is building up at a ridiculous rate on the boxes. He'll need to get them on to the hoist to drag them up the cliffs, then get them and his nosey guest home before they were buried for good in snow and all that potential goodness is lost.

More questions. "So you said you work for the Union?"

He shakes his head. "I don't think I said that at all. Anyway, I don't work for the Union, I don't really work for anyone. They're way up north the way they tell it. Most they do is tell me to… keep an eye on the Channel and make sure that…"

He stops.

"People like me don't come across?" All sweetness and light.

"We all do our bit. There's a war going on over there."

"I had noticed. Do you want me to do something with these?"

"Go ahead."

She picks up a box that must weigh half a ton with one hand and moves it to where he directs."Do you know anything about the barriers then? Are those your work or the Union's or…" she laughs, it is oddly harsh coming from such an elegant form. A sound that resembles a set of choking coughs and is nearly drowned out by the howling winds. The sound a dead thing might make if you caught it unawares with an unexpected birthday gift. "You know I feel I may be throwing out things to which you don't know the answer but indulge me, please. My crew, rest their souls, said the glow was dangerous and looking at those," she points at the half-melted wreck of a bulk carrier up the coast, sat half in and half out of the glow. "I strongly concur."

"The orange blur? It's a barrier I think. No idea where it came from. Been here for months. Long as I've been doing what I do. I just collect stuff from wrecks and keep away from it." That and sink bastard Vampires. "You can leave the boxes. I can manage."

Delight, unbridled. "Oh. Disingenuous! You do a little more than that Mister, and you know it." Narrowed eyes glint red from blue. "I saw your light. You're a warden of some sort. You guard the gap in your employer's defences."

That is what he is. Denial would be a waste. "You got me. I still can't tell you about the glow though. It's there, it's dangerous and it's been there since I've been here. Not," he adds quickly. "That I have any link to it."

"Coincidence?"

"Yes." He starts shifting the boxes towards the cliff winch. "If it were me I'd have extended it the whole way round and let you Continentals throttle each other to death. Block us in, or block you out. Leaving a gap seems dumb if you ask me."

She laughs again. "We have a theory on that."

"You're going to tell me, I'm sure."

"Unlike me and mine a lot of things need to breathe. Countries mirror their creators I suppose. Had it been me, I'd definitely have closed things up good and tight, same as you. Hunkered down. Seen who won and come out swinging!"

She waves a fist with controlled force.

"Not you it seems." He replies, earning a glare which he counters with some box shifting up to the cliffs. Crunching across the sand. "The blur though. I thought it might be a side effect of those things up there." He points upwards.

She looks at him steadily. "That does not seem likely to be correct. The foundations that project the effect have been the subject of some study by our teams and they posited that although 'the blur' as you name it does draw its power from the nightmare above us, it is a directed creation rather than a side effect. After all," A smile. "Do you not find it just a little suspicious that it appears to defend the approaches to a single political entity whilst your neighbours find themselves held at arms length, save for this one section of coast? And then there is the similarity between the foundations and the concepts underpinning the runes under your own skin. They are..."

"What?" He shakes his head. "What runes? Tattoos..."

She gives him a knowing glance. "Alright. You may keep your secrets. For now. You can tell me about them later when we are better friends."

"Yeah." He picks up the last of the stowage boxes and carries it up the beach to the sharp-edged concrete that underpins the coastal road where the rest are stacked, ready to go up the cliffs. "If you're coming you should follow me."

"Oh. That sounds very nice." She shuffles her way up the slope of the beach, gingerly. "Sand is a terrible invention. It gets everywhere."

He pulls a face and loads the winch, one box at a time. Heavy gauge rough-to-the-touch rope pulls against the callouses on his hands as he wraps it in place around his windings.

She's interested in the winch. She seems interested in everything. "Is that how you move your ill-gotten gains up to the top of these very large cliffs? A little primitive but the execution is admirable. Practical, even."

He grunts assent.

"I had rather expected you to throw them up there.

You seem remarkably strong for a human." She estimates the height using her thumb and a serious expression. "If you need some help I could do it for you?"

"No! Stop offering to help!" He has an unpleasant vision of his new possessions arcing their way up the cliff face, and then shattering on impact into a pile of useless garbage at the top or worse still teetering on the edge amongst the thorn bushes before bouncing back down the cliff to clip him one over the skull. "I'm good. Thanks."

"Your loss."

She seems to be chewing over another question as he works. "You have more questions?"

A grimace that reveals those sharp teeth once again. "I always have questions. It's a natural condition for us."

Wonderful. That wasn't in the stories.

"Though I would suggest that this is a more 'natural' question than the ones I've been asking previously, so I hope you forgive me." She waits for an assent that will never come. "I've been wondering what I should call you, we can hardly become friends if we do not know each other's name."

"I really don't see that as a problem." The last of the boxes is loaded. He gives the ropes a pull to make sure they're secure. "And you seem really obsessive about names. I don't get it."

"Do you even have a name I wonder." Her face becomes fox like, eager and cunning, giving away some hidden intent. Whatever else they might have said about vampires the Radio and the Union appear to have left out the fact they are truly awful at controlling their facial expressions when they remember to have them.

He chuckles. Up goes the last of the boxes.

"What?"

"Are you going to run one of those 'if you don't tell me,

you're lame' sort of arguments?" He starts to make his way slowly up the cliff-side stairs, taking his time over every step. The ice and snow are treacherous and the stairs are steep. He doesn't want to slip and fall in front of this monster. He'd feel… ridiculous.

"No." Her lips droop down into a parody of a pout as she sashays alongside him. No issues with the snow for her despite the fact she's basically walking on a pair of ice blocks at this point. "I just can't see how we can have a civilised conversation without some degree of familiarity, and I'll tell you mine so we're even."

The stairs seem to last forever.

"Promise."

Step. Step. Step."

She growls in irritation. "Are you absolutely sure you have a name?"

"'Are you absolutely sure you have a name blah blah'. Of course I have a name. Quit it."

"I mean you have runes all over your skin which you cannot acknowledge, I'm not sure what you think they are, the usual answer would be tattoos or scars if someone were hiding them. You have eyes that force me to look away when I try some of my cleverer tricks and you don't even seem to notice, and me being what I am, and you seem oddly indifferent to the fact you are carrying a Vampire Master back to your home despite my assured belief that my tricks are failing." She smiles gently. "You don't seem the sort of thing that would have a name. Maybe a stats bar and a description in a game of sorts."

He gives up. "If this is what having you around is going to be like long term I'm glad the Union will be along soon to take you off my."

"So…"

"My name is."

They reach the top of the stairs. Before them the ice-fields stretch out as far as the eye can see, wormed through with his paths. Up to the big houses along the road the drifts have reached the tops of the ground floor windows and the cars, even the Bimmer, have disappeared into their cold embrace along with the blade grass outcrops.

Even the routes that he's lined with heat runes are struggling to hold, with water trickling down to be caught by the bloodsucking blackberries pressed over the edge by the weight of snow.

"Ahem." A cough from behind him. The Vampire is staring at him again.

"What?" He slides and twists the load from the pulley on to the ground and digs his sled out of the snow.

"You did not finish your sentence." That look of concern. She should be afraid of him. This is his place, not hers. She's a guest.

"I'm." He gives the sled a kick to check that it's ready to run and then after securing the straps to his shoulders starts on his way back along the faintly glowing path back to the Flint Lanes and the Tower. "We need to move. It's dangerous here."

She watches him pull the sled, six foot and a half of cloth wrapped monster hauling a couple of tonnes of salvage. Then she blows a single flake of snow that's settled on the end of her nose back into the storm. "I think I agree."

23

The Bravery of old-age

He's old. Nearly eighty years and years off the sea and look how he's having to spend his golden years? End of the world. What a joke.

And all on a Petty Officer's pension. It was shite, but it was something. Could even treat the ladies and gents and everyone else to a nice kebab once in a while from up the road when it wasn't that grumpy young plant-fucker serving.

Shame there didn't seem to be any fucker willing to pay his pension recently, not after this whole Catastrophe kerfuffle. Shame about California, and Japan, and all that bit of South America that slid off into the sea. Some of it had been pretty nice to visit when you were off that way.

Ah well. Best get on with things.

The weather's the same bloody snowstorm it's been for nigh on a month and it's taking him longer and longer to get the trolley around to the lads and ladies, get the gruel ready, nice cup of tea, help the ones that can't eat it to get a bit of sustenance in them.

Stick around and keep the ones that are going

company. No reason anyone should die alone. That's basic humanity.

Hadn't expected he'd end up doing this. Bloody young people, all running off and leaving him to shift for the residents. Typical. Should have brought back national service when they had the chance. Hadn't done his dad any harm. He'd been Navy for a while. Cut when the frigates had been cut back. Shame.

Though the missing leg did get his dad grumbling when he was gardening. Good old dad. Would have thought the world now was a right old shambles.

He'd seen two young 'uns heading past them into town earlier that day, before he'd finished the first floor. Bloody weird. No one's out and about if they can help it, a couple of those council types popped in once in a while to provide bedding and a bit of dried supplies, supposed by in the tunnels he'd heard.

Hmm. Should bring all the ladies and gents on to a single floor. The handcrank on the lift is good exercise but it'll be the death of him one day.

Oh the kids. He didn't recognise either of them. Same lean streaks of nothing in winterised gear that reminds him of the Norwegian lads he used to transport on semi-rigids back when NATO had been a thing.

Those had been the days. Speedy run into the beach. Exhilarating.

They headed into town. Looking to get off this icebox of an island. Sensible kids.

He's settling into his armchair, bundled up in blankets with a cup of cocoa, tot of the good stuff, when he hears the sirens go off.

Oh fuck me. That's just perfect. Air raid? No dust storm. Or something of that fashion. The sirens have gone quiet recently. Mercy to be honest. No one's doing anything about 'em.

Oh no. But this is something. He can recognise that rumble. Armour, it's the bloody army. They've finally come to help. He jumps up, or nearest thing he can manage given the arthritis.

"Ladies! Gents! Everyone else! Relief's arrived!" His knees are fiery hell, but that this needs a proper wake up call. Those who'll understand it can help him get the squaddies attention, those that can't, well they can wait and get picked up, soon as. Fucking hell. Who'd have thought he'd ever be happy to see the Army? Ground pounding twats, the lot of them.

What? What is it Sim?

Fucking Army my good lad. They've made it through the snow and we're getting a ticket out of this prison. He chuckles. Shame those little care-home shits ran off. Could have stuck it out and would have been okay I bet.

Not that he doesn't wish them well. Who'd want to be left with a house full of invalids when the bloody world looks like it's falling to pieces? Horrible the stuff they'd heard about America, China that side of the world. Had been bad enough here in Blighty well away from the volcanoes. Shame they'd got rid of the news with that shitty slowed up music.

The clanking and rattling continues. He pulls on snow-boots and his good coat, still got his veteran's card and ID in it. Nice. Coat had been a present from the granddaughters, the bloody stupid one, if you'd asked him back then, global warming not cooling, ladies.

The look she'd given him. Daft bint. Still she was family. So you did what you could. He'd managed to scrape together enough to give her a holiday. Didn't hear any thanks of course but she'd put up pics.

Cor, the weather down on the Coast was bloody lovely back then.

Not now. The world provides if you put in the effort. He steps out into the snow to hobble his way up to the main road.

There's figures up the road. Soldiers.

The soldiers see him. They don't wave.

He peers at them, picks out his glasses, slips them on.

There's something wrong with them. He didn't recognise then. The flashes and the insignia looked almost like the good old UK but had some boxy crap around them. Were those goat heads?

Weren't marines. Maybe Special Forces or some spooky bunch.

He glances behind him. Shit he's forgotten to close the door. Old Albert's sticking his bald head out. "Back inside you prat, You'll catch your cold out here…"

"Is that the army?"

"Yeah, see if Noreen's got the others dressed if you want to make yourself useful."

When he turns back the bastard squaddies are pointing rifles at him and there's a tall looking fella giving him the stink eye.

"Oi, haul it back lads. Bunch of survivors down this way." One of the soldiers looks at the man in the long trench coat for instructions.

He served his time. He recognises that look. Volunteered too.

Why is the tall fella covered in tattoos?

The tall fella shakes his head. Not at him. Fucker's not interested in him at all. That shakes of the head's aimed at the soldiers in their pantomime gear. No good ever came of that sort of uniform, nor that sort of head shake.

A moment to do something. Give the others a chance. Maybe. Best he can do.

Albert's still there.

Sotto voce. Hissed. Just loud enough. "Shut the fucking door Albert. Now! Shut the Fucking door and…"

There's a volley of shots and he's in the snow looking upwards. He gets the weirdest feeling that tall fucker's looking at him from above.

He's c…

———

24

Guest

She follows him home, lagging slightly as she examines the heat runes on the path. He gets the impression she's judging his workmanship and he's not entirely sure he likes that. He can feel irritation biting away at the odd passivity which has held him in its grasp since he sank the woman's ship.

And then rescued her.

Like a part of him is rebelling against the idea of someone telling him how to do something of which he is more than a little proud. He's defended the Union against the Vampires for months and here is this monster silently judging his rune craft.

Silly. He's barely a dilettante at the magical arts. Still, he knows he'll feel better if he says something.

"Getting a good look there, lady?"

"Yes," she replies. "Who taught you to put these… things up? Heat runes, obviously. Not a pattern I recognise, and I thought I was rather well versed in the various schools, there are those who know better, not many though. I am, after all, a Master."

"Not some of yours? Vampire stuff? You're supposed to be better than us at magic?"

"We are. There's virtue in practice. Not to put you in your place, but we have simply been doing it a lot longer. As Serah would say you're awfully young," a smile with sharp teeth. Not fangs exactly but a very healthy set of dentistry. "These are not something we would create. Very – wasteful. There's a hint of Fae magic around them." The smile morphs into a grin that fades in the same fluid way as every other of her facial expressions, a constant rate of change where her face melts into its new forms rather than organically switching on a dime, like a human expression with all its leftover facial ticks. "Maybe that's it. Serah says you had been engaged with the Fae in the time before, some of you longer than others."

"Fae?"

"Oh. Nothing you need to know about. Not anymore."

What did she mean by 'says'? There's no one else around.

They reach the roundabout where a patch of blade grass has managed to push its way out of the snow. He tips his hat to the deep-covered bodies outside the biggest house in town as he always does.

She gives him a look. "Dead people?"

"Yes."

She waves back. "There seem to be a lot of others around hereabouts. Did you know these ones specifically?"

"Not that I remember. It's just good manners. Hey don't go there…"

She is edging her way towards the house, sniffing the air. "Sorry. There's something about that place. Do you mind?"

"I do! Come back here, right now. If you're going to get awkward, I still have the shotgun and I don't think you'd like that, Vampire or not." She's still sniffing, shuffling towards the house. A bloodhound catching an interesting scent. "What the hell are you doing?"

She's turned from the house and is sniffing her way towards him!

"Keep away, you crazy…" He raises his hands to ward her off and his arms start to itch terribly.

She seems to realise how ridiculous her behaviour is and stops, though her eyes flicker between the house, the shotgun strapped across his back, and the two piles of snow under which the bodies are buried.

That fox-look again. Some piece of information has been filed away in the vampire's brain. Given enough time she'll have dug up all the secrets of this place.

"Alright. My bad, your house, your rules. I am Alyson by the way." She holds out a pale hand with inhuman grace. Each movement is just so. Her fingers are long and elegant and unprotected from the elements. He hadn't thought about that up till now. He's been having a completely insane conversations with a woman dressed in a soaked business suit in thirty-below-zero weather and with a snowstorm blowing.

He glances at the offered hand. He suspects it as cold as the dark side of the moon.

"I'm not sure what to do with you Miss, but I am not shaking your hand. Not yet."

"Fair enough. That's the phrase, isn't it? We can perform the formalities and then we can be friends. Until your bosses send someone to collect me and I can be on my way, that is. My name, as we have been having so much difficulty with yours, is Alyson."

"Alison? Didn't you just say…"

"Ah-LEE-zon," he pulls a face. "It's a different name.

You know, you can call me Aly if you're going to insist on mispronouncing it."

"Fair enough, Aly."

"Would you like a name too? It would make conversation easier. We have some thoughts on options."

"Quit it with the name thing. Okay?"

"Okay." She runs her fingers along the start of the alley of flint walls. "This is interesting. Quite warm to the touch."

"You get cold?" The thought makes him feel bad, huddled up in his plethora of clothing.

"No. Not in that way. I do have a preference for warmth so I'm hoping that we can get out of this biting cold sooner rather than later. Do you happen to live in that Tower up ahead or is that more of a base for your piracy? Is it warm?"

"Piracy is conducted on the high seas," he ventures as he gives the reins of the sled a jerk and starts his load moving down the lane once more. "I'm a wrecker."

She sighs. "Yes. My poor crew."

The Shrine is up ahead. The Vampire, Aly, seems very interested in it, taking in its structure with a professional eye. "How pleasant. Pugin, isn't it?"

The *Shrine* is up ahead. He stops.

"More stopping, eh? I really need to come up with a name for you, even if it is just so I may comment on how you are the most appalling laggard sometimes. What is delaying us now?"

"I live in a Shrine under the Tower."

"That's nice. Which Saint? I've known a few in my time. Pleasant people if you could keep them off the ergot. Always wondering where their messiah is. It's a universal constant, you know. None of the promised ever…"

She's not getting it. He tries to emphasise the point. "A

shrine. Baptist. Quite an important one I think. The gift books they sold at the gift shop were very clear about that."

She taps her foot. "Yes. You said that."

He growls in irritation at her obtuseness. "I'm asking if you have any issues with holy ground? I can't remember the Radio saying anything about that and I don't want you turning to dust the moment you set foot inside. I'd have to clear that up and you might get into something important."

A bright smile. All those teeth. "Oh. That's very thoughtful. The answer is none, none whatsoever. So your home care routine will remain undisturbed by my poor ashes. I do have a healthy appreciation for the architecture of your chosen abode though so I'm quite excited to see what's inside. And the lions are quite lovely if a little worn." She narrows her eyes, whether from the snow or some irritation he cannot tell. "I even quite enjoyed the lines of the Tower from the banks. Squat. I had a wonderful view of it while you were shining that silly little light on me."

"We're good to go then, Alyson?"

"We are indeed, man with no name."

"Don't bring that up again. I have a name.

"Yes. Everything has a name, even if it does not seem able to articulate it. And anyway this place has not been holy for a while, I suspect that might be since you took up residence."

He glares as he opens the gate to the graveyard. "Is that a dig?"

"Observation." She looks around. "Is this a graveyard? Why aren't we going in the front?"

"Can't you tell?"

"Not really. Everything is a little snow-robed and I

think someone's been building snowmen." She snorts as if in memory of something funny.

Locks undone, he opens the heavy door and waits. As does she. He lets the wait extend just long enough to answer a question that's been bouncing around at the back of his mind.

"Need an invite?"

"If you wouldn't mind." Bemused grin. "That bit is true. We're sticklers for protocol."

"You're invited." Promises. Get her to make a promise. "Don't make a mess and don't try and kill me."

"Super." She rushes past him into the warmth and faint stench of his lair leaving him to move the boxes inside.

25

Guests are welcome

By the time he's finished bringing his new possession inside and loaded them on to a trolley for sorting, Aly the Vampire has set herself up in a deckchair next to the heat rune stove and is flicking through one of the piles of 'trashy' novels he reads in his spare time when the mixed magazine pile is too depressing.

She flicks through the pages at speed with a faint air of disapproval, then carefully places them in a newly constructed packing box.

There is steam rising from her clothing as the runes do their damndest to dry them off. She looks like a demon with a book obsession.

And she's nearly filled a box by the time he's clambered out of his soggy outdoor gear and stowed his shotgun. She is writing the names of the contents from memory on the side of the box in black felt tip pen.

"Make yourself at home, why don't you?"

She holds up the next of her targets. "Not good. You have terrible taste in books."

"Very good. Can't beat a 1950s spy thriller." He pulls

the trolley into the main room and unloads the boxes one at a time. They are surprisingly heavy. Should be some good stuff in them, he can run them off to the appropriate store when…

There's doings afoot behind him.

"What are you doing?" It's actually pretty obvious what she's doing. He's just not sure why she is doing it.

"Clearing up. Mess is the sign of a lazy mind. You can leave the boxes in the corner there," she gestures absent mindedly from her seat as she sorts through everything within the reach of her hands which move with blinding speed. "I can open them for you if you want. Easier to get everything nautical and ship shape if they start that way rather than being scattered about by a one-man howler monkey troop."

Howler monkey? "My place, my rules. Thought we'd agreed that. And I'll put them where I want and, and… I have this," he waves a crowbar, "when I want to open my boxes. You are a guest for now. I'll decide later what you are longer term based on how you… stop messing with my stuff!"

She raises thin eyebrows at him. "Oh, you will, will you. I'll have you know I'm quite the catch, young fellow, so I doubt you'll have much say. There have been entire expeditions launched from these shores with the intent of catching one of us. Your chiefs will be delighted and you will get a pat on the head and then it'll be planned obsolescence for you. Incidentally, when are you going to tell them?"

"How are you quite the catch, oh it's a sea joke. I caught you at sea and now you're here." He gives a fake laugh. "Funny."

"I suppose that is correct and has some degree of humour, but I mean that I am quite an important person amongst my people." She pulls herself up, hands still flicking back and forth, summoning forth organisation from chaos, and stares imperiously down her nose at him. "I would therefore suggest you treat me in a way appropriate to my station."

That earns her a proper laugh. "Aren't you a heap of funny? I've watched your lot getting their arses handed to them by the Russians for the last couple of months so your station is 'refugee' far as I can tell and maybe you're a runner at that…"

"Oh." She looks genuinely sad, eyes downcast. "There is some truth to that, although we all agreed I should see about setting up our little family somewhere safe. Not so much a run as a tactical retreat, yes? Time is on our side in the normal course of business." Aly pauses. He recognises that look from personal experience. She's listening to something. "Then there is the alternative point that I am quite strong. I doubt that you could stop me doing anything I wanted were I to take umbrage at your unpleasant attitude."

She smiles and lightning plays over across her fingers. He can feel his feet lift off the ground. A delicate piece of magic to make a point.

"Okay. You've made your point. Though," he adds, "that would leave you wandering around what's basically a wasteland without anyone to call in the people you really want to talk to. So that would be pretty fucking stupid."

She puts him down. His arms sting. There's a pattern to that sensation he's not liking. "Yes. That is a problem. And it's probably going to make you wary of calling them in. That's… I won't do it again. Honest."

He tries to work out if she's being sarcastic. Best he can tell, she doesn't do sarcasm and is entirely serious. "Good. Ground rules."

He goes back to his boxes. The first one opens to reveal tinned goods, carefully stacked. "Not bad." He picks one up, a tin of peas and checks the expiry date, "Wait." Then another. "Seriously?" He throws the tin into a corner. "Who would waste their time porting this crap about? It's all expired years back!"

She is talking to herself. "It was such a lovely plan and then someone insisted on sinking my boat and I'm beginning to think the plan was not so good after all. Strange. We all agreed it after all. I could… no. No. That wouldn't work. We'll work with this fellow and… He's listening."

He waves another tin at her. It's so old it's bulging outwards and the paper wrapper is faded to nothing.

"What?"

"They're all out of date."

"Sounds awful. Not a huge issue for me. I thought we should bring something with us in case it was useful. Maybe they were ballast. That's a thing isn't it? Anyway. Here I am and this place is a disaster so I suppose I should do something useful. Keep busy until we've… settled in my aims," She looks pointedly at the mess. "Have you considered organising any of these things you have stolen. I mean salvaged?"

"They are organised." He points. "Different piles have different purposes and the world's a lot less crowded now so I have space and plenty of other hidden stores if I did."

She sighs a long suffering sigh as she scrawls a series of marks on the box of books. "I really do need a name. How am I to scold you when I don't even know what to call you… Good idea. We'll try that." She draws herself up like a snake rearing and before he can do anything she shouts in a voice of roiling thunder that hammers at him from a thousand directions at once.

"I demand to know your name."

He staggers back, dropping the tin of expired peas with a dull thud.

Compulsion tugs at his brain, he needs to tell this dead thing what his name is, that's clear. He understands that. However, as the compulsion pushes its way deeper into his mind it is channelled into a dozen dead ends. A raging torrent of obligation is split into multiple streams that slow and then ebb backwards into a vaguely irritating ache that seems to pass through his body and out of the tips of his fingers.

And from the back of his mind comes a bracing wave of contempt.

"Hmm," her eyes widen. "Interesting."

The last puddles of compulsion begin to evaporate among whatever part of his brain deals with minor irritations and finally find purchase. After all, there's nothing in a name.

"I've told you before. I'm." He coughs. Odd. It feels like he should know this one. Then the urge is gone entirely and he returns to his glaring.

"Have it your way. I shall call you Carlos." The Vampire smiles. "I had a good friend called that once."

The smile twists into discomfort and she drops her head. "No. I know. I… what do you suggest Serah? Isn't there… William. As you wish, we'll call him William."

"All done?"

"Yes."

"Can call me what you want, don't expect me to answer." He is overwhelmed by the ridiculousness of his situation and pinches his nose, then kicks out at a wall. He needs to get a warm drink in him and spend a bit of time up in the Tower, check if the Radio's saying anything, watch the fighting. Something other than what he's doing now. "Here I am arguing names with a Vampire who seems to be having some trouble with her own. Which are you? Aly or Serah or something else? Or is it a big in-house argument?"

"That's not what's happening, William. It's more complicated. I have a suspicion you understand at least subconsciously. I have a theory…"

"You have a theory. You're dead, you drink blood and you're making up names for me. Absurd."

The Vampire frowns, he's hit a nerve. She manages to do this without a single wrinkle appearing on her face, the effect produced by the alignment of eyebrows to nose. "Drink blood? That might be true in the abstract. What of it? You eat dead flesh. It is not something I do very often and I positively affirm that I have no such urges now, thank you. I prepared for this journey before I left, and," she waves a finger metronome style. "From entirely renewable sources. If you are offering refreshments which would be the civilised thing to do however I would be very interested in a nice cup of tea if you were to have any? My throat is full of salt from my enforced time on the banks, after someone sank my boat, and I am aware that I sound like a sea lion at a circus."

She does the barking cough again. "You should have some too. It's cold out there and I think I will have more questions for you before I decide what I should do next. This place is very odd. As are you. I am intrigued!"

The Watcher pinches his nose. He's being rude. Aly has done nothing to earn his enmity other than being what she is and that is really, really odd. No one can help that.

"A cup of tea?"

"Please?" Toothy grin.

"Okay. I can do that. Let's start again. No more magic, no more shouting."

"That sounds very acceptable." She shivers. "Magic is such a horrible thing and a cup of tea so very pleasant."

He turns on the lights, it's been that sort of day, and runs the kettle while the Vampire admires the flashing fairy lights, stepping carefully around the room and tapping each in turn. "I have a question, Aly."

"Ask away William." She's got another box up and running and is sorting books once again.

"Lets say I don't call in the Union. What do you do next?"

"Hmm. Thoughtful." She ponders, chewing her lip. "If it wouldn't inconvenience you I would like to take a quick look at the tunnels hereabouts. We had some friends down there and I hear…" She stops, listening to some otherworldly voices. "I hear that there might be something interesting down there. Some information. Our intelligence people were very sure that there was a command post there and I don't understand what could have happened to it or some of the people we were going to speak to…"

He gives her as blank a look as he can manage, remembering throwing the inhabitants of the tunnels into the sea a few days earlier.

She tilts her head. "If it's not too much bother?"

"We'll see."

This is not turning out at all how he expected. The reality of this Vampire Master is that she gives the impression of being precisely no threat to anything except his peace of mind and his dubious storage practices. There's a physical menace but it's directed mostly at his stash of novels.

As if on cue she sees something that interests her and before he can raise a finger she has grabbed it and returned to her deckchair in a sudden burst of speed, holding another of his favourite novels.

"This one is also terrible." She stacks it with infinite care and marks its name on the newly packed box. "Peace, Camelle. It is a very poorly written work even if you like it."

Steam rises from the kettle and there's a click as it switches itself off. He makes the tea, adding a dash of condensed milk from a carton and passes her one. "You aren't exactly what I was expecting."

"Oh." A flicker of attention. "How?"

"No one mentioned how – weird – you things are."

"I'd prefer, different. There's a big change in viewpoint when you become one of us." She ponders for a moment. "Lots of changes actually. Everything matters a great deal more, some of us theorise that it's an adaption to eternity. You humans are always running around and… Where are you going?"

He's on his way to the Tower with his tea. "Checking on stuff."

"Okay. Well. I'm going to see if I can make a dent in this den of horrors." As he pulls down the ladder he hears, as if an after thought "thank you for the rescue William. It would have been difficult to get away from that horrible sand dune. You did a kind thing."

"Don't need to thank me. Not sure why I did it."

"Oh, I think I know." She looks sadly at the discarded tin smashed against the wall in the corner. "I'm sorry about the peas."

"Thanks?"

Her gaze settles on his botanical garden. "Oh! Are those plants I see over there? How delightful!" Narrowed eyes. "They should be labelled."

"Definitely not what I was expecting," he mutters, clambering up the ladder, pulling it up behind him as the Vampire hums some lullaby to his plants that he can hear all the way to the top of the Tower.

There is no calm here. No sense of home. It feels oddly bereft this evening. He opens the windows to watch the sea, but all he can see is snow and a reddish fog that reduces visibility down to not much further than he can wave his hand. The seagulls have come back after their bravura performance of what feels like a year ago. Cawing quietly to themselves up on the roof and sheltering.

The Lamp sits on its runners, immobile. There's no point to turning the thing on as even if it could see something in the pea-souper out there, he couldn't, and anyone stupid enough to go sailing in this weather would quickly end up with a stoved-in hull, washed up on the shore like the container ships that litter the shores of the world, watching the sea recede back to the poles behind their broken backs.

He drinks his tea, wincing a little as it burns the tip of his tongue. It's cold up here and even his nest is strangely repulsive. He examines the blankets and notes how filthy they are.

The bin in the corner is overflowing and there's stains across most of the floor. Is there any reason to spend time up here? It's actually pretty revolting.

He walks over to the Radio and gives it a tap. Still silent, still dead. Even the flashes of light are gone.

He'll give it an hour or so. Then he'll head back down and see what Alyson is doing, maybe take her to the tunnels. There are plenty of boats up in the outer harbour if she wanted to move on. Wasn't that her original plan? If the Union didn't want to collect her there was no reason to keep her here and the Union's not being communicative this evening.

Maybe he could go with her? There's a world out there.

He hears a whirring noise from downstairs followed by the sound of a small drill bit at work. He decides to let that little bit of uncertainty go for now and settles back into his nest with visible distaste, pondering whether he should bring up one of the deck chairs from his stores, so he could sit without having to use this nasty little nook.

Still, it is home, and there are worse places to be in this world. He's suddenly very aware of the piles of dead buried in the cold earth and the lights of the fisher flies dipping down.

He dozes, hunched up on himself, waiting for instructions from the Radio he is beginning to doubt will ever arrive before leaning a little further into the stale softness and keeps going, falling deep into the past.

The chair has a hard back and Carlos is lolling around in the comfy seat. The man was alright provided you didn't get him on to the subject of soccer, food or politics and they'd been on the same break rota for the last week. Best option was to leave him to read the fashion magazines he had glommed from their last port visit and ignore any sudden departures to the head.

He would spend his break the same way he always did. Putting together one of the complex jigsaws in the break room stowage lockers, the company's idea of entertainment since the satellite network had been shredded in the last war and his break time had become a lot less interesting.

He was glad he'd cashed out before then. The merchant marine was a cushy billet now that cargo ships with working mag-line nav-comms were like hens teeth.

He spreads out the contents of one of the boxes across the table, the pieces tiny and difficult to get a handle on in the dim fluorescent lighting here, deep in the bowels of the five-hundred thousand ton beast. Best he can tell today's entertainment is a pastoral scene and best he can tell it suffers from the usual problem of missing a dozen at least of the corner and side pieces.

He tries to figure out from the box what's missing. He turns it around a little and ignores the sound of Carlos heading out of the room, muttering to the accompaniment of rustling paper.

Looks like there should be a ruined tower at the right-hand side. He brings the box closer and squints. There's a figure up there. The top bit, anyway. Half the shadow of a head turned to look down at the farmland with its hedgerows and outcroppings of trees and the distant sea with a yacht passing, its triangular sail seeming to shift impossibily as he watches it.

He shakes his head. Trick of the light.

Probably for the best that he can't complete the jigsaw. Feels like the figure in the Tower is best left where it is, in pieces, somewhere else. There's a whole world to build beyond its confines and even in pieces the figure seems to brim with malice.

He jolts back into consciousness. It's past eight. No news at seven today, that's a first and there are pins and needles playing up and down his arms. There's no singing from below, he wonders if the Vampire has gone exploring outside. It's not as if the dark would hold much of concern to her.

No. Light pattering as something climbs the stairs.

"Car-William? Are you awake?" There she is. Slightly muffled, waiting before climbing the Tower. "Do you mind if I come up? I have some thoughts on your supply situation and our future plans?"

Why not. Other than being disgusting there's nothing at the top of the Tower that she shouldn't see. He might even be able to get the wind-up radio working and let her know what's happening across the Channel. That would be helpful wouldn't it?

"It's fine. You need to pull the…"

Clunk. The ladder slips its way down and drops to the floor. He can hear her coming up, clumsier than he would have expected.

"Watch out for the…"

"Oh. Grenades. Interesting." Some shuffling. "I've put them in a bag. Are those Russian grenades? They look very scary up close. All that death in a nasty little metal casing. Humans…"

Then more clunking before he guesses she's below and he undoes the trap door to the main viewing platform stepping back from the brink. A moment later a thick head of black hair bobs above level of the floor like a fishing lure attracting the catch of the day, to be followed by the rest of Alyson now wearing a comfortable jumper and jeans combination.

"I took some clothes from your stores. I hope you don't mind. Mine were still a little wet and it was uncomfortable. Business wear is not hugely practical. Particularly when wet. From being in the water. After someone sank my boat." Laser powered glare, amplified by the blue flame in her brown eyes.

"It's fine. Welcome to the Tower." He brazens out the glare and studiously ignores the mounting horror in the vampire woman's eyes at the sight of the mess in the Tower's top. It's better than the Shrine anyway, if you ignore the faint smell of spilled soup and noodle fragments covering the floor.

The overflowing bin. The stains. The smears at the edges of the windows where he didn't quite get rid of the Seagulls' leavings…

"Thank you." She gives it a once over. "This is quaint.

Very you." A pause. "Should your wireless be doing that? It doesn't look like it's plugged in."

"Doing what?"

He turns.

The Radio's information panel is flashing red. "No. That's new."

She hisses through her teeth. "Oh dear. Do you think it would stop doing that if I went back downstairs? It stinks of the same nonsense as the runes hereabouts. I don't like it."

Maybe. It's not a good look.

"Tell you what Aly, you head back down and we can talk tomorrow."

"Alright. Not sure why you would stay up here, but your place, your rules as we have clearly agreed. " Aly gives the Radio a hard stare. "I hope it stops. It looks like a very distracting piece of machinery if you ask me."

It doesn't. But for tonight there doesn't appear to be much that can be done, so he decides to lock up and catch some sleep. He can't afford to be dozing so much during the day.

His sleep is undisturbed other than the wispiest dream that the ghosts of the snowmen are back in the graveyard.

Some of them, anyway.

26

Echoes of another story

Another morning. It's different though, starting with a jump scare. He's startled to find Aly standing at the window of the Tower, head cocked to one side. Apparently listening to something.

The Radio's light has stopped flashing. It could have reset, ready to forward messages again, or it could be that the Radio is finally on its last legs and losing function. That leaves him in two minds over whether it would be a good thing or not. The great horror it has been shouting to the veiled stars for the past six months has arrived and she's nothing worse than confusingly goofy.

"Hey Aly? What are you doing here?"

"Seems quite misty out there. Doesn't look natural to me. What's going on do you think?"

"Aly?"

"Yes, William."

"What are you doing up here?"

"What does it look like, Carl…?" Narrowed eyes. "William. William I mean. And I'm keeping an eye on your new guests." She points out towards the town.

"They're very eager to get somewhere. I think they're headed towards that big half-built building down by the sea rather than here though. It was a pleasant surprise as it meant I didn't have to wake you up. Isn't that where the Tunnels are?"

"What?"

He jumps out of bed, stumbling out of the cocoon of blankets and sending pillows in all directions, grabbing for the binoculars next to the recumbent Lamp.

"Where?"

"I'd say…" her index finger floats from point to point as if bobbing on water. "About there."

Sure enough there's unwelcome guests in his little domain. At least a dozen. He can see them moving with clear purpose around the part-built development, next to the tunnel entrance. Not the stagger of dead things, or the furtive point-to-point subterfuge of a band of destitute survivors. Straight of back, purposeful of movement and signalling to others of their ilk that he cannot see with confident waves like they own the place.

He shivers. They remind him of something from before.

"I wonder what they're doing. Anything interesting down there, William? Something you'd like to tell me maybe?"

"No." He lies.

"You're not a good liar, William. We're the same like that." She favours him with a blankly pleasant look, eyes wide and lips quirked at the edges into a cheerful smile. The effect falls deep into the uncanny valley, a china doll, a mannequin, something pretending to be human without a great deal of skill, for all its apparent beauty.

"Don't do that."

"I can't help my expressions, William. Can you? Shall

we go and meet them? I believe I mentioned that I'd like to see what's in those tunnels."

He ponders the thought. It's possible the red light was an alarm. Watch out humanity, Master nearby. They could be here for Aly and think he's down at the Tunnels. If the Tunnels really had been a base of sorts, well. That would explain a lot.

"We'll go."

"Good, good. Would you mind if we went and saw the Marina on the way?" She ventures. "Can go and meet your friends down there, and maybe I can take a look at these boats on the way back." She stops and does that head tilt, then changes tack. "It's always good to have options."

If they do leave without her, or turn out to be hostile he supposes it would be another way out of his dilemma. Though he is enjoying the near-human company. "Okay. But keep back. I don't think you'll be welcome and I'll need to… introduce you."

"I will." She tilts her head. "Do you hear a helicopter?"

He gives her the look. "Of course I don't hear a helicopter. There's a storm blowing Aly. All I can hear is that and the seagulls. Have to be insane to use a helicopter in this." He points upwards. "Or that."

"I think I can hear something. Do you mind if I check it out? Give me a moment up here?"

"Knock yourself out. I'll get ready. Assume you're fine to go as you are?"

"I am, William. Thank you." She points at her boots. "I borrowed these too. Very stomp."

As the Watcher slides down the ladder, she waits a heart beat to let the top of his head drop below the level of the floor. Then she moves to the rails on which the Lamp sits, glares at it and does something to its casing, twisting hard and crushing. Then the same to the Radio.

"Awful dirty machines."

Through the Flint Walls and down to the town. Aly seems lost in thought as they walk, flicking a pack of cards between her fingers. muttering conversations with her own inner monologue. Fighting battles and discussing failures.

He leaves her to her thoughts as he tries to put together a plan. He has no proof the men and women working at the Tunnels are Union. If they aren't then, well. Between the two of them they should be able to handle anything, however confident they might appear.

If they are Union, then that's more difficult. Bordering on complicated. Does anyone even know he's here? There were the people who gave him the Lamp. He remembers that. But the Radio's not working the last couple of days and he'll be turning up with a Vampire. Or nearby at least.

If they'll listen to him, know who he is (one up on him), then will they take the Vampire off his hands or just try and kill it?

Does he even want them to?

They wend a stealthy way through the ruins of the town. With every step he has a building sense of foreboding which, try as he might, he can't shake off.

Would he really want to meet whatever it was that speaks from the Radio? Would anyone sane want to meet the stilted thing that has been directing him to sink escaping refugees and ranting about a state he'd never heard of till six months before? Where did the population go? He's been alone for so long he can't remember.

They duck into the cover of the Marina with its light engineering works and concrete walkways, and the vampire tilts her head to one side.

"Boats interesting?"

"Maybe in a moment. I honestly think there's something coming this way."

"Good hearing, vampires?"

She gives him a conspiratorial look. "Terribly good."

"Okay. I'll bite. Are they coming this way? The ones from the Tunnels?" He reaches for his shotgun shells but stops before his fingers grip the fat metal cases.

"No. I don't think it's them unless they've decided to make sandcastles. It's something else." She chews her lip. "At a guess I'd say it's a small convoy of sorts. Two or three vehicles with big wheels, driving along the beaches from up that way," She points up the coast, the beaches extended by the receding waters like badly cared for teeth, "and headed this way."

The odds were rapidly getting worse. That many vehicles meant two dozen of the intruders at least, and maybe some heavy weapons. "Can you still hear the ones at the tunnels?"

"Oh yes, they're clunking around, moving things about. Noisy fellows. Surprised you can't hear them – they must be using drills to make that sort of din." Her gaze is wandering across the Marina with its forest of masts set at crazy angles. "Goodness, there's a lot of boats here. Do you think any of them would still be solid enough for a jaunt somewhere a little more tropical?"

He frowns. "Not those ones. Anything in the water's generally got a cracked hull from the ice." He watches a shadow of irritation pass across her otherwise statue-like face. "If you're seriously considering leaving – and don't let me stop you – I'm sure I can find you a hull that'd suit you. I've had a lot of time to find the good ones."

"Rather the least you could do given what you did to my previous vessel." She pouts, pauses, and listens to something unheard. "And not yet. I feel like I want to see a little of the world hereabouts before I decide where to go next. Plus I want to see who's come for dinner."

He nods. "First things first, this isn't all under our control, Aly."

There's at least two groups making up the initial intruders and they definitely look like they could be Union based on what he's seen. There's something old school about them. They could almost fit into the world before.

The first team is swathed in outdoor gear. From their stance at least some of them are military, though it is difficult to see exactly which branch given the sheer amount of fabric covering their uniforms, bundled up like polar bears in the cold.

They carry a mix of weapons, assault rifles, light machine guns, carbines covered in rags to break up their profile. He suspects there are others hidden up on the cliffs, watching, with longer guns. Professionals, military. Special forces maybe even.

The other team are civilians, running tests on the entrance to the Tunnels and drilling around the locks. They want in. One of them has come across the remains of the broken goat's head that he had destroyed days before and is engaged in earnest discussions with one of his colleagues who's wearing a thermal parka and an armband with a square that looks like a stylised barbican.

In all, there's maybe twenty of them. It's the largest gathering of people he's seen since… since this all started. Maybe the crowds looting the supermarket… when had that been?

"I think they've heard their friends. Silly wrapping yourself up in all that padding. Ruins your hearing."

Aly is distracted, barely present. Occasionally words escape her lips running a narrative for unseen viewers.

Things like "I know," "What good will that do," and "How near are they?" Whoever she's talking to is in a rush and is barely giving her a word in edgewise, just instructions that never seem to quite take into account reality.

"Oh, they've definitely heard the others."

One of the civilians gestures off towards the slope of the beach and distant sea-splashing sluggishly despite the winds, and two of the military types head that way, heads bowed as they push their way into the wind. The storm, if anything, is worse than ever and the visibility is awful.

He's brought the Vampire to the top floor of a 1920s style hotel that should have provided them with a good view over to the half-completed flats and the Tunnels, whilst still remaining inconspicuous from above and below. It hasn't turned out that way. The dust and ice in the air gives the whole scene the logic of a nightmare and the noise of the drill is burrowing into his skull.

There's something both fascinating and disquieting about the scene playing out below.

It reminds him a little of that Antarctica documentary, the clothes, the military types watching over the experiments. All that's missing is the helpful voice-over explaining what's happening and why and goodness but he misses that right now. It's difficult to make decisions when you can't hear a word of what's being said.

Given the way their attention is focussed entirely on the tunnels he'd think they weren't even interested in him or his guest. Wouldn't that be nice?

"Aly?"

She looks up from the broken bed on which she stands, perched on one leg in some bizarre yoga pose. "What is it William?"

"What are you doing?"

"Listening."

"To what?"

"Important things."

"Could you tear yourself away from that for a moment? I'd like to borrow those ears of yours."

The Vampire remains silent.

"Aly?"

"Yes, yes. I can help." A flicker of sadness, then back to passivity. "Wait a moment. It might understand what's happening. I know. I know. What do you want to know, William?"

"What are they talking about?" It's like pulling teeth. He hopes she's not like the all the time.

"Your friends down there? They seem pleasant enough." She stands and peers over his shoulder and shivers. "They are looking for friends who are in those Tunnels but some 'idiot' seems to have locked the entrance tight. Hence the drills. I wonder if that's the clade our intelligence people mentioned down there?" She brightens. "I think we should go and help them. We had friends in there."

He frowns. "Any clue as to who they are? They look like Union types would look…"

"Um. Okay. Always happy to help Carlos." She playfully whacks him on the shoulder which sends an unpleasant tingle down his arm. "Silly man, we're a team. Even if you don't know it yet."

He waits as she starts to mutter to herself again. He coughs.

"Oh. Now. Yes. Sorry. Do you want the gist or what they're actually saying? I can do either."

"Gist!"

"Right. Well, they're from the MDR, which is a Ministry of your old government. As you would expect they work for a Minister of some sort who's up at the 'Castle. Whatever that is. There's some soldiers," she points at various places and then up at the cliffs, stabbing a finger and revealing a pair of cunningly concealed snipers perched in the houses at the top of the cliffs, "and there are some Assistants…"

"What's an Assistant?"

"Seems to be what they call Agents now. Silly term. Maybe they're new, and haven't qualified yet? And they smell better than I'd expect given the circumstances and past experience."

"You're commenting on their personal hygiene, of course you are."

"No, no. I'm sure they're clean, relative to your kind as they seem to have a lot more cleaning facilities wherever they're from. Even a bit of deodorant." A deep breath. "Axel Forest?"

"Aly!"

"I'm talking metaphorically. I've found a lot of your sort recently have smelt awful, on the metaphysical level. Even you, dear William have a nasty whiff to you on occasion." She sniffs theatrically and he growls as his irritation mounts. "I suppose you want to know what they're doing and if they're here for me?"

"Yes!"

"No."

Silence.

"No?"

"I believe I was very clear on that, if you're going to complain when I tell you everything then…"

"So why are they here!"

"That." Another finger jab. "Now that place does smell bad. I have a horrible feeling we all may be a little late to the party. That horrid seal looks like its done its business and you don't lock people in with one of those with the intention of making it easy for them to get out. How long can humans survive in the dark? Is that a thing?"

He looks at her.

"Not a thing?"

"No."

The two civilians working on the remains of the Goat's head have produced a strange contraption of crystals and wire which they are twisting into various configurations that make the item hum. The one looks at the other.

One of the soldiers runs from the beach up to the two civilians standing around its broken pieces. A crackle of short range radio.

"Oh, and I think they're about to have unexpected company." Aly is peering down the coast, off towards the cape then wrinkles her nose. "Coming from that way. And they smell horrible, lots of civilians and a few soldier types I think. Balance is very 'assistant' though."

Figures at the very edge of his vision, visible mainly due to the faint orange glow surrounding them. A mirror of the team at the Tunnels. "Can you see any insignia? This lot have a square."

She squints. "Umm."

"Aly?"

"Goat!"

Why had he thought the Union was one thing? He feels like that was something he should have known wasn't true. Nothing was a unity anymore and everything had scattered to pieces. "Aly?"

"Yes, William?"

"Lets move a bit closer."

She claps her hands. "Oh, a jaunt! If we're picking sides, I say we go with humans with the weird tunnel obsession and the squares. They remind me of the old ones we had to speak to, and they could be quite reasonable once they stopped trying to kill us. Those new ones look like they're…"

She freezes in place, halfway through a step. Eyes wide, blue flames engulfing the brown of her eyes. "Carlos! There's…"

The train of her words are derailed in an instant as an indescribable explosion rumbles across the Isle. It seems to emit from somewhere far off to the south-east, deep in the Continent. It is followed by heat wave that melts away the ice on the windows facing that way, and a wind that rattles the few remaining planes of glass.

He's thrown himself to the ground, blowing all the air from his lungs. Some inbuilt reflex, more than a little redundant as the explosion is so far away.

When he picks himself up Aly has sat down heavily on the bed frame, hand over her mouth, eyes no longer blazing with blue fire but plain hazel.

"What the hell was that?"

"Oh." She is all she manages. Then her head drops and she seems to shrink into herself.

"Alyson. What was that?"

Nothing. She's frozen up entirely.

He leaves her be, she'll either snap out of it or she won't and he needs to see what's happening below.

Whatever the explosion was, it appears to have taken both teams at the Tunnel by surprise.

One has recovered its bearings earlier than the other. The group making their way down the coast are waving at their apparent compatriots by the Tunnel entrance, from their side the military types are dropping into half-hearted cover whilst the civilians wave back at the approaching team with an air of confusion.

Shouted words in the storm, greetings, challenges. Questions over the explosion.

He looks at Aly. She's not moving anytime soon. Whatever it was that happened has left her basically inert. She looks more like a waxwork model than ever.

He shakes his head. "Probably for the best. At least until I've worked out what's what." He jumps down from the Hotel window and creeps up to listen in on the intriguing meeting that could be the key to a lot of the questions he has and prepares to introduce himself to whomsoever seems to be the most reasonable.

27

Pick a side

"Ho there, lads. Looks like the war's over doesn't it?"

"Think that was Paris?"

"You get the same report as us, Childs. Can't see it being anywhere else. Advance team has done the Union proud."

"Yeah. Well. That's on us more than you. What are you doing here Flaught? Haven't you got a camp to clear out for kicks?"

"Oh, that's all done now. Bit of a fuck up on the numbers but you live with the consequences. Don't give me that look. None of us would be here without Last Light."

"That's your line."

"There were other ways."

"You keep telling yourself that, Ix. Sound like fucking Thespian…"

"Anyway… why are you here?"

"Brooker's asked us to check up on you. Dangerous along the gap. He's wandering about and unsupervised and, ah, so are you."

"Brooker? Don't make me laugh. I know who you really work for. What are you doing down here. Following us?"

"Maybe a little. Need to keep tabs on where the pieces are. I

wouldn't bother with the digging though. No one there anymore. Seal's broken. See?"

"I can see. Question is why there's a seal at all. There was a support team based here and Ministerial orders were that..."

"Gods, you and your Minister. When are you going to get that that stuff is done. All of it. Time to move on. Same with the team down here. Relics."

"Archaeology."

"Relics or not, we're supposed to find them and..."

"Excision or recovery? Which was it?"

"Recovery of course. With the war over we're going to need everyone to help rebuild. Even the stick in the muds."

"Yeah. That'd be worth it."

"Why are you here, Flaught. Other than overwatch. We're all supposed to be on the same side. Or not pretending anymore?"

"Excision. Then hang about and catch a couple of little fishies"

"I thought you said they were all dead? That we're wasting our time?"

"Excision isn't for them, my man. It's for you. You picked your side."

All hell breaks loose.

The Watcher is taken aback by the fight that ensues. That there's a fight. He can get that. Nothing's been simple for a long time. But he's still expecting something resembling a skirmish from the old days. The sort of fights with guns and explosions and men and women dropping for cover and grenades flying.

The shoot-out at the okay coral, urban combat 101 from the training manuals the army wrote.

Instead.

Well this is not what he'd expected at all and it's all he can do to keep up with the ebb and flow of the fight.

Everything has changed since… whenever he was last involved in something like this.

One of the 'Goat' assistants has launched herself up the cliff in a single leap and is wall crawling almost vertically to kill the sniper teams atop the cliffs. Another has lunged with arms made of fire and is gripping the man with the crystal and wire contraption close, holding him close as he burns alive with a horrible grin playing across his face which has too many eyes.

Childs, the leader of the 'Squares' is making more sense, crouching, caught in the act of throwing a grenade at the main body of the Goats who seem to have missed the memo that they should attack. The burning monster is screaming at them to engage and they break into group and scatter and suddenly Childs can't seem to move, grenade held at half throw.

The cliff runner nears one of the Snipers. Bullets aren't stopping her but the sniper keeps his cool and shoots an outcropping of chalk under the attacker's feet as she rushes impossibly along the cliff. The Assistant stumbles, falls and lands with a crack on the rock below.

Gunfire erupts from the soldiers on both sides. The squaddie who had warned the first team of the approach of the second knocks over the frozen Childs. The grenade tumbles away and the man begins to rise as the burning thing, Flaught, drops the barbecued remnants of his victim and jumps at Childs, catching bullets in the air with a whoop as he attacks.

It is chaos. Flames and ice fly from the attacking goat team and are absorbed into spinning shields that spray the attacks right back in the faces of the shooters.

A sniper topples from their position, rigid as a plant and drops by the fallen Assistant. The woman picks herself up on broken legs and slices into him with arms that are suddenly scythes with a howl.

Explosions erupt. A machine gun opens up, catching Flaught as he charges another scientist, sending him tumbling backwards with multiple impacts.

Childs is down and bleeding.

The Goats are winning. More of the 'Assistants' hurl themselves up towards the Snipers whose fire is the only thing making this close to a fair fight, one jumps impossibly at the hidden Machine gun, tumbling in midair.

Half the Squares are down. Maybe a third of the Goats.

Fuck it. He's helping the Squares.

There's a giggle from beside him.

"Hello, D. Long time no see." It's the woman with scythes for arms. She's edged around the battlefield to catch a pair of squaddies preparing a missile launcher, and found his hiding place. "No orders about you." She grins a bloody smile, legs twisting themselves back into a semblance of structural solidity, waves of agony swim across her face and her teeth splinter. "Guess that makes it dealer's choice."

She jumps at him faster than he could believe possible. He raises his arms in a futile attempt to ward her off and his arms burn in patterns. Scythes extend and are poised to slice him in two, the edges still bloody from her murder of the sniper as she spits bits of enamel in his face.

She never makes it.

She runs straight into a storm of debris that flenses her to a bloody mess in a moment, throwing her up in a blast of force, then keeps going and going until the remains splatter to the ground.

He turns to look behind him.

"William. You have the worst taste in friends." Alyson is pale. Paler than usual and her eyes remain dark hazel, lacking the blue fire of her previous self. But she is here and she's saved him. "Squares, then?"

"You bet."

They are too late. The battle has passed across the ruins like a flash fire across dry prairie and in practice neither side has won. Magic and technology have cancelled each other out. Dead bodies litter the ruins in various forms of dissolution, burnt, frozen, peppered with bullets. They catch the last two Goats, including Flaught crawling towards the Tunnels, coughing blood and looking for shelter after taking a direct hit from the missile launcher.

Aly finishes them without a moment's thought, a neat snap of the neck between two fingers of her long hands.

"Aly…"

"What? He was suffering. I don't hold with that."

"We could have questioned one of them."

"I don't think either of them would have said anything interesting, William. They don't seem to be that sort of people." She lifts up Flaught's arm, gripping the limp hand and examining the etched runes across his skin. "Yuck."

Fires from the fight light up his way as he stalks the battlefield looking for any other survivors before Aly can continue her mission of mercy.

Surely at least one of the men and women must be alive?

28

Unravelling

Are you Childs?

That's the name. Don't wear it out. Head of the Baptist, is that you D.? They said you were here still.

Do I know you? No. Just hold still. We might be able to save you. There's a lot of damage but I've got help and they seem to have some skills. You're Union? I've been waiting for you to turn up…

Ministry. Union. Whatever. And don't make me laugh, D. I've seen how you help people. You're the worst. Always have been, always will be… just my luck…

Why do you all keep calling me that?

Not fair, man. Try to be honest. For once in your life. I'm dying here and you're messing me around. It's you isn't it? You look like seven shades of shit.

I'm… I don't know.

Fuck me. I almost believe you. What a disaster this has been. Whole thing. Almost wish we'd all just died and been done when it hit. Saved a lot of… the unnecessary.

…

D?

If you say so.

There's someone coming. Flaught and his traitors had it right on one thing. You need to stop them. Witches… not witches. Carrying something…

After Childs dies, he opens the Tunnels and lets Aly take a look around. She returns with an old style thumb drive and a glum look to her.

"Find what you were looking for?"

She holds up the drive. "None of my people but… I have what I have. Odd place to store it and not sure it matters much, now. A recording from a broken communicator. Did he have anything interesting to say? The Square guy?"

"Nothing interesting. Some regrets."

"Lots of those floating around at the moment."

"You could have helped him."

"Probably not. And I'm not feeling very merciful just now."

"You seem different."

"I am." She grimaces. "I'm alone."

"What was the explosion?"

"End of the war. End of us all, bar me. And do you know what the last thing my family had me do before they went out to fight their last fight?"

"Get that drive?"

"Get that drive. And the comms device too, if it were working. Which it wasn't." She hobbles off towards the Marina. "I don't think any of these fellows will be taking me with them and I think I can live with that. I think your Union might be having a Civil War and that's too much bother for me right now. I'm going to hang around a while to get my bearings again and then you can help me find a boat and I am out of here."

"Yeah." He follows the Vampire woman past the boats. "What's on the drive?"

She chuckles. "Isn't that just the question? Best I can tell? Impressionistic art."

"Seriously?"

"Series of stills. Of a little red teapot. Maybe something else. I can't tell." She snorts. "I don't really care. Time to go home William. I think we'll fix you before I leave, people matter. I suppose. Things, less so. Got to hold to our principles even when there's no 'us' anymore."

His sleep that night is the best he's had for as long as he can remember, which given the nightmare of the day is as surprising as it is welcome.

It is deep and refreshing. Brightened by dreams of duty-free rum, sandy beaches and sunshine filled days. There are highlights of music festivals and ice cream treats, food tents with hissing woks laden with noodles and fishing trips on quiet seas.

What unpleasant elements there are drift away. Fights with drunken yobs, checking ministerial briefing papers past midnight, cooking up a mush with arthritic fingers in a cold kitchen, they all melt away into a dream of nautical life on a grey hulled warship.

No one is watching him. It's liberating. And he feels like himself.

The question with which he awakes is, who is that? He doesn't feel like he's the 'worst' but there's still a lot to clarify before he'll be back to whoever he was before the world collapsed and he lost himself.

He wonders how Vampires are at counselling. His

guess is they're shitty but are sure they're pretty damn good.

When he comes down the next morning it's clear that the Vampire has been busy. Her natural inclinations towards order are in hyperdrive, he suspects it's due to the loss of her family, though the exact nature of a Vampire 'family' escapes him. Do they have blood ties or is it all about the… blood… ties.

Whatever it is, she's taking the loss badly.

Each of his plants are now meticulously catalogued with ties notifying the reader of their scientific and common names, date of planting (how did she know that?) and feeding schedule. They are also arranged in an optimum pattern to best make use of their time under the lamps. If plants could be spoiled, his pre-Catastrophe darlings are now officially spoiled plants.

She's even set up what looks suspiciously like a clockwork water sprinkler system hanging off hooks attached to the ceiling that release light sprays of clean water mixed with plant feed in perfect rotation.

"I suppose that explains the drilling last couple of nights."

She looks up. "Good morning, sleepy head. How do you feel?"

"Confused. But better."

"That should hold a while, though I think we're going to need to get some remedial work done on you to keep you that way. When everything is a mess, the best you can do is help others, William. That's one of his favourite aphorisms, though not exactly one he lived by."

"Who?"

"Doesn't matter."

She is carefully cataloguing his stores again, sipping at sweet hot tea. Piles of neatly stacked packing boxes neatly labelled are set up against the wall next to the map showing St. Augustine's travels from Rome to Thanet to speak to the King of Kent and his Frankish wife whose street nearly proved the death of him a few days before.

Aly has taped a master-list of the contents of each box by the front door, noodles, water tablets, biscuits, novels (trash), novels (classic), maps (local), maps (archaic), make up bags (velvet) and so on.

"What did you dream about, William? You may think it's a silly question but in fact it's rather important if we want to get you back on track. Which we do." The tea has mellowed her voice into a soft burr of warmth. It's ever more difficult to match up the horrors of the Family's occupation of Europe and their disastrous coup in China with the softly spoken, sweet of nature, helpful near-woman sorting out his scavenged stores.

"The usual nonsense."

She looks dubious. "That sounds evasive to me, William. The usual nonsense is very uninformative and I think you might have enjoyed better dreams than usual."

"Okay. The dreams were fine. Confusing, but fine."

She nods. "That's good. I've kept myself busy as you can see. Yesterday was not a good day for me."

"Did you sleep at all? Can you sleep at all?" He's not sure how much he should dig. For all her kindness, Alyson is, well. A Vampire.

"I don't. I could, but I don't. Too much nastiness lurking back there. I must be the first Vampire in millennia who's got no one watching over her and it is a bittersweet feeling. They always say that you can pick your friends but not your family. In my case for all their faults, my family picked me, and I've had them around since forever." she puts down her pen and paper and stares at the ground, whatever she's thinking of, it is not pleasant. "Anyway. I've been making a list of the things you have here. They're almost all food and books, no electronics, no spare clothing other than that box where I found this get-up. Do you have other places you store your items?"

He nods. "Yes I do, and why would you be asking that?"

"Given what I saw yesterday I'm not going to be staying, so I have a long journey ahead of me once we're finished here, and I would like to take some of your stuff to replace the store you have stolen as it is indeed all of a sort."

He shrugs. He has enough trash for a lifetime.

"My colleagues do not seem to have understood the remit of my instructions for my initial voyage. I have some tolerances, but…" She waves her hand around the room, where the contents of her remaining cargo have been neatly stacked.

He suppresses a snort of laughter. "That's a lot of expired peas."

"And a surprising amount of Tartan goods. I should have been more clear in my instructions. They seem to have taken 'trade goods' to mean whatever they found in the nearest shop, whilst my request for canned goods. Well. You can see for yourself. It was all quite a rush. No good for travel though."

"You don't eat."

"I don't think anyone eats those, William. And I have no use for Tartan right now as I'm aiming for a warmer clime. However wherever I end up I will need some leverage and this, we can agree, has limited value."

"I see your problem."

"You might have some spare things you could… lend me? Or we could trade. I'll help you with your identity crisis and you can get me stocked up for what's to come." A dead eyed smile. "You could even join me if you want?"

He splutters, that's a step too far. "I'm not sure about that. The Union…"

"The Union, whatever it is, looks to me like it's falling apart." Aly shakes here head. "Goats and Squares and whoever it was who was in those Tunnels. I suppose that's what happens when humans finally get what they want."

"What was that?"

"Power. I saw those unpleasant types waving their magic around like mad idiots. I, for one, wouldn't want to be anywhere near those people are. Children with… nukes and nukes powered by death."

"Yeah. Seems that way. Still got killed by the guys with guns though. If it is a civil war the goodies might win."

She raises her eyebrows at the thought of their being 'goodies. "Practice makes perfect with the guns. Even the 'goodies' tend to shoot first and think later and I think you're overestimating how 'good' Mr. Childs and his friends were. They seem the sort to look the other way. No. I'm done here."

She goes back to arranging stores as he looks for something to eat. He has quite an appetite today and everything has changed, however whatever system Aly is using it is quite beyond him.

He finally identifies where his food has gone, the corner nearest the Tryptych and furthest from the rune-cooker, and shuffles through one of the boxes of supplies to a hiss of irritation from the woman. "Breakfast biscuits," he apologises.

"I had thos nicely arranged." She crosses out an entry on her list and hisses again like a steaming kettle.

"So, why do you do that? I didn't ask you to." He looks at the bar. "Hmm, strawberry. That's okay I suppose."

She takes up her pen and paper again and starts to slot the now disordered breakfast snacks into carefully arranged piles, three tall. "We all have our quirks. For my own peace of mind? I like order, I like to arrange and when we like something and we've been around for a while we can get more than a little obsessive."

"You don't say."

"Something to do with an eternity, and it increases with age. I read a monogram by one of the lost masters that it's a side effect of time with what is still basically a human mind. Though we like to pretend we're much better than that."

"Huh."

"William. I thought you would have some understanding of this, but without self-knowledge. I will cut you some slack. If you think I'm bad, you should have met some of the others in my little family. Or some of the greats of the past. Or I suppose you could just look at the debacle across the Channel. We do like our rules and regulations and somehow it never quite worked out when we fought that stupid war. Damn Albrecht and his nonsense."

She holds up a hand as an apology. "Sorry, that wouldn't mean anything to you."

He's eating his breakfast chewing on oaty goodness. "Can tell me if you want. I've not had anyone much to talk to for longer than I can remember."

"Well, William," she begins.

"Not called William. Apparently."

That earns a sharp toothed grin. "So you know your name is not William. That's progress of a sort. Maybe you remember what it is then? Or is it just a negative that you can't prove."

He ponders, the ratio of strawberry to oats in the bar

was proving a disappointment. "The Union man yesterday. Childs, he said I was called D. Or he called me that."

"D is not a name. It is an initial," she sniffs.

"Woman with the blades too. And I think…" at the edge of his memory. A car and warmth and a female voice.

"Would you rather I called you something else? D would be pretty barbaric but I'm sure we could make it work?"

"Gods no. I think Child's exact description was that D, whoever he was, was 'the worst'. Honestly, until I remember what I'm called William will do as well as anything. Some good kings of that name."

"If you like history you'd have got on with Albrecht." She holds up a hand. "Story for another time. Suffice it to say we buried him alive."

"He sounds like the worst."

"An arguable position, William. He would have argued it for eternity, given the opportunity."

He glances at his watch. "Do you think I should check out what the Radio says about yesterday? There was.. maybe you…"

"Concentrate, William. Words have meaning only when put into grammatical structures. Even in English."

He is unsure whether he should tell Aly about Childs' last words. The warning. If something were coming this way and it was something that both Goats and Squares thought should be killed then surely…

"Witches."

"Witches what?"

"Childs said there were Witches coming here. And they need to be stopped. They were bringing something."

She stops what she is doing. "Witches? That is interesting. Haven't heard from them since the Catastrophe. I wonder if they're waking up. Could do with the help, honestly what with…" her voice trails off.

"He said they should be stopped."

"He would say that. I don't think there's a single group of non humans that your Mr. Brooker likes. Witches." She smiles. "Witches are excellent news. In fact…" Her smile has some human warmth to it. It's the first time he's seen that.

"So they're good?"

A snort. "What does that even mean, William? They're witches. They vary just like everyone else in the world. Bar us. We're all very similar, all copies of an old lunatic copied over whatever was there before. Or we were." She shakes her head, "Odd that something so fundamental is now in the past. I wonder if this is how humans feel all the time? I'd ask you but I'm not sure you'd know anymore. Anyway. They're better than good. They're helpful. If we catch them at the right time and they don't decide to drag us into the world woods and leave us there."

She returns to her organising leaving the comment hanging.

It is at this point that William notes that all she is doing is shuffling already arranged items. That doesn't seem to be a positive sign.

He decides to leave her to her own business for a while. Whatever had happened, whatever her relationship with her 'family', their destruction had knocked her down pretty hard and he was beginning to develop a soft spot for the monster in his home.

Though is this still his home?

The Tower is empty. The stones cold. He sits up there as long as he can as storms blow themselves out across the

Channel, watching the tips of icebergs as they nudge southwards.

William spends his time assessing and reassessing the past that is beginning to reveal itself to him. Reassess how he has spent the past six months. It is an uncomfortable experience. He bounces between trying to account for the over abundance of memories he has of the time before the Catastrophe, the way nothing seems to fit together, the way everything overlaps and contradicts everything else.

When that becomes too difficult he tries to justify what he had been doing since. The Radio and its bizarre nonsense dead in the corner. The Lamp, a lump of metal of rails that sits forlorn at the end of its tracks.

Even if he wanted to continue this life, which he does not, was there any need? The Union men had said the war was over. Alyson's torpor seemed to point that way too.

Would he be expected to guard the Channel against the Easterners next, or had they too been swallowed up in whatever had happened at Paris the previous day?

He felt like a man who was coming up for air after a deep dive into the abyss. The problem being that he wasn't sure he could hold himself together without the pressure.

At least the voices were gone.

When he comes back down to the Shrine, Aly is sitting in a chair with a notebook. The pages covered in frenzied scratches of words linked one to the other by lines that jump across each other.

"If that's a plan then it looks a little overcomplicated, Aly."

She closes the book. "I know. No matter how much I try to simplify my plans they spiral off into the millennia and I lose track of what I need to do right now. I'm beginning to suspect that we were all created to fail, William.

Carlos, your near namesake, said something to that effect once, just before he ended. That would be strange, would it not? Why create something flawed, surely it would have been better not to create at all."

"Do you want more time? Your plans look… detailed."

"No. I have all the time in the world." She gives him a faint grin. "I find having someone around to keep me focussed useful and that someone looks like it's you, William."

He picks up another of the deckchairs and sets up opposite the Vampire woman. "What's the first step in this plan of yours then?"

She seems to chew the question for a time. Then takes a deep breath and speaks. "I'm going to repair you. I don't owe you anything, it does seem the right thing to do and you know what they say about who you are in the dark?" She sighs. "Even that was a carriage crash of words wasn't it?"

"Um. Okay." He wasn't aware he needed repair. Maybe a little therapy. And everything is dark. That was how things are. "Nothing unnatural I trust?"

Big eyes stare at him. "I'll explain as we do it. Otherwise we'll be here all night. Nothing to worry about." And she gives him the most unconvincing grin he has ever seen.

"After that?" She opens her mouth. "One step at a time…"

"Get away from here. And I've had some thoughts on that subject that I wanted to run past you, based on what you told me."

"Oh?" She goes to open her book and he closes it quickly. "Maybe keep it simple?"

"I can do that." Though it comes out more as a question than a statement. "The Witches you said were coming. They might be my ticket out of here without a stupid boat.

They have a network they use to travel about and I might be able to hitch a ride if I ask them nicely. Unlike humans we can all be quite reasonable."

A pause.

"Not the Fae."

"Where do you think you'll go?"

"Farthest place from here I can. Sit out whatever's going on here and keep away from where he's buried in case they wake him up." She picks up an atlas, opens it, traces a line down from a point in Northern France and across the Atlantic, veering away from the Americas and heading round the Cape. "Goodness that would be a disaster."

He chuckles. "Far as you can go? Australia then, or is it New Zealand? Was that your original plan?"

"Yes." She holds up a finger. "No. It was our plan, then something got in the way."

"And you were planning on getting there using a patrol boat with a marine diesel engine and nowhere to refuel? How much fuel were you taking? A dozen better boats for that up at the Marina!"

"I left in a bit of a rush. I've mentioned that. There were a lot of very angry Russians and other assorted Easterners trying to stop me." She harrumphs. "I accept that things could definitely have gone better, and it's not like you had nothing to do with the issues that arose. The Patrol Boat seemed a good bet, and we had some extra fuel in the hold I believe. At least I hope it was fuel. Knowing what those idiots pulled it was probably jet fuel or vegetable oil. So literal minded."

He chuckles at the look of distaste playing over her face.

"Anyway. If the thing with the witches doesn't work you can show me the 'better ones' down in the Marina. You could help me sail it if you'd like? I don't know if you're still welcome here."

"Neither do I." He sits back. "Big decision though. I'll have to think about it."

She looks him up and down, appraising. "Lets get you working again and you can decide then. In the meantime are you feeling peckish? You still seem to need to eat given the way you messed up my perfect little system earlier."

His stomach rumbles, a remnant of the old compulsions tugs at him. "A little? I should really patrol though."

"William. Go on your patrol. We can talk more later." She opens her notebook and starts scanning, adding more links. "If you are lucky, I may even make you dinner. I have missed cooking, it never occurred to me that I could still do it. Isn't that strange? How imperatives can push you away from the things you love? Though I may scavenge for some better ingredients, these are a bit… dry."

She's tapping disconsolately at some of root vegetables with her telekinetic powers, and throws a rotten garlic clove into the trash with a flick of her wrist.

Thinking of cooking is making her lick her lips, those sharp teeth. The predator is a little too close to the surface. A shiver down his spine. "What will you eat?"

"I'm sure I can find a bite to eat somewhere near." That sharp toothed smile is out again. "I may even try some of my own cooking, it may not be any use for sustenance but I have a hunger to see what's happened to taste in my time away from myself."

She gives him 'the look'. "It's not like I can eat you, William. That's something we're going to have to talk about."

Time for not William to leave Aly to her hungers.

29

Outside context

The Patrol is uneventful with traces of disquiet. He takes the wind-up radio with him but has no reason to check it.

He finds no trace of the Union teams when he returns to the Tunnels. The bodies are gone, though a little further up the coast he does find a series of beach huts that have been adapted into a facsimile of a fort and daubed in runes that turn his stomach.

No vehicles.

In the middle of the fort, the second team have raised an obelisk of unfamiliar design. It generates an endless heat that is melting the ice around it for nearly five hundred yards, without becoming scorching even when he presses his fingers to it.

And when he looks he thinks he can see the faintest hint of something being drawn down from the clouds above.

He shakes his head and moves on. What was it Aly had said?

Powered by death.

Something deep inside chuckles.

When he returns the promised dinner has not been prepared. It seemed a bit of a throw away comment at the time. Instead Aly is waiting for him in a set of outdoor gear, wielding a walking stick.

"How about we go out of town?" She asks. "Kill two birds with one stone?"

"Why do you have a walking stick?"

She waves it in the air. "Not for walking, dousing. We have to find a nexus point for the World Woods."

"You mentioned that. Do I want to know what it is?"

"It would make the trip we're about to take a great deal more intelligible to your sadly deficient arcane education, William. I saw those heat runes you drew. Rather crude, if you don't mind me saying."

"You'd love what I found earlier." He mutters.

"Can't get distracted. Have to keep on point." Aly replies in a mantra-like intonation. "Yes I'm sure I would but that's not the issue. If we're to find those witches before they fly off we need to get to the nearest World Wood entrance point. They use it to travel from place to place. Sort of a motorway through time and space and some less savoury things. Can get nearly anywhere if you've got the right invitations."

"Including Australia?"

"We can ask!"

"And the stick?"

She levels it. Mutters something in a guttural, creaking tongue that makes him think of stone tables and overgrown graveyards, like the one he lives besides. The stick pulls itself forward with a jerk directly towards him, and he nearly jumps out of his skin.

"No, no, no. Don't be so jumpy William. You happened to be in the direction of the nearest nexus."

He's not sure about this.

"Come on, William. It will be fun. And the witches really are quite delightful." Her voice drops to a whisper. "If you don't get on their bad side that is."

He gives her a glare.

"It'll be fine and we can do some work on you Mr. Fall-Apart on the way. Plus you're all ready to go right now, be a shame not to seize the moment."

Deep sigh.

"Good!"

They head out the front door to the Shrine, the Vampire with a skip to her step and a pat to the flanking stone lions, and he with bad grace and a grumbling stomach.

"I brought you a breakfast bar for the journey."

"Thanks."

He'd known this was a bad idea from the start. Alyson leading them at speed with her ever twitching walking stick guiding the way.

They head along uncleared roads all the way up to the Railway Station via strange paths."What happened here?" She asks as she sees the ruins, and the pulled up tracks that lay twisted along the embankments.

"I…"

He doesn't know. All the various threads of his memory seem to terminate at the exit of… of a military column that cleared the town of its people to some kind of refugee camps.

They left him here. He remembers standing outside the Tower and the panel van with the…

"It's not important," Aly sniffs. "I was interested as to why anyone would waste this much effort breaking up the rail system. Thinking about it I suppose it was in case you failed in your watch. We could have used these tracks to move supplies forward for our inevitable Vampire invasion of this snowbound dump."

He gives her the side-eye.

"Blarrrghhh." She wiggles her free hand at him and bares her fangs.

"Don't do that."

A chuckle. "Come along, William."

They're at the edge of Town and the stick is pulling them along the main road out towards the countryside. This is as far as he has ever come in all his time as the Watcher. He doesn't like it. He feels like a crab out of its shell, skin shivering where it's missing the protection of its home.

"This feels wrong, Alyson."

"I know. That means it's working." She tilts her head to one side and brushes some snow away from her hood. "Come on, this could be my last chance to take a look around this green and pleasant land." She smirks. "All I've seen so far is off-grey snow and burnt out ruins. Don't you have more to show me?"

"I'm not a tour guide."

"Not sure you're anything, William. Not really. You could be though. Take a chance!"

She has a point. At worst, if he did take a quick recce a bit further out then there could be new materials for when she is gone, and if there is some kind of danger lurking out there, well he was going there with a Vampire who had demonstrated a little more than basic proficiency in combatting threats.

Plus, if the road were mined or something ate her then it would solve his problems in a very real way.

He doesn't mean that.

"Lead on."

"Good. That's the spirit William. Adventure!" She sets the walking stick down and lets it find its head, then raises a finger and lines up a big hazel eye along the route set out. "I think we're headed this way," she says.

Then she produces a novelty map of the local area, the sort with pictures of local landmarks and very little else from her pack. "All becoming very familiar. Nothing really changes you know. Nothing real, just people."

"Is that a tourist map? What are you doing? Those are crap, baby's first map." He reaches for his own thumb-eared map, a good ordnance survey set which he uses to keep track of where he's scavenged clean, he picked it up from… a backpack.

"No need for that. Like you said I'm a tourist and I have places I think we should see together." Aly rotates the tourist map in a manner which does not inspire confidence, double checks her bearings from the stick, and points. "That's the place. We should go there."

He looks a couple of times at the map. "You want to go to a replica Viking longship?"

Wide eyes. "Umm. No. I must have misread the signs." Another part turn of the map. He shakes off a little snow and growls. "There. The ruins up the coast at a place called.. Regulbium? Reculter?"

"Reculver. The Roman fort?" He taps. "The one with the cartoon Roman Soldier waving an eagle standard and not the one with a Viking in a horned helmet waving a battle axe?"

"Exactly. That's the place. I remember it had a very good nexus back in the day. Soldiers looked a little different. More mail and less… Lorica Segmentata."

He snorts out a puff of steam which carries off in the chill wind. It looks like cotton candy.

"Are we talking when it was a Roman fort?"

"Yes. But also we are talking the mobile home park just outside as I needed a quick chat with a fellow we had at the AIA spying on the Director and the AIA counter-intelligence types were far too snobby to go to a caravan park without an excellent reason." She frowns. "Really nice guy, very thorough. Wonder if he survived?"

She stares blankly at the map. "Any idea which road will take us there?"

William grits his teeth and pulls out the actual map. Reculver… If they followed the London road up and then took the route up to…

"You do realise this will take hours?"

A nonchalant shrug. "I move very quickly and I think you may surprise yourself."

"Okay. Just this once. We should get back in time for the Radio broadcast."

A grimace. "Just when I thought you were making progress, William. When will you realise what a dreadful contraption that is?"

He breathes better the further they walk, the feeling of transgression melting away like the snow and ice around that odd monolith left by the Goats. He's almost enjoying the feeling of freedom. Of picking a place and going there, no ties, no Tower full of dead machines to janitor.

No ships full of people to sink. No hungry sands to feed.

They swing through the little village of Cliffsend and then along country lanes till they reach the north coast of Thanet, lit up by the orange glow of the barrier just offshore, marked with the stumps of a melted wind-farm. This is past the edge of the conurbation made up of the three towns, and out towards where a rail journey would be brightened by the green between the picturesque little coastal towns that had yet to be consumed by the march of in-fill.

No mines and no people either. His bodyguard is out of a job.

If anything Alyson seems more uncomfortable than he.

"There's no one around, William. Not one solitary soul."

"I said I was alone."

"You mentioned it."

A traitor thought suggests that she might have been expecting a snack or two, but she seems honestly concerned, darting into empty homes and shops that retain enough structure to provide some cover had anyone been there, other than them. Standing on abandoned truck-tops and hallooing, to no response.

Every so often she looks up at the sky and shakes her head.

"No one here, Aly. I told you. Whole area was cleared. I remember that." He corrects himself. "I remember that ending."

"Do you happen to know where they went?"

"No. Maybe north? It was after the food ran out. Army took them, at least I think it was the army. Same people who shot those two at the corner."

"Who?"

He promises to show here when they get back home. It's coming back.

No more railway trips for a while. The lines along the coast are as thoroughly destroyed as those in the Town itself and bridges have been blown as well leaving piles of brick and steel in twisted piles blocking the frozen streams.

It doesn't stop their stroll, this route from Thanet along

the coast to Reculver and onwards had been a popular hiking route back in the day. He remembers watching the great ships at rest along the estuary that led to the Port of London and bright days with ice cream at the Italian cafes that dominated the treats-trade along the coast.

Alyson gently pushes for more information about him as they walk, particularly when he needs a quick rest, unlike his undead companion. It is an interrogation of such silky softness he wouldn't have picked up on it but for the fact that he was talking to a nosey bloody vampire.

When he queries, her only response is that it's to help him.

"So, were you married, William? Do you remember?"

A little too personal. He remembers a lot of being married, and he can't unpick it. He deflects. "Don't see how that's your business. Were you?"

"On a number of occasions." A wistful toothy smile. "We had our own rules around that, no humans, and no dating outside your age bracket. For me that was limiting towards the end. I am," She preens, "a Master after all." A giggle. "And if you'd met my peers you'd have sworn off marriage of all kinds for good."

"Hmm."

"What are you thinking." She kicks away some wreckage into the sea. "Go on. Ask."

"Did you…"

"No. We're not really that interested in that physical stuff."

"I watched lots of Vampire TV stuff, couldn't avoid it in the end. Isn't that supposed to be your main thing? Blood and sex? And lesbianism," he adds, with a wince of embarrassment. "That was in a lot of the TV too."

She gives him a wry look. "Really, William? I suppose you're still mostly human after all."

"Sorry."

"Well. Let me put it that way. I'm not sure what sort of 'TV' you were watching. The first bit, not at all, when you're as old as I am it's all a bit silly sounding and I am, of course, entirely dead. The second bit? Well female companionship is preferable as you don't get into conversations like this."

He blushes like an idiot. Maybe. Who could tell.

"Joshing with you, silly. People are people. You're all quite dull and my experience is most people find us rather dull too. Order, order, order. If you want that sort of thing you'd have to talk the Fae." She pauses. "Did you notice something else about the vampire characters in TV? Books? Now, knowing we're real?"

He thinks as he walks. The roads here are more overgrown than in town, no one around to keep them clear, for much of the way it's easier to walk besides them where sabre grass pokes through the snow, quiescent due to Aly's presence. "I think I've got something."

"Do tell."

"The old programmes and films you're all raarrrrgh and drink your blood and have lots of weaknesses."

"Quite correct."

"Later ones, you're shiny and friendly and passionate and seem to quite like humans, depending on whether you're talking like or 'like'." He coughs.

"And that means…"

"You were softening people up for you to actually appear?"

She claps her hands together. "Jolly good. Bingo in fact. Give that man a blood milkshake and a season of Veritas in the Blood."

The clouds overhead are scudding faster, drawn north

by some unknown attractor. He thinks to mention this to Alyson but that just triggers another set of questions he's almost afraid to ask.

They walk in silence for a while until he gets together the courage to raise them.

"So."

"So."

"Was it you who did this?" He raises his hands, palms open. "I'm not going to try and do anything if it was, you'd probably just rip my head off."

A moment of silence where he thinks he's crossed some invisible line and then the tension drains away as she laughs like a cloud-bursting. A deep laugh emitting from somewhere near her underused diaphragm. "You know what, William. The more I see of you the more I suspect that that would not be as easy as I had thought at first. Your head seems to be very attached to your shoulders by some very interesting binds." Then serious. "I also think that it would attract unwanted attention from at least one of the factions of your friends in the Union, whichever side they might be on. We made too many mistakes underestimating what humans are capable of and I am not going to fall down that rabbit hole again."

"You didn't answer my question."

"This isn't us." She points upwards. "We wouldn't have done anything as mindlessly destructive. Believe it or not the Masters had… I have a lot of time for humanity. Before all of this we spent centuries being told to think of ourselves as shepherds helping you achieve things and saving you from the dark…" She stops. "You know what I did before I died?"

"Of course I don't. I met you two or three days ago."

"After you sank my boat…"

"After I sank your boat…" he mumbles in a sing song

voice. Gods of the Baptists she was never going to let that go. He was different now.

"I repeat it, because it is true. And what I was was a poet. Many of us were. Creatives, one and all. In my case I wrote fine lyric poetry about love and joy. I even dabbled a little in the epic forms, I wrote the definitive poetry of the Lelantine Wars if that means a thing to you." She waits for a response, but he has nothing. "And that's how I ended up as a vampire."

She declaims in some oddly rhythmic language which may as well be Greek to his ears.

"That's… odd."

"Depends on how you look at it William. We were selected for a very specific personality type and skill set. And I know how our Father looked at it. I'm third generation down from him so I understand him very well indeed. It's part of the reason I need to get away from here as quickly as possible. Without the Masters he's going to wake up sometime and if he does then… well. There's bindings with which I would prefer not to comply and honestly I don't want to see what he'd do given this to work with."

"He sounds a bundle of fun."

Coldest look she has every given him. "I know you're joking, William so I'll forgive you that. He can be fun I suppose when he's inclined that way, but it's the fun of a madhouse and he can't see it." She continues. "He picked people like me because he had an aversion to creating vampires that were warlords, soldiers, sailors, no offence…"

"None taken. I didn't do much sailing exactly." Couple of lifetimes, tops.

"Or military types overall. He said we should be the sorts of people who could step out when we decided the world was ready for us and say 'remember that great love story from two thousand years ago? I wrote it, hi!"

She waves at him with a gawky smile on her face that drops away like a stone into a bitter set.

"Okay." He thinks it through. "Isn't that a stupid plan?"

"As it turned out it was an extremely stupid plan. No one cares about the things he cares about, celebrity is fleeting and" she taps her head "my Lelantine epics are just up here now. There isn't a single manuscript anywhere left in the world and if I were to create one the world would think it a fake. Allowing for all of this of course."

"That's tough."

"And to add insult to injury the process of becoming *this* destroyed our creativity anyway. So we… we're just voids of nothing floating around." She shakes her head, "ask me to make up a poem."

Dubious look. "Make up a poem?"

"Okay."

There's a Watcher up above, he's been watching for a while.
The Watcher's being watched, by a wrecker with a smile,
The Wrecker's being watched, though by whom he doesn't know,
The Wrecker talks to him…

He hisses through his teeth. "Ah. That's plenty. We should probably…"

"It was bad, wasn't it."

He grimaces.

"And that's all we can do. How were we ever going to

save the world? Would you want anyone who produced that in charge, no matter their history?"

She's on a rant. It's as if his questions have opened a dam and millennia of bile is pouring out of the dark-haired creature with her sad hazel-eyes missing those inner fires, and quirks.

"Then there was failed secrecy, the Governments of the world found out about us centuries ago so we were never able to get it together for the big event. Too busy dodging hunters and a variety of nasty little tricks which got nastier year on year and which most of us considered funny. Building up what we could and arguing about what needed to be done to keep up. Poor Carlos." Her face fades back into the blank passivity that makes her so uncomfortable to be around. "That disaster over on the continent is the closest we've ever come to stepping forward and it took a hundred years and a lot of good people dying to achieve."

"Straight into a right hook from the Eastern Alliance." He waves a fist to the air. "Pow."

"Yes." She says, dryly. "Pow."

They keep walking for a time.

She seems deep in thought, though it is hard to tell as she takes up position a little ahead of him, maintaining the distance every time he tries to catch up to point out something she might find interesting.

Her head is slightly turned down as if she is studying the ice before her and there are no more scampered excursions to look for the missing population. He gets the feeling this walk is more for her than him.

After a time the signs on the road stop declaiming the distance to their destination and instead confirm their arrival. A welcome sign that informs them that they are entering the historic site-town of Reculver.

She stops by the sign, and lets him catch up to her, finally.

"You know, William. I had expected this walk to benefit you, help us get you back to yourself but I was wrong. I suspect it's been more of an aid to me. Things have been stewing in this old head for quite a while and it was lovely to get them out."

No shit.

"Learnt something?" He offers, brightly. Hoping to draw the Vampire out a little more.

"I think I've decided that wherever I go, I shall keep my head down and maybe stop being quite so concerned about other people."

"Sounds sensible."

She taps the sign. "Are we there yet, dad?"

The comment isn't aimed at him

——————————-

30

Internalisation

After all the travel and for all her previous enthusiasm, Alyson seems disappointed by the reality of their destination. The sea foams and freezes around a low headland on which they stand and she casts around for anything to get her witch-seeking investigation started.

The dreaded stick even makes a reappearance.

"It's pretty small" he explains as she frets. "More of a village than a proper town. There's a trailer park down there and a pub and that's about all I know, only visited a couple of times for a change of scenery though I did float past it a few times going back and forth from Tilbury. The old fort's that way and there's an Anglo-Saxon chapel by the sea, or what's left of one."

He's remembering as he speaks. Interesting experience.

"Good." An icy rain has started to fall replacing the snow driven by a strong North wind. It's like standing in a really shitty power shower and its worsening by the minute. "Fort that way you say?"

"Yes." He yells.

The stick twists and its direction is clear. He groans.

"That's the place. In fact we should get there right now. No time like the present." She grins. "See? I've learnt a lesson, William. Don't put off to next year what you can do today. The opportunity may pass."

That does not appeal. He is cold, he is hungry and his legs are aching again, plus it is getting darker by the moment and if he stays out much longer he's going to be soaked to the skin despite the trench coat and rags. "Hold up. I know you don't feel this but is there any chance we could find something with a roof and get into shelter for a bit, maybe have something to eat." He produces his thermos, empty given their rushed exit. "Have some tea?"

She stares, porcelain pale in the scarlet light of the clouds.

"You didn't make me that dinner. You owe me, Alyson."

She weighs up his request then nods her head with that strange up/down motion that resembles a guillotine. "I have been a little unkind, I suppose. I concur that you deserve a little rest. I will make a conscious effort to cease being quite so wrapped up in myself all the time. Being an individual is strange."

That earns her a chuckle. The rain is falling more heavily and his trench coat has stopped dripping and is instead running rivulets of ice cold water into his boots. "That's the most self absorbed thing I've ever heard anyone say."

She snorts "Says the man who hasn't spoken to anyone for three months."

"Six." He points. "This way."

They find the pub which appears to have experienced a second life as a shelter for a refugee family, an area cleared in the public bar and sleeping bags and tins of food scattered around. The toilet blocked.

The family had left in a hurry, maybe when the toilet facilities stopped working.

Still, the roof is in place and there are the materials he needs to set up a heating rune to dry himself out and heat the place up a little. The Radio encouraged scattering them around to deal with the pervasive icing. He starts to mutter the rote incantations until Alyson rushes over and shushes him.

"Hey, it's cold in here."

"Could you… not. If you need to keep warm maybe light a fire, there's bags of firewood in the corner." She's right there are. "Firelighters too."

"Thought you liked magic and stuff?"

"There are different kinds and that sort is increasingly distasteful, particularly after meeting your Goat friends. I have some theories"

"Why distasteful?"

Her mouth twists into a ouroboros of disgust, just for a second and then she her face resumes its statue like quality except for a deep stare of utmost meaning. "You don't know what you are using to power your magic. And it isn't what you think it is."

That's interesting. He's not sure he's ever even thought about it. What was that thing about death? The Radio had said… "The runes and the stuff in the sky isn't it? The stuff that's not wriggling around and knocking down planes, that is?"

"Yes. The question we never really got answered before, recent events, is where that came from in the first place." She sighs. "We had an idea, and at the end the others felt we had to use what we had as our armies and air force, oh that stupid air force. Such a waste… they weren't able to stop the Russians. Even then we only used the absolute minimum it was too much."

"I heard that explosion, that doesn't sound like the absolute minimum to me."

"That was the Easterners, William." She sniffs. "Our powers are more subtle even when we use that."

He erases the elements of the heat rune with the damp rags hanging from his wrist. The cold water cleanses them to fragments which dissolve into the floor.

"Thank you, William."

"I'll get a fire going, then." He checks his watch. Nearly seven. If he can find a Radio then maybe he can catch up on what's happening? That would be useful to then both. "Silly question, Aly. Do you mind if I check the radio?"

She chews on this. "Well. I'd rather you didn't. Though, you did stop with the runes nonsense so you're in my good books for now… and I suppose I can see if there's anything useful in the nonsense it spouts. Small steps. Okay, William. But you need to tell me what you find out if you do find a radio. Deal?"

"Deal."

"I would get the fire going first. This building is not, entirely, structurally sound. Carlos would have been very disappointed. He was quite the architect. Big gaps and you'll be very cold otherwise."

"Not as cold as you."

"Ha ha. I'm actually a good two and half degrees Celsius above ambient temperature at all times." She wanders behind the bar, and tries pulling one of the pumps. Nothing. "And I'll have you know we invented Celsius and a whole lot of other useful things so don't give me any lip on temperatures."

He scans the shelves behind her. Every pub had a music system somewhere… how else to play 'careless whisper' for the Christmas crowd.

There it is. Another of those old ones with a tape and CD decks that had been popular as a Christmas gift a few years back.

She pulls a face. "Silly me. I was rather hoping there wouldn't be one of them."

"I said you can listen in and you can listen in, fire first and then we c can resume our chat about how it feels to be a pleasant, but dead lady who sucks blood."

She carefully raises her middle finger with utmost care and rectitude.

"Where did you learn to do that, young lady?"

"No one you know. I'm sure you might get to meet him someday." A glare at the radio. "You know what? I think I'll take a look upstairs. You do what you have to do. I trust you'll tell me anything important."

"Alyson."

She turns back to look at him from the stairs, a vision in marble. "Yes William?"

"This is just what I've needed. I feel sort of… refreshed."

She smiles, almost convincingly. "I'm please to hear that. Now don't go taking anything the radio tells you too literally you hear?"

The fire's crackling.

He unplugs the Radio and waits as the minutes tick away to seven. Given the lack of communication in days past he's not surprised when the assigned hour passes and there is silence in the bar, save for the tip-tap of the rain against the tape-reinforced windows and the equally light step of Alyson above him as she investigates the night's shelter.

He tries the other beer pulls which nets him a stinking stream of sour brown liquid which he hopes was once beer.

The bottles of spirits along the shelves are empty, though stacked carefully back in place other than an outlier, dust covered and wedging a fake book block in place.

The bottle has a pear floating in it. He's on the path towards finding a bottle opener when he's nearly blinded by a crackle of blue light and the Radio erupts in a stream of near gibberish far louder than seems possible.

"**) AD IASDO- (A(SD IS THE !!!!!! SCREEEEEEEEEE... attackonMDRHQ as predicted. Wars end... Paris. Brook...ERRR absent. SCRRECCCH-HHH... Them engaged in maaaaaaa..... Revetments expect THIRTEEN, escape. Done done done. ASASD ASDASD ASDAD SCRRRRRRRRREE.... rebels suppressed. Operative control restored... Scramble to... RECALLL SCREEEEEEEEEEE. Thespian battle group... No no no no..."

Then a click.

And a calm voice, one he has never heard before makes a simple statement.

"Temporal distortion detected. Normal service will be restored on all Watcher Services prior to Excision of Corrupted Operatives. Long live the Union. Long live the Provisions of Oxford."

Now what, if anything, is he going to make of that?

Aly has no more idea than he when he explains what hapened, and simply suggests that the Radio is a busted flush, whatever that might be.

He gets the gist, and is inclined to agree.

The next morning dawns red and dreary, with flights of birds swooping around just below the clouds, taunting the monsters within to try their luck, before elegantly cutting away from the grasping tentacles. Corvids the lot of them. He watches the show as he eats a couple of packets of crisps he found in a shopping bag by the door, along with one of his hated strawberry breakfast bars.

She does not eat, declining the offer of a gruel bar with a graceful shake of her head. "I like the taste of exceptional food, William. I will tolerate the taste of something new. That *item* barely qualifies as 'nourishment'."

However her batteries have clearly recharged, whatever she did while he was sleeping and Alyson is bouncing with energy as they head out to the old fort. Sure enough her trusty walking stick pulls them over once again to the old Saxon Chapel.

And that is where it seems to stop. For half an hour she stomps around the place, conducting a variety of what are either experiments or interpretive dance moves to a constant muttered litany of confused mumbling and occasional prods to the midriff to move William from place to place.

"Where is it… goodness… nearly… oh Hecate this is weaker than it should be… maybe here. No. Let's try… move would you William, you're disrupting the lines, oh no! Not there… better. No. Worse. Goodness me!"

"Would it be easier if I stood somewhere else, maybe the pub?"

"No. You need to be here."

Ten minutes later and he is becoming irritable, even watching the birds outsmart monsters could get boring after long enough and his arms are tingling from the cold.

"Alyson."

"Yes, William." She's aligned herself and her stick to a series of large Oak trees which remain strangely unaffected by the incipient Ice Age. In fact, but for the cold, this could almost be a really terrible day on the English Riviera.

"Why are we here? If that's the World Woods I'm not impressed."

"Well, William," Her walking stick fizzes with energy as she raises it to the heavens and she releases a cheerful chuckle. "Not that the wonders of the arcane world are there to impress you, but as I mentioned before there are different sorts of magic so we are here to tap into a little of the witchly kind to contact our approaching friends."

He sighs. "Does this involve crystals?"

He seems to remember an aunt who had an obsession with the things. In the end it had been what killed her. Though that was a story for a different time and involved a very large and ill-placed crystal and a very small and ill-timed earthquake.

"No, William. It does not involves crystals." Exasperated sigh, and as Alyson had to inhale the air to perform that act of derision it only added to the weight of it.

"That's Fae magic. Crystals. Shiny things."

"Okay." Consider me schooled, he thought.

"Witch magic is ley lines, and so on. This delightful relic is an ancient crossroads which is part of the reason the church and the fort and indeed the chapel were placed here back in the dark and misty past." A beat. "Though probably brighter than today."

"Okay, so what are you going to do? Summon up a monster or something?"

"No William, that's not it at all. In fact… monster summoning? Where would I get them from? I suppose if I were insane I could try and call down something from up in the clouds. Yuck. Just yuck. And that would involve different um. Power sources? Have you learnt nothing William?"

"Not really."

"Then maybe you'll understand this given our previous conversations and your obsession with listening to those horrible Radios. I'm here to see what's what as you always put it before making me want to vomit - and I don't have a working alimentary canal so you can see how bad that must be."

He leaves her to speak. It boils down to a very wordy explanation that she's basically going to see if there are any Witches around, as she doesn't entirely trust anything anyone around here says (with an apology to William himself) and then see if they'll take her somewhere at a reasonable price.

It sounds to him like she's using the Witches as a travel bureau. He wonders in passing if that's a good idea. Vampires seemed to combine an intense level of self-absorption with a very limited ability to understand other people's problems and, hadn't there been a big die off of witches just before the Catastrophe?

Isn't that dangerous? After all, here he was in an abandoned fort, in an ice age, about to contact the very people that two almost reliable sources had informed him were exceptionally dangerous.

"… then maybe I can call in some markers and stop bothering you so much."

"Okay."

She taps a foot against the ground, not part of whatever ritual she was running. "Were you even listening, William?"

He tries to smile but his face won't comply with his instructions. Must be the cold. "Mostly."

"Whatever."

"Well I'm ready. You keep quiet. And don't move. This is like sneaking across a spider's web so I need to take appropriate precautions." With which exclamation she very carefully and with great solemnitude, stands on one leg and begins to hop.

It is faintly ridiculous. He cannot suppress a rough laugh.

Which earns him the fury of the Vampire. "I know how this looks but it's important. You don't want to get too attached to a spider's web... If you can't control yourself you may face the other way and stop your shenanigans, young man."

"Fine."

He turns, looking out towards the town and lets her do her thing. It seems to involve a mix of humming and snapping her fingers and he is ever so glad he is not watching. Earlier this morning he's sure he would have expected something more impressive, however it is what it is and who is he to question such an august practitioner of the arcane arts.

"So you'll really go if you find one of these witches? What about me?"

"Well I should be able to travel to where I want to go from here, or somewhere nearby, it would be quite the effort and I'd need to give up... a lot. That doesn't mean I'd forget my promises, William. I am not going to leave you in the lurch, I will aim for... an advance ticket." She laughs, then goes back to clicking her fingers.

"Great." He faux grumbles. "You can tell me more about ancient poems and whiny vampires. That's a lot of help. You said you were going to fix me, whatever that meant."

"Unworthy of you." She continues bouncing on one leg. He can hear the thuds from her landing from here and her shadow is sliding along the grass of the fort's interior. He has to admit she has exceptional balance. "But I will anyway!"

Boing.

Boing.

Boing.

Really this is getting… she's humming a bloody pop tune from the 70s. He's sure of it.

"I am fairly sure you are taking the piss at the moment, Ms. Vampire. This cannot be how you do magic, it's ridiculous."

A raspberry from behind him. Long and redolent of disdain. "Oh one of the things about witch magic, it involves lots of bargains and ritual and takes bloody ages. The standing on one leg? That's real, the rest, I just like humming and I like to practice my balance. You know there's nothing stopping you going over there and taking that unpleasant hiss from all that garbage you have written on you to watch the sea or whatever it is that sailors do."

"You told me to stand here."

"That doesn't sound very much like me, William. I think you're mis-remembering. You should think on that."

"Fine." He takes her up on her offer, walking then standing, looking out to sea. Ice patches float against the low cliffs, and the sea calls out to him. It would be nice to be travelling again even if Aly won't take him across the world. He remembers his times fishing with his father, the motorised whir of the nets, the weight of the fish and the sliding gasping death in the holds.

The loans, the restructurings and the graphs on a spreadsheet going the wrong way and the man from the Bank coming round to sell up for what they could get.

He wasn't cut out to be a fisherman, but he had never stopped loving the sea. Navy. Merchant Marine. Needing to escape on that boat.

He wonders for a moment if the fish have survived the catastrophe.

Of course they have idiot. You've seen them in the Channel. And you were never a fisherman. I'd know…

And with that there is a screech of pain from behind him, something that shouldn't be able to feel anything, suddenly feeling a pulse of dry torture and unable to stop it releasing in a single agonised sob.

He turns from his reminiscences and rushes to Alyson who is laying on the ice and mud, holding her head in apparent agony.

———

31

Pursuit

"Aly? Aly? Are you okay?"

"I'm… fine. It'll pass in a moment."

"Did you find any witches?"

"One, maybe two. And they're moving fast this way. That much was true."

"That's good news, isn't it?"

She sits up and shakes her head. "There's something following them that's… That spider's web metaphor? Imagine if a stag beetle or a big dog was racing through a set of cobwebs, or better still a fire, think of a fire, one running along a net of gunpowder that leads to an armoury. Hissing along, destroying and burning everything before it. The witches are running and they won't be helping me. I'm not even sure they can help themselves and they're carrying something. Oh your friends are doing horrible things William. Horrible in every way."

That doesn't sound good. "Here? Are they coming this way?

She looks at him. "Yes. They are, and falling over themselves to get here. I think that your little piece of heaven is the only place anyone can get in or out of this stupid little island. World Woods or otherwise. That glow goes everywhere."

"And you can't get out yourself? Jump on and sneak out?"

"No, William. Vampires aren't particularly welcome in the World Woods. If I were to go in there on my own," She thinks of a metaphor, it's not something that seems to come naturally. "Have you seen what happens to ants when they attack termite nests? The ants are big but the termites gum them all up and eventually the ants stop moving and that's that? That's what the inhabitants of the World Woods do to us."

"Glue you up?"

"The mental equivalent. It would take a greater Vampire than I to even think of such a thing."

A pause, her gaze has not wavered from him all the time they have been speaking. There's a very inhuman look to Alyson right now. Something of the progenitors of her kind who he now imagines as giant ants with equally over-sized pincers. "How very important you must be to be trusted to guard the one exit from this hell, William. I think we need to move our little recovery project forward more quickly than I had thought, and how awfully lucky you're a sailor."

"I won't like that will I?"

"Lots of necessary things are unpleasant." She drops her gaze. "I'm beginning to learn that now that I'm having to deal with things at your level."

"I…"

"What, William."

"At the same time you screamed I heard a voice. Like the ones before you arrived. Do you think it's related?"

Her eyes flare red, and she throws out her hand

towards him like a whiplash. Long elegant fingers balled into a fist.

He steps back, Arms raised and his arms flare.

She slowly releases her fist and lets out a held breath, leaning back against the damp earth.

"We are all creatures of our past, William. And that might be the cleverest thing you've ever said. Those runes you write off as tattoos are of the same nature as the ones in the clouds and I think akin to whatever is coming here, destroying everything in its path. Then there's your revolting Radio and that Lamp, and the heat runes that burn power like billy-o from a source I think I don't want to understand."

"I'm sorry."

"I know." She holds out a hand. "That's why you're still here. I'd say alive…" A giggle. "Oh William. Help me up would you?"

He offers his hand. Has it always been so wreathed in rags and bandages? And she picks herself up. "Soggy down there," she offers, sheepish. Brushing away mulch.

"Looks it. Though at least it's grass and not blade grass."

"There is that." She scratches the side of her head. "Do you mind if I try something? It'll move us forward immensely in the project of getting you whole, which I need pronto given what's coming. And of course, if it goes right."

"And if it goes wrong?"

"I shouldn't worry about that, William." Her smile is bright and febrile.

"I should probably say now, but if I did you'd use my corpse anyway."

"Don't be silly William."

"Stand there, hand on the tree." He obeys. They're over by the unnaturally natural oaks. He doesn't like the way that the grumble at the back of his mind has started up though. Not one bit. "Thank you. This does involve physical contact, so brace yourself.

"Well you said you're not ice cold so that's not going to be too bad."

She tuts. "I'll have you know there were entire cantos devoted to my touch." She gently clears the rags away from his forehead, steps forward, and places her index finger on his forehead. "Not this, of course!"

It is not exactly cold, more room temperature.

"This is weird." The birds above seem to agree as they've started croaking out their disapproval.

"It's about to get weirder. I need you to close your eyes and think peaceful thoughts."

"Peaceful thoughts?"

"Like, meditation. Think on the nice bits of the past and things that matter to you and… nonsense. Remember we're intruding in a Spider's web, just on a smaller scale, and we're trying to avoid attracting something's attention whilst still getting a good look? Do this wrong and you'll wreck it. And us. Maybe."

"Don't see how this is worth it."

"Shush."

He tries. For an endless moment nothing happens.

"Nearly there. It's attuning you to…"

Then there is a blasting pain through his mind centred right where his spine attaches to his skull, and another agonised scream from Alyson as she is thrown backwards, like a cannonball from some medieval bombard. He opens his eyes in time to see her crash into the side of the church sixty feet away, having splintered at least one oak on her enforced journey.

The birds above screech one last time and hurl themselves into the orange barrier, burning like comets as they cook themselves alive.

"Holy crap." He rushes to her side under a rain of frazzled feathers. The ancient stone of the wall is shedding mortar and stone fragments, centuries of history going the way of the Dodo, yet she is already picking herself up and brushing the settled snow from her clothing.

And laughing.

"What the hell are you laughing about? That was fucking awful! And I saw precisely nothing other than a flying vampire and a bird cook off. And you said you couldn't fly…" He begins to chuckle himself. "Shouldn't you have turned into a bat before you hit the wall or something?"

"Well well well. It looks like I've completely misinterpreted what's keeping you together my William." She is racked with coughing for a solid minute before she speaks again. He offer her some tea from his flask, refilled in the morning, which she gratefully takes. "Wow, that was a doozy."

She spits out a feather. "Birds gone?"

"Birds gone."

She winces.

"What just happened? I didn't see anything other than stars. Not the good sort. And I have a blinding headache coming on."

They slump down together against the rock wall of the church, out of the rain and wind as the smell of frazzled avians fills the air. They sit there and gather their thoughts.

"How was that helpful!"

Alyson sighs a deep deep sigh. "Would you like to know

what you are William? Really? I was wrong myself so I can't imagine you've guessed."

"Because I'm a stupid human?"

"Not at all."

She tells him. He does not like it. Nor does he believe her. It's not very funny and neither of them are laughing by the end.

32

No one likes reality

They walk back to Thanet in silence. They've agreed to make some stops on the way.

For confirmation.

He does not feel like speaking. He has a worm in his chest and it is eating away at his heart, his courage is draining away and he wants to be anywhere else but here and now.

The Vampire is also silent, whether from concern at his reaction or from a basic disconnection from human emotions, he does not know.

"Look, William. It's just a mirror. Nothing to be afraid of."

"She says having told me… Look. I've seen myself in a mirror. I even shave once in a while."

"Not really, you've seen what you expect and you think you do things you don't. That fun little experiment will have shocked out a lot of the things that limited your perception even if we didn't do it intentionally."

"You first. Vampires have history with mirrors, don't you?

"That is true and I suspect a similar issue. Do you know what I see when I look in a mirror William?"

"Nothing?"

"No. I see a shadow."

"At least you know you're still real."

"It's not my shadow, dear man. I don't know what it is, and every century it gets closer. At least I know that. You need to look and tell me what you see. Once you know the truth, the healing can begin."

"Healing? How can I heal?"

"Poor choice of word. Think of yourself as a fine mansion made up of wonderful parts, gone to wrack and ruin. I'm going to be the architect of your renewal, and we can all live happily ever after."

"Mirror?"

"Mirror. Please."

She looks up at the clouds from time to time as if trying to solve some riddle she is playing through what passes for her mind. His view of her is soured by the onset of reality, as one element of his world view is not what it had been.

Her last words to him before they left the pub are still curling and uncurling across his mind. "I would not be averse to checking the flat about the restaurant for you if you don't want to go there yourself?"

"It's a kebab shop. Not a restaurant." He manages, "and there's no point. There's nothing there. Nor any of the other places."

Then silence and walking. He winds his radio absent-mindedly and checks it obsessively every couple of miles but all he can hear is static and scrambled communications from across the channel where the last of the Vampire resistance is ground down by the remnants of the Eastern forces. Broken backed war, neither side the winners.

They are hugging the coast road on the way back. Aly doesn't know it but that way they won't pass the shop on the way back, the one with its two doors, one into the shop itself and the other with its brass door knocker and box for mail that leads up narrow stairs to the flat above.

The shop isn't the problem.

A set of stairs which was half blocked by the mountain bike he rode up to the station every weekday and then had to fold up and stick by the door when he started his shift. Or the person that forms part of what he is started it.

How many other memories were happening at the same time?

He looks across the estuary, no land visible on the other side but the clouds are angry and the orange of the barrier gives the whole the same hellish tint as the Tryptych. The King marching his way down to hell to suffer for his sins.

There is definitely something coming south, if the Vampire is to be believed, it's a witch and her pursuers.

He ponders the possibilities, moving on from the unpleasant reality he is supposed to confront in order to become a whole person if he is to believe Alyson, seeking protection in abstraction.

Who would be chasing after a witch? Or given what he knows, who wouldn't?

The actual question is why they are chasing witches. There are two, not one.

"I haven't missed you."

Always here, idiot. This isn't your place, no matter what Ms. Vampire might think. This is mine.

"Shut up."

"Did you say something, William?"

"No."

What do witches actually do to escape pursuers? Were they hugging the nape of the earth on high-speed brooms pursued by bug drones, shark tooth missiles being swatted from the air by toad decoys? Puddock defence system engaged.

Too fanciful. If that had been the case they would have been here already. Ground pounding. Longshanks pony. Leg mark one. Chased by an old man and some soldiers.

They're reach the boundary between Westgate and Margate. A non-descript slice of English seaside with red-brick three-level houses and roads sloping off the main road down to the sea.

He stops and looks down one of them. They've misspelt the name on the old-style sign and it bugs him. A thing is known by its name and if you can't get that right then what is the thing?

The sea is like blood and the clouds are lashing it against the seawall as whatever comes from the North drives it forwards. The ice melts as it passes the barrier and it steams as it hits the ice on the shore. There's a thaw coming. He can feel it. The north wind, is warm and angry. His head, aches.

He looks over at Alyson.

The Vampire is watching him. She is perfectly still, the buildings move more than her, roof spars swaying where the weight of snow and ice has broken the flat roofs and cambered ones alike. Her stare is as distant as it had been when she was watching him from the sand banks amidst the wreck of her ship.

Where had her crew gone? The sands usually left them behind, like that tricky captain from all that time ago. Dead and sat in the skeleton of his ship. It's a defining feature of the dead. They are still, it is the living that shift from place to place. He wonders if it would be peaceful to be that still.

He remembers what he saw in the mirror.

The faintest of smiles from the Vampire woman. Maybe her distance is deliberate. Giving him time to digest his trauma just like he had when she had been hurting.

"What are you thinking, William?"

The sea hisses and the ice melts a little more.

"I'm thinking that I should take a look at the shop. And the other places too."

She pats him on the back. "I think you are right about that."

When they reach the shop he lets his muscle memory guide him. He picks up the key from the inside left of the letter box, snapping away the ice, a copper coloured twist-lock key with serrated notches along its length, and tries to unlock the door.

A short struggle and a little cursing as either the lock, or the door, has warped over the months, before the key turns with a satisfying click. It's dark in the flat, that same old mould and death combination that haunts all the properties in the area, other than the Tower and the Shrine.

He takes the stairs up, using his torch to light the darkness and avoid the bike fallen haphazardly at the bottom of the stairs.

He opens the door to the studio apartment.

The air in here is foul, biological. A fatty soup and a sweetness that coats his tongue. The roof hasn't held and what's in the bed has not aged well.

He winces.

She waits outside until he's back down. He looks calmer and more relaxed, though he spits upon exiting and locks the door behind him, placing the key back in its place.

"Anything?" she asks.

"Yes," he replies. "Not nice up there."

He is still. "Not really sure what to make of it. That's not me up there though."

"It's not. Not you William. Like an organ donor I suppose but for up there." She taps him on the temple.

He shakes his head. "Could you not do that?"

She steps backwards. "I won't. Sorry, William. Feel better?"

He shrugs. "Let's walk up to the civil servants. I'd like to see them. Same deal?"

"You tell me. If you remember anything about them then I guess it's the same deal. This was the work of a talented amateur, not an expert. I think he or she simply took anything they could find lying around and patted it into shape to fill in the gaps."

Gaps from what?

The rain and warmth has melted away a lot of the ice that held the bodies next to the roundabout at the top of the Flint Alley in place and he is able to pull away the pack from the man although he cannot quite reach the woman.

The contents are ruined except for a mottled wallet and a couple of credit cards.

"Steven Archibald." He holds the cards up. "Steve I guess. Worked for the MDR of all things."

He looks at Alyson. "What's the betting the dead guy in the bed in the kebab shop was called William?"

It is her turn to shrug, although her shrug is somewhat more emphatic. "You could be correct, there'll be others about, anyone who died about the time our unknown friend conducted their botched repair job. I understand if you don't want to use the name now though? Could have a fresh start? How about…"

She eyes him up and down. "You look like a Martin to me."

He sighs a deep, deep sigh. "No. I was kind of hoping that I'd remember my own name, I mean there must have been someone in this body before I was and that was the base of who I am so…"

"Maybe that's one of the things that got lost. Look, I know this is a lot to take in, but if I asked you, the person you really are, who or what you were before all this, I think you'd say that you were a sailor who sailed the seven seas and that's the core of who you are. That's the body you're in and it's perfectly… um. Okay? Then, because the people who did this were incompetent buffoons with more power than sense and they filled the gaps from their own screw ups with a lot of other memories like the ones where you're an accountant, or a salesman, or a civil servant even. It's up to you to try and make sense of it and forge yourself into a person. If that's what you want to do of course. I don't get to make decisions for you."

"That doesn't sound easy. I mean was I always on my own here? Who the hell was the guy who shot Archie? I remember him pretty clearly…"

No. No he doesn't. Who the hell is Archibald? Archie. "Argh."

"Oh this could be very difficult." A bright smile, the usual array of fangs. Alyson was not very human when you got down to nuts and bolts. No more than he. "If you were on your own and did not have someone who knows what they are doing to help you, that is." She grins. "If you want I can speed things up. Like what we did back at the Chapel. Think of it as, lacquering a table."

"That is not a thing."

"Silly human, of course it is and it makes wooden furniture far more durable." She frowns. "You really don't know that you use varnish on tables?"

"No."

"That's almost barbarous."

"Great." He mutters. "Now I'm a table."

"We could say we are lacquering a night stand if you like?"

"Why can't you just be normal? And stop saying lacquering."

"I like furniture." She frowns. "It's a thing. We'll get you sorted tonight back at the Shrine." A screech as something enormous twists in the cloud and fire jabs down just beyond the town limits. "I think whatever's coming is nearly here so I think you should take me up on the offer."

The walk back to the hideout is slow, the meltwater is streaming along the roads and taking with it a lot of the debris from the past months. It's necessary to dodge some unpleasantness.

The drains are long clogged. They talk as they walk. He has a lot of questions.

"If I were what you said I was. Some kind of revenant made up of bits and pieces of the dead. What does that actually mean. Am I dead? I don't feel dead."

"I'm a bit of an expert on the subject, William. Ask away."

"I get cold, you don't, I breathe, you only breathe to speak, I eat and drink and get hungry and thirsty and I remember being alive. I remember a lot of being alive."

She picks her way over bits of wood and unidentifiable scraps of cloth as they make their way along. Dodges a dead rat. "Well William, I think you're one of a kind. Baby's first revenant, and they caught your body just after you'd died so they could keep a lot of what made you human and then brought you back with borrowed parts so… technically I suppose…" A grimace. "You have no idea how it feels to be truly dead. I would give a lot to feel some of how I was before all this."

"Not great for a gate guard."

"You're more than that. My guess is that someone or something did try to make a guard for the gap in the orange wall that's here. And they tried to bring someone back to do that but they got it all wrong. You're the end result and all we have to do is plane the edges to get you back to yourself. More furniture eh? Get it?"

"I get it." A question arises. "What would have happened if they hadn't done that?"

"You're asking what happens when a person dies, aren't you? Quite profound." She waves a hand. "Get that one a lot."

"Well?"

"Dissipation, ending, nothing. Have it on good authority." She tilts her head. "Maybe being a Vampire isn't so bad after all."

They stop outside the door to the Shrine, Lions watching them impassively.

"Shall we?"

He shakes his head. "Am I real or am I just a robot or some zombie or something else?"

Alyson closes her eyes, the tiniest hint of impatience breaking through. "Getting a bit stuck on this huh?"

"I found out I'm alive but dead and made up of spare parts. And apparently programmed to guard a gate and sink ships. It's a lot to take in. And I'm still a bit concerned that there's a real person under all this trying to get out. And that he's…"

The Vampire shakes her head, chop chop. Emphatic.

Cutting off his musings and glancing towards the marina. "Now, William. I'm a rather good judge of character. And I can tell you that the person I'm talking to is real. Due to a mix of stupidity from your creators and the various 'issues' we've had, some intentional and some… less so, we're lucky enough to have my lovely William, Navigator extraordinaire, with us today."

"You make me sound like a recipe."

"Soup? I could use different metaphors if you don't like the furniture?"

He spits at the thought. "Come on Alyson."

"A really good soup?" She raises her eyebrows. "Sorry, isn't that a human expression? Or is that eggs?"

"I have never heard that expression in my… life. Though what would I know. I'm a gestalt entity made up of bits of dead people's minds."

He stands undecided. She pushes open the door. "Would you like it better if I said you were a poem made up of other people's words?" She smiles bright. "I quite like that idea. It suits you."

They head back through a section of the Shrine that he's kept boarded up to perform the 'lacquering' 'varnishing' or whatever furniture related simile has taken Alyson's fancy at the time.

He stands by the windows and rubs one clean with his damp rags. The ice in the graveyard has melted away entirely and the water is draining down towards the sea along with unidentifiable bits of ice that might once have been snowmen.

"Well there go the neighbours" he comments as a wizened body is drawn down the hill towards the marina below.

"I almost preferred it when it was frozen solid." Alyson

watches as the 'camel humps' of bodies that have dotted the Town since the Catastrophe are released from the ice that held them, and newly open to the possibilities of rot and motion, slide out into the sea. "This town will stink soon unless this rain keeps up and washes it all away."

"This town always stank." He says. "I'm not sure why anyone ever stayed here."

It wasn't all bad, lad. It was quite a nice place to retire.

Alyson nods. "I quite like it, it is quaint and some of the buildings are pretty. England has always had such a strange melange of the new and the old, the beautiful and the profane sat side by side. No structure, things dropped higgledy-piggledy, individualism run riot."

You would have loved the old power station down the road.

"I would?"

"No."

"You need to lay on the table, and off with the rags. I've got some cutting to do. Can keep the pants. Please. Keep the pants."

He does as he's bid, shivering in the cold of the abandoned gift shop. "I think I preferred the lacquering analogy."

She produces a small set of what look like brushes and a set of large needles. "*Now*, he knows what lacquering is!"

Pain.

"Ah William this is interesting."

What is. She's been working for an hour, tracing the tattooing over his hands, nails and knives and needles correcting and adding, the implements like an ice scalpel, sending prickles of discomfort across his skin.

Where there is a subtraction there is a ripping sound and a warm feel as his skin grows back under her ministrations and soft chanting.

"I had thought I could discern something of your nature before from the work of the one who set you on this path," her eyes narrow in concentration, "but now I have the chance to look at the work in detail I can see this is not a single artist's hand."

"And?" He winces at a long incision across his thigh. "Plenty of people use more than one tattoo artist."

"Not tattoos, William. But yes. There's two. The first the work of many years. The mind behind it as sharp as this scalpel."

"Ouch."

"Sorry. The work is interesting. Always looking to cut corners to get to a goal. All the fat trimmed away. His earliest work is clumsy, a match for the early agents we encountered back in the day. Trying to do a little too much with a little too little by way of knowledge and power."

She giggles.

"I'll leave this one. A charm against Fae, well. Most Fae. I suspect he did not realise it would merely divert attention from you to those around you. It works in a way. I suppose."

"Fae again? OUCH HEAD OF THE BAPTIST WOMAN…"

She tosses away a reel of skin from his lower left arm leaving behind a greyish-green strip which she works on with needle and thread.

"Don't worry William. They've gone. They have other places to be." She works along the incision, from elbow to knuckles tracing invisible patterns and the sting becomes more pronounced.

"Could you…"

"Oh. Sorry. Of course, William. There's an awful amount of feedback here. Both in the original work and the later artist. Is that a sanctuary rune? Tough one. May leave it." The humming resumes.

"So the first one is done by someone working over years, I'd think I'd remember that."

"I'd think you would too, William. Here we are though. Trying to do a little lacquering!" A tap of her toe on the ground and his arms light up like a fireworks parade.

"Holy shit."

"Yes! There's a lot isn't there! I bet you're covered in these." She laughs, joyous. "Lets see. I don't think I'd like to meet the man who created these, William. You know that diversionary effect? There's a lot of that. I think he did it deliberately. That's quite cold."

She slides into his vision, peering into his eyes. "I'm going to knock you out for this part, William. It's important to integration and really not for the squeamish."

"I'm not…"

"And its faster this way."

He feels a cold deadness creep over his body. Through numbing lips he manages to raise a question. "What would happen if there were someone in here, still. The original one. Who did. That. Stuff."

Darkness. "Don't worry about that William, with what I'm doing he'd have to be quite remarkable to pull himself up again."

"If…"

"If, then he'd eventually eat you alive. I suppose."

Life closes up.

Silence.

He opens his eyes. There's lightning flashing and Alyson is holding up his face, examining it in the light of the approaching storm.

His eyes and his face are not proximate.

"Just need to put this back on, silly. I think I may have been hasty in my appraisal of your rescuer, dear heart. They were an artist. Many of the errors are actually suppression. All self taught too. The first of your benefactors was working from treatise, books some of which we wrote. I can see the deliberate errors replicated – we never really trusted where those would get you, I'll tell you! If he'd worked with us then we'd have told him where they were, but… he's done a good job."

"The second gentleman was working from a different set. And he was working very fast."

The world outside is suddenly very dark. His voice gurgles in his throat. Liquid. "We need to finish up, Aly. They're near. We need to get you away from here." What? He needs to…

She ignores him, shifting the face-skin mask from hand to hand.

"If I were grading I'd say there's about eighty percent of a decent job done here."

She turns to watch the clouds. "You are correct however. Let's get this back on you."

She twists her fingers and runes across his chest light up. As they do he slides back into darkness.

What has she done to him?

33

Success

I wake.

My skin is flame, and it seems that the patterns etched across it agree, as they are glowing like fire flies on my grey skin. I lay on a cold table and outside the window the world is insanity.

I blink. Once, twice, the fire on my skin gutters out and I see a note left by my hand. I grab it, and it all comes flooding back.

William,

We were running out of time and you were ever so sleepy. I hope everything has turned out as expected (of course it has, I'm very good at what I do!) so we can begin our big new adventure together.

In pursuit of that, I have decided to save a little time and get a boat set up for us to make our escape. Our friends from the North are awfully close and they smell very bad indeed. Don't worry about helping, I've arranged for some assistance.

After all, you didn't think my crew were permanently

drowned did you? I think we've come far enough for you to realise that the world is full of wonders, many of which I intend to show you.

That's assuming you don't decide to stay of course.

If you do decide to stay, I wish you well and I'm going to have to learn 'piloting' rather on the fly.

Awfully inconvenient, but new I'm almost enjoying new things again.

Isn't it wonderful?

Your friend, Alyson.

I pick myself up off the table, muttering about Vampires and their impatience. There's set of cold weather gear, fleece, jeans and rubberised fisherman's outers by the door which I slip on. They feel odd against my skin. Maybe this is the first time I've actually felt them there.

I remember that my sense of touch had been dulled in the dark times before whatever Alyson had done. Given the damage it was likely a mercy.

A glance out the window confirms that the weather is not looking great for an untrained crew to get anywhere bar Davy Jones' locker. The storm outside is lashing the sea into foam and the cemetery is dark and puddled, in this, my first late-afternoon as a person.

I head upstairs and collect the things that matter to me. Some books from a box labelled 'Trash, tat and nonsense' in the same carefully crafted handwriting as my note. She has no taste in novels. A compass, a set of charts, an old magnetosphere locator - I can hope - the shotgun in its…

No. There's a twinge at the back of my head. The shotgun can stay.

I've got a vampire on my side now and I work.

I look around my former abode. It is emptier than I could believe. I switch off the fairy lights that are running their cycles, burning through the last of the battery power, in the absolute darkness of a dead place. I can't say I'm going to miss it.

There's a crackle from above me. From up in the Tower.

"Ho boy, that's not good."

Maybe I should check. For old time's sake.

That's when the screaming begins.

"This is the Voice of the Union, broadcasting on emergency frequencies. Listen."

The old, cultured voice is gone. The new voice is distorted and there is a chorus of screaming just underneath its words. It sounds like a man in the last extremis of his life pasting together each syllable and throwing them out in a second stretched out into a day.

It is the sound of nails on a chalkboard, personified, and is trying to shout as loudly as possible to get my attention.

I cannot move.

"This is the Voice of the Union. You must listen. Now. There has been a terrible mistake. The Door is opening. The degraded World is reaching in with steel claws and teeth. Darkness is coming. I don't care if you hate us you fucking construct. You were always the.... Screaming... worst."

"LISTEN. The Union cannot allow this state of uninterrupted anarchy to maintain its grip on the throat of the nation. Stop the witches. Then leave. That is all you... Thespian? Can you hear me? You need to do it. I'm trying to get you help. LISTEN. I'm trying to get you some help. Kill the witches. They cannot escape. IT's The OLDER. Two doors, both need to shut..."

A crack from below as the grenade bouquet explodes

as someone in a rush forgets to disarm it, and the Radio spits sparks and flashes red.

The transmission garbles into nonsense and the screaming increases in volume.

"What are you doing with that thing?" Alyson flies out of the hatch and pulls away the plug. "Why are you even working, nasty thing? Why are you talking? William... Help..."

I can feel a strain as whatever is at the other end of the Radio struggles with the Vampire Master. Alyson's face contorts into a mask of stress and the lights begin to flicker as she suppresses the signal.

She freezes, everything freezes.

The Radio continues, nothing but the new Voice.

"You think you are so very clever... clever don't you... missy. But we are on to you. We have been watching, You are not welcome here. You will be annihilated like your brothers and sisssssssters across the water. You will burn as they do. We are stronger than you now and you are not welcome. Listen."

"You will end here in the ice and the cold and you will listen for once in your damned half-life. So clever always with your we know best for you. You lose you lose lose lose lose if the witches... What an ending. I was a patriot..."

A crack.

Whatever power has been holding her is broken by her insurmountable will, and the distance from which the Radio's operator is acting, for all his strength. With a snarl she breaks the Radio apart with a short controlled chop of her hand, its mechanisms flying apart and scattering across the room.

A printed circuit board hits me on the forehead.

"Ouch?" I offer.

She looks around the room for any other transmitters,

taking a moment to topple the Lamp for good, stomping the box like centre flat. “Oh that felt so good. That man was a horror.”

I feel nothing. It is almost sad.

She continues. “What were you thinking William? We have to go. There’s a whole war coming this way and I don’t think either of us want to be involved.”

“How did you know to come here?”

“I got handed that stupid wind-up radio of yours by one of the crew when we were packing. It was spouting swear words at me and I thought something similar might be occurring up here.”

She pats him on the back. “How do you feel?”

I feel fine. I grin.

“Glad to hear it.” She hurries me along. “You need to meet the crew.”

I hear gunfire as we head down to the harbour area. There’s a large yacht decked out and ready to go. Whoever’s done the preparation work seems to have known what they were doing and picked the perfect vessel for a long distance journey.

It reminds me of…

Warm seas of the Mediterranean? That’s not you, creation of my enemies. Those are mine. You can’t have them. Keep to your freighters.

I bounce off the memory hard.

“Okay?” Her voice is concerned.

“Yeah.” I pinch my nose to get rid of the iron taste at the back of my throat.

“There might still be a few side effects of the work we did earlier.”

We walk down the stairs, ignoring the thorn bushes as

they claw away at a few rats. Past the businesses under the road leading up to the cliffs.

The firing is getting closer. We stop at a jetty where a small skiff awaits and she gestures at the 'Wind Runner'.

"What do you think, William."

"It's a good choice," I nod. "We can make this work."

"Crew now?"

"Crew now."

I can see figures on the ship. They seem oddly stooped, bloated. I have a feeling the crew might be a little different to what I'm expecting. "Aly."

"Yes."

"Are you not telling me something."

"Always." I get to row the boat across the harbour. Somehow that's not surprising. With a clear escape route, Aly's helpfulness is subsumed into her drive to leave.

Who remembers now the jousts of St. Inglevert?
Goodbye Mr. Brooker.

34

New friends

"So, William. I'd like you to meet your crew."

She's nuts. Completely insane. The crew is something from a horror show. And I say that as a monster myself. Yes, I have seen myself in the mirror, and my reflection in the sea.

I can live with that. This, less so.

"This is my assistant, Camelle."

Every last one of her crew are dead and clearly so. Camelle's the best of them. He's obviously a vampire, given the fangs in that slow smile but at least he still looks human enough to avoid triggering my gag reflex.

Camelle's in Vamp military garb, straight out of the manuals. The cloth is soaking wet and stiffening into ice.

"Heard a lot about you, Will. I'd say it's good to meet you, but ah," He gestures outside "… I have things to do and there's a Union special forces unit barrelling this way along with a couple of nutso-witches, so if we could do this chop chop I would simply love it." He taps at his collar. "At this rate I'll be a fucking icicle before I can get off the dock."

"Language, Camelle." Aly frowns.

"Sorry Master." A hint of defiance. Interesting.

"He's the one who taught me about this finger thing. A rude devil."

"Seems the sort?" I manage, gagging from the smell of the rest of the crew.

The rest are of a type, and that type is 'things scraped from the bottom of the ocean that should never be moving'.

The raw material is obvious. Each of them clearly started as a person, mostly sailors and they wear a variety of uniforms, salt encrusted and bleached by long term immersion.

The best of them are from the Patrol Boat I sank. The worst might go back centuries.

Their flesh is grey, loose and bloated with veins of salt that pulse. Bone gleams red at the joints I can see. They have boiled egg eyes. White and blind but they watch me none the less, heads swinging on drooping necks as they adjust to the world above the brine.

"And these are my jolly jack tars," Aly smiles. "They're all volunteers of course."

One vomits a stream of seawater, before saluting, its uniform the faded black of the German U-Boat fleet.

"They stop doing that after a while." She pats it on the back. "Better out than in."

She smiles brightly, a mannikin's smile from a shop window. Hazel eyes shining. "What do you think William?"

What else can I say. "All good, Aly. All good."

35

All is as it should be

The clear up was going poorly. That fucker Archibald is proving to be like a tick, hiding out somewhere in town with the Q box transmitter and a store of data from Tony.

Including the calculations. Arithmetic hypothesis, disproved. Geometric, next best guess. Well that would be fun.

It was, however, not something he could have going to the Vamps, even if it were only a hypothesis at the moment.

The Vamps weren't stupid, if they worked it out then eyes would be turning this way.

Where is that fucker hiding?

"Agent?"

It's that bloody Lieutenant. Andrews. Distracting him with details. That and the old shit who'd just wasted more than a minute of his time.

"Agent? We have a problem."

Of course we have a problem. Everything's been a problem. "What is it?

"The old geezer, you shot. We shot. He's military."

He snorts and shoves his hands deep into his trench coat pockets. “He was about two hundred years old. If he was military he’d have been working for Queen Victoria. And you know what the rules are.”

“Those are civilian rules, not ours. You wouldn’t get it.” Andrews is frowning. Gods above save him from the military.

“You seemed happy enough to shoot at him when you thought he was a civilian, corporal.”

“Lieutenant. And Captain said you’re in charge. That makes it your responsibility but we’ve got our own orders and that doesn’t include killing our own. We bring back any veterans. That’s straight from Devonport whatever you Goat F… gentlemen, say and I’ll send it right up the chain of command if you don’t… They don’t go to the resettlement camps and they sure as hell don’t get shot down like dogs on the fucking street.”

He can feel a headache building. Would there ever be a time that the Military were less of a fucking drag on efficiency? He doubts he’ll live to see it, if it were true. “Are there more of them? Is that your problem?”

“Whole bunch of old geezers in the house down that road.”

He bites his knuckles. Gnawing at the pain from the new tattooing. And the internal irritation at this interruption. “We’ve got a job to do, Andrews”

“Rescue and recover. That’s what my job is.”

“That is not the fucking job. Excision, direct or via extraction camp. That’s the rule, your team agreed to it.”

The Lieutenant stares back at him. Usual blank disobedience from these overly orderly fucks. He hates them almost as much as the fucking vampires… Time gentlemen, time!

He needs them. For now. And he doesn’t need to be

stuck on a Q box to some attenuated Admiral sitting in a bunker down at Devonport.

"Fucks sake. Go ahead then. Take a squad. I'll sort this out myself." Never trust the fucking military. He should have learnt that by now. When the chips are down, off they go down some shit for brains procedure that leaves everyone with a pile of….

There's a surge in the sky. The pain in his hands dissipates and he's filled with a sense of intense well being.

Not that he needs them much longer. Time for a test. Scientific method. It's what sets him apart from that idiot Thespian. The world beyond this nonsense belongs to him and his kind, not these relics.

"Andrews?" He shouts. For a moment he thinks the man didn't hear him. The dust storms are still messing up everything and the screaming on the radios is getting worse. However the man stops, turns. "Can take the APC too. Load up any of them you're keeping and get them back to the base for recovery."

"What about the dead man?"

"Leave him here. We can bury him with proper ceremony if that's what you want, once we've got the living out." And lock up the fuckers Archibald is trying to reach.

The tension in the Lieutenant's shoulders drops away. "Shitty mistake but no way you could have known. And there's been a lot of them getting up again recently. Give him a good send off."

"Do what you need to, Andrews." He picks the rune lock out of his pocket and tosses it in his hand. "I'll do the same."

36

Cutting it close

Alyson leaves the cabin, along with the crew. The stench of sea water and rot goes with them.

I lay the charts out and start to plot out our journey. I can hear the engines starting up. Space saved by having a dead crew in the holds has been filled with marine diesel, though I'm not going to ask where they found it but it looks like it might get us to…

"Hey."

I turn around, it's the other Vampire, Camelle. His hands are different from Alyson's, they seem part formed, the definition lacking at the base of each finger so that they meld into the palms in the faintest hint of a marine mammal in the mid-point of a radical adaptation to a new environment.

"What is it?"

He tilts his head towards the rest of the boat. "Bit of a baptism of fire huh?"

I chuckle. "Could say that."

"Lot of people feeling that way. Been a kick in the nuts for everyone the last six months. Living or otherwise. Same for our Master Alyson. Course, she's doing just dandy, what with all her compadres getting the chop." He leans in, the smell of a charnel house, images of carcasses hanging upside down from hooks, arms lolling. "How you finding her? Really. Bit of a trip, yeah?"

"Aly's just…"

"Weird? Yeah I know. The older they get the odder they get. As with people. So with us. Aly especially. Jumped the queue on Master status, not that she didn't deserve it. First and last of the ones picked by the dearly departed Council with an eye on the future rather than tickling the fancy of some old nutsack. Course that was back in the June days. Shit I hate this drifting crap."

June days? A half-remembered history lesson springs to mind. "How old are you?"

"Couple of centuries. Paris born and bred and then whack. I get to be this. Help your people, can do that better like us. Bullshit. Always some hook. Came up with Babeuf, rest his bones. Fucking wonderful. All the time in the world and the world filled with hooks you can spend eternity staring at if you're not careful." He gives me an appraising look. "Guess you understand that now."

I ignore the jibe. "Is that Family military uniform you're wearing?"

"Good eye, kid. Suppose the guys who made you probably built all that stuff in. Feeling the need to smash in my skull or stick a stake through my heart or has she been working on you too long?"

"A little."

He shrugs. "Think that's pretty normal reaction to a vampire on your front lawn. Know you agents don't like us much."

"Agents?"

Camelle starts to pace. "We're not that bad really."

I raise an eyebrow. I have eyebrows again.

"Really, sport, you're gonna have to love us."

"You drink blood. You keep people as cattle. Most of you seem to be a bit more… and don't take this the wrong way… You, and a bit less…" I nod out to the Captain's berth.

"Yeah to the first, but a lot less than I used to, prefer chewing on gum if I can get it. That's all fucked up too. A straight no to the second. Not that I'd be averse, free-range fuckers are taking a piss on my hometown right now, but we're stuck listening to her sort."

"Her sort?"

"Masters. You're a vampire? You're bound to them and you have to do what you say? Yes Master, No Master, Three bags full Master."

He laughs, a bleak sound that reminds me of the Seagulls, or the crows before they all committed suicide. "Yeah Master. Sure Master, you want to take a day trip over the Channel? I'll leave my unit to get torn apart by those Russian shitheels, can I get a bag? Oh. right his instant. Off I go. Poor bastards."

"Where's your unit now?"

"Probably caught up in some Russian tank's treads if I'm being honest with myself. Paris was gone and we were traffic control for the rout." He opens up a porthole, looks out to sea, over at the opposing shore. "Whole war was a clusterfuck from start to finish."

"I'm not sad you lost."

The finger. "Nice. Classy. Allowing for the fact you're a corpse too I think you'd have got on with some of the guys on our side. We weren't all bad, not when they weren't in charge."

"What do you mean?"

"Lots of normal people fighting on our side. And

they're probably doing better than whatever your shitty Union's been up to. The stench from up there? You smell it too? Glad we're off soon as you get your finger out of your ass."

"Lovely."

"Hey. I am who I am."

I go back to plotting a course, ignoring the younger, relatively, vampire.

He comes in close again. "You never answered me. How you finding Aly?

He deserves an answer. "You hit it on the head. First time. She's odd, weird. Doesn't seem to understand people and then says something that hits you like a gut punch. Seems to be a lot of that sort about recently."

Camelle smiles. He's not even close to getting it right. It's like looking down the path to hell.

"Yeah. Preach on brother." Camelle spits out a piece of something unidentifiable. "Pretty lucky you were about. We lost our boat guy on to the water pumps the night you got us. Without you she'd be stuck here or running about in circles. She wouldn't like that. We'd have been down there for good. Until she found a replacement."

My blood runs cold.

"Or made one."

Camelle stretches. "Yeah. Think on that if you'd like." A bloody grin. "I don't have a choice. For now. You might. See you around, D."

37

Sailing

The Boat is about to sail.

I look at the Vampire woman, weaving wards around the boat as whatever horrors approach us fight their private war.

"What do you think, Will? My bet is that the Witches will make it." She nods approvingly. "They're making good progress. I can feel it. Be a miracle if anyone can stop them. There's something very attractive about the older one. Feels like one of us!"

She stands elegant as ever on the deck of the yacht which she plans to use to travel half way around the world. It's a good yacht, I'd have recommended it. The question is whether I should help her get there or not.

Her appearance is deceptively mundane, a slim woman in her late twenties, dark loose ringlets of hair that drop down to her shoulders, twisting at the ends into tight curls in the fashion of a bygone age, brown eyes, wide spaced, the intensity of them unnerving when they're turned my way.

Worse when she has plans. And she has a lot of plans. I've seen them.

Her eyes right now are those of a hellfire preacher hurling damnation out at a cowed congregation.

A general declaiming the need for flawless victory to his devoted soldiers.

A fanatical devotee of a forgotten writer directing her students to the subtler points that drive meaning in a story most have forgotten to study.

But what she is clashes with her accoutrements and her voice, manner and I cannot get the two to gel.

She's dressed for a sea voyage. Or so she thinks. No more pants suit. Now she is accoutred in a bizarre, colourful pastiche of the Pirates of Penzance glommed from a fancy dress store.

A pastiche of a pastiche yet one she seems to believe is ideally suited to long sea journeys.

It is part of what it makes it so hard to abandon her. She is like a child in some ways. Gaps in her knowledge, gaps in her awareness. Were she not so powerful she could almost be pathetic.

A preacher with a flawed book, a prophet waiting on a god who never comes, A general with a single failed strategy which he clings to like a rock.

There is something wrong with her, an insect caught between instars. He wonders for a moment what she will become in time.

Of course it does not make less deadly. Her inhuman stillness gives away what she really is, her head frozen at a half tilt, listening to the fighting up above us drawing ever closer to the harbour. The hand raised to point, unmoving and alabaster pale. Poised on a rocking deck directing my attention to their shared predicament.

I feel I can hear the voices of women, raised in defiance, bullets spoofed and evaded, a cultured man shouting out threats and promises and explanations that he doesn't want to do this.

It is oddly familiar. A sting at the back of my mind that's always there.

I am following the silent echo of a person who died millennia ago, a purported poet whose works have been forgotten and who has in turn forgotten how to rhyme. Yet enough remains of her to make me miss warmth and company that I have never truly known.

For all that I remember, none of them are my memories. All borrowed, all stolen from oblivion by a poet of a new poetry.

And she spins a plausible lie.

Pace Radio. Pace whoever it was who controls it. Pace Brooker if that was you. I can't say you didn't deserve whatever was happening to you.

But will I follow?

Vampires are users. It's in their nature. They can't help it. For all their purported good will, those who work with them never seem to come to a good end. Thanks for the heads up Camelle. You're one odd bastard.

But what's the alternative?

There's a war going on up there. Maybe if the witches are losing I might try and intervene. Maybe if I understood the threat they posed I would step up and take my place beside the humans doing their damndest to stop them. What did they bring with them that's so dangerous that a man with a reputation like Brooker's spent the last moments of his life screaming that they had to be stopped.

Okay. I don't know any of that stuff.

On the other hand I know her well enough to understand all the problematic elements of her existence and all the reasons not to jump off the edge of the world for a trip into the unknown.

Those sharp teeth are the least of it, she claims to barely eat, and I believe her.

But there's that intellectual curiosity uncoupled from human feeling which leads her to treat me as a laboratory experiment. That's led to my very existence, but it is that of a lab rat, with a specific purpose in mind.

It will take six months more to get where we are going.

How long before she decides to dissect me or see how long I can swim, or tries to lure up some deep-water beast to speed her journey and sacrifice this crew of the dead.

I shiver at the thought. The depths are as dangerous as the skies.

Then there's the kindness and concern that can turn in a moment to a cold calculation of future worth.

Emotions spinning on a dime, if such a thing can even be said to have emotions. What would I have been if I had lived a thousand years or more under the thumb of my peers.

And then there's the mistake. I understand that now.

The voice is back and it's happier than its been since I heard it first.

"She's running away from a war that her kind have lost, she is fleeing something that is coming but she says it's not soon, yet she seeks your assistance to go halfway around the world with a man whose experience is captaining a yacht and it's not even your experience and you can't have it, fucker.

Why do you think she has done all she has done, why do you think she wants you there really? Can you believe a word she says?"

"What do you care?"

"I don't. I have all the time in the world now. Nice to have someone repair Thespian's fuck ups. Surprised at who, but I'll roll with it, you sad piece of shit."

"I'll fight you."

"Let's see how that turns out for you."

I look down at my new boots, the red light makes the damp mud on them glisten like blood. When I look up she's standing there.

"Tick tock, Will." Her voice is musical and sweet, except when she laughs.

I take one last look up the road to the dead town.

Not dead now, there's life scattering around, diving for cover, scurrying away from explosions, more life than there has been at any time since the evacuation.

Engines revving. Hollow pops from automatic weapons, centered on the Monastery.

The place that had been my refuge since the day my new life began and someone has decided to use it as a fortress of sorts. I wish them well.

It's time to go.

A minute later the boat casts off and behind them in the port, as they race away, a desperate figure rises high on wings of red scarlet to strike down at a threat to the existence of everything brought into the now by a protective mother.

But that is a story for another time.

Epilogue

Time distortion detected - month two of Catastrophe. From records of AIA Agent body camera and post action reports.

Codename Darwin

Darwin's eating a toasted sandwich. It's cheese and ham and came out of a plastic baggy, heated into a lukewarm treat by the Track's boiler unit. It's his one concession to physical need after the debacle earlier that day with Andrews and his soft hearted crap.

He's not even angry. He'll make Andrews pay eventually. Patience. He wishes that virtue on the team locked down in the tunnels.

Really the sandwiches are supposed to be for the Scrapes, there's separate food for the operational team but he got hungry and as an Assistant he can do what he damn well chooses, half the soldiers here wouldn't have been alive if it wasn't for him.

They've set up the mobile command post at an old service station, signage still declaiming the price of gas and with a thoroughly looted convenience store attached.

There's a small hive of MDR and military types co-ordinating day two of the Thanet sweep from a set of tents and vehicles scattered around that he's assigned his command to, the sigils on the vehicles providing a little protection from the howling winds which drive the dust clouds into everything.

The Thanet clearance has been moved up so that they can help him catch Stevie and his little lady. Bitch had somehow got hold of the early feeds from Tony and a Q link direct to the source, and that was not going to stand. When he got through with this he was going to shoot that little Vampire traitor who had passed it over and who had holed up in the old HQ.

He's got big plans for Archibald, a former MDR Director who seems to have acquired a love of blood donation and continental breakfasts. A bit of fitting justice. If he and his girlfriend wanted to betray the Union then it's only fitting that he have the opportunity to serve it in another form to make amends.

The woman he'll just kill. Or keep back if the first run of the Watcher protocol doesn't work. It's all as one to him.

After all, there needs to be a way in and out of the Union's territories and that means someone's got to guard it. And that someone ideally isn't a person. His faction of the Union won't be staying once its business here is concluded. Bigger fish to fry, like making sure the right people are in charge.

A slice of ham slips out of the bottom of the sandwich as he bites into it. "Shit."

Harrison looks over from where he's watching drone footage of the rails being torn up. "Want another one of those?"

"No. I'm good." Darwin gives the sandwich a dubious

look. "This is shit. Cheese is like snot, the ham's just water and fat."

"It's food." Harrison, the Assistant assigned to the second day of the clearance, shrugs. "Lot of people would kill for that."

"Debatable." He walks over to where the other man is sitting. A modified Track is twisting and breaking the rails. If there had been sound he'd have been able to hear the snapping and cracking of the Victorian age's finest form of transport meet its end. The feed's unstable due to the crappy atmospherics but he gets the gist.

"This is going well."

Harrison nods. "Sweep's looking good too, D. We've got most of the survivors loaded up in the lorries up by beaches, usual scrapings but they'll do fine and they're not complaining about the sandwiches."

He gives the man the stink eye. Harrison's in on the joke. One of the Goats rather than a sheep. "Any sign of the targets?"

"Not yet, but it's just a matter of time. We've closed the girdle up so no one in, no one out, till we say so and Thespian's on the trail."

There's a warning bleep from the terminal and the camera view suddenly shifts as if it were being yanked up at speed into the clouds above. "Shit shit shit." Harrison hits a button. "Get me another drone and can you tell the Manston guys to keep the things low. Lower. Yes low. The opposite of high. Know it takes longer but those things don't grow on trees."

"We lost the entire complement getting down here. None of these military bozos seem to get the fact they'll get their toys eaten if they go high." He spits. "Got any coffee? This tastes like farts."

"Thermos over there, I'd ask you to refill but that would be a waste of breath."

"Yup." He takes the thermos and sits down on a camp chair to watch the orange glow of the girdle on the northern horizon, past the airport they are using for drones. He drinks the coffee but the sandwich defeats him. He dumps it on the ground and treads it into the dirty snow. Then spits on it.

"No fucking refugee will want to eat that now."

There's a yell from behind him. Harrison again.

"Thespian's team."

"We got them?" He hands over the empty thermos.

"Thanks. And yes. Thespian's still got some moves." Harrison passes the thermos to a waiting administrator, one of the new hires, she rushes off to the temporary canteen for a refill without prompting.

Darwin snorts. "Old gimp."

"Not a fan eh Darwin?

"He's the past. This…" he points upwards. "That over there, that's the future. He either wakes up or he takes a dirt nap, near future. Excisions all round." He chuckles at the thought of the Government team in the tunnels scraping in the dark at dead controls. Some people weren't meant for the future.

Trucks start to roll past. Slow and steady, fuel's limited until they can get the new engines working. The loading beds packed with ragged looping scrapes. "And those fine people are going to help us create it."

One of the dumbasses waves at them as he passes.

"Thank you sirs. You're a blood miracle!"

"It's what we do! Don't worry about it," the truck is gone. "And you'll be in a resettlement zone before you know it."

"Still, better than this ah, shit hole sir?" says a trainee assistant holding out the thermos to Harrison.

Harrison gives a tight smile. "Very much better, could you go get me the progress reports on the loading please, Miriam?"

"Yes sir, right away sir."

Darwin giggles when she's out of hearing range. The wind helps. "Jesus, they're dumb as a box of spanners but you've got to love the scrapes."

"Yeah. Anyway…"

"Anyway. What's our dramatic pal got to say."

"See for yourself." They head back into the command vehicle and Harrison fires up the radio. It crackles and fizzes, the signal boosted by crude glyphs etched into its casing to cut through the cloud interference. He's not sure he likes the way the clouds ripple when the system is used nor the way that the vehicle shakes under his feet but it's necessary. Plenty of time for refinement later.

"Thespian. You have news. Over?"

"Sorry Sir, it's Andrews of the support team. Thespian's gone out for a smoke. He told me to say that we've got them surrounded so the kill team can mosey on in whenever you're ready."

They look at each other. "Wanker."

"Sorry Sir, didn't catch that."

Harrison leans in, "We're on our way. Thanks Andrews."

Darwin heads over to a suiting up station, "Well he wangled his way out of guard duty I see."

"Numbers game."

Darwin sighs. "You coming or got more important things to do? Either way I'm going to need a driver, need to find that box."

Harrison nods, "You know how this works, the Minister's asked for a confirmation so I get an outing in this dust storm. Right-hand left-hand stuff."

"That one's tricksy. We'll need to keep an eye on him."

"No one said he's an idiot."

Darwin suits up as Harrison arranges transport over the radio.

"Check check."

"Radio's working good."

They head out to the road ignoring the lorries rattling by.

"Where's that transport, Harrison?"

"Should be here any minute. Provided the bloody thing doesn't break down."

Darwin can taste dust in his mouth, "Baptist's head, is anything going to go right today?"

"What is it?"

"Filter's clogged. Some shit stuck a used hood on in the station. No fucking professionalism in the military guys. Hold here." He pops into a nearby command crawler to change the filter, a twist and replace that he's done a hundred times before. Inside there's an NBC suited infantry squad huddled around a heat sigil.

"Afternoon gents. Liking the new heater are we?"

"Yes sir. Freeze our bollocks off without it."

"Lots more good stuff to come. The Organization has you covered. We're going to keep this country together if it's the last thing we do. You should see some of the new shit I'll be doing today."

"Love to see that, sir."

"Can't if I can't breathe though. Some scrape's left me with a clogged filter." He looks around. "Anyone got a spare?"

"There you go sir. New one from stores."

"Thanks lads."

He quickly fits the filter and leaps back out of the car into the icy winds. Harrison is waiting for him with a four by four.

"Hop in, Darwin. Don't want to miss the main event,"

"Wouldn't miss this for the world." The engines starts up and they bomb down the dual carriageway outside of town, past lines of lorries. "Not a bad harvest. We'll be head of quota on SACRIFICE/LASTLIGHT sure as sure." He grins. "And I've got Andrews running guard duty."

Harrison gives him the look. He can tell even through the lens of the NBC hood. A crinkled eyed look of disgust.

"Necessary evil. All agreed well in advance…"

He's still looking.

"Look somewhere else, idiot. This is survival of the fittest and if everyone was half as efficient as us then we'd already have the SIGIL protocols in place."

"I know, I know." Harrison might not be up to snuff after all. Soft hearts, soft minds. Not a long term survival trait, fortunately. "Just beginning to realise how you got that codename."

They pass a roundabout and veer left. "Coincidence. There's was a random generator at old HQ set up by the previous administration. Think it was originally used for weapons prototypes."

"Hmm."

The winds buffet the vehicle as they advance past the rundown houses of the town. The road is surprisingly wide right up to the point where they reach the roadblock. A soldier with a rifle waves them down.

Harrison leans out of the window. "Thespian's up at the next roundabout. The ministry bloke's hiding out in the house on the corner. He's going nowhere."

Harrison nods and the soldier gestures up to his mate

who moves the APC blocking the road forward to let them through.

"You ready Darwin."

He grins, white even teeth, prominent canines, a predator's smile.

Not that Harrison can tell, the Noddy suits hide a multitude of evils.

They pull up a little before the final roundabout. The house in question is obvious, a couple of army vehicles are pulled up outside with marksman aiming rifles and mounted machine guns at the windows.

Thespian is leaning against one, smoking one of his disgusting cheroots. He's using some cantrip to repel the dust, the same as Darwin copied and improved on on the way here, and there is a slight crackle of static electricity as he waves languidly at them.

"What what. It's Darwin. And is that Harrison?" He rubs the back of his neck. "Come to show us all how it's done eh Assistant Evans?"

"'Bout the size of it Thesp. And stick with code names, be professional for once in your life. You've done your bit. Bloodhounding, a bit of containment. Can leave the kill to the big boys."

"Not what I've heard, but you go knock yourself out, my lad." He clicks on a laser pointer and runs it along the sills of a couple of windows. "Our friend is up there, first floor and he's got the feed. Not sure if the girl is with him but he's armed so..."

"Not a problem. Been some advances since you were gone." Darwin slips off a glove and shows the red lines running in waves along his fingers. "If I can see it, I can stop it."

Thespian feigns interest. "My, my. Such fast progress now you have all the power swirling around up there.

Same effect from, well, you know. Stealth and a bit of brain power but you big lads go and do your stuff. I'll be sure to be particularly amazed."

He blows a smoke ring at Darwin. Annoying arsehole.

"Harrison, you stay here. I've been waiting for this for a while."

"So you keep saying," mutters Thespian. "Mr. Harrison, can I interest you in a smoke?"

He leaves them to their nonsense and strides up to the gate. The garden is full of plaster-work figures. Gauche horrors, they make him sick with disgust at the sort of people who thrived in the world before. So much better now. A clean slate.

A shot rings out from above him, he can feel the shock-waves approaching as if in slow motion, the structure of the bullet, lead, propellant the sonic crack, the casing falling. He catches it with his mind and pulls it apart into a cloud of dust to join the dust of the dead world it came from.

"Oh yes. This is the good stuff," he chuckles.

There's two more shots before he's through the door. Neither comes close and he is up the stairs before the man can reload. The traitor's still fumbling with an old fashioned Webley when he kicks it out of his hands and the traitor down to the ground.

A little TK goes a long way.

He puts his foot on the man's neck.

"Good to see you again Steve. Where's Angela?"

"Fuck yourself, Darwin." The man coughs out. That earns him another kick. Good solid metal tipped boots crack ribs.

"No thanks. Think I'll fuck you up instead. You good with that Steve? Then we make some modifications. Time to be useful for once in your life you fucking Traitor. Now where's..."

There's a tingle in his fingers, the sigil's supposed to work in 360 degrees so he knows that the nasty little bitch has snuck up behind him and even has time to grasp at the projectile before it's halfway towards him.

Something is different though.

The projectile is just a ball of lead, it disintegrates with little effort.

But there are more. Lots more. Eight more to be exact. He may be good, but this is a new trick for him and he only manages to catch three of the little fuckers.

He has time to think 'shotgun' before he drops to his knees from the impact. The second blast hits him full on, he can feel his face fragmenting and the soul grips cutting in, trying to hold him together.

"Run Steve, run."

The world darkens around him and he coughs. Blood splattering against his respirator lenses from his perforated lungs. His last thought as he topples to the carpet is that Thespian was right. It does not make slipping into the darkness any easier.

The two escapees don't get far, barely out of the door and on to the road.

One of the soldiers catches the man with a single shot to the head dropping him face down, leaving his ridiculous green backpack exposed. The woman is caught a moment later in a burst from the mounted machine gun.

Thespian shakes his head sadly as he examines the bodies.

Harrison and a couple of the soldier boys have gone in to look for the overconfident Darwin.

"Darwin is the worst."

He never had much time for the man, they'd worked together on that god awful mess with the Fae, and ever since then the man had gotten mixed up an ever worsening crowd. Worse still, he never seemed able to understand that some things were better off not knowing.

Still he feels rather sorry for him none the less when he sees what the rampaging civil servants have done to him.

"Thespian? He's still alive… but he's really messed up." Harrison is panicking. Losing an Assistant would be quite the black mark against him with Brooker. Reassignment awaits this young man unless something is done.

"Bring him to the APC. I'll see what I can do. If anyone can survive this it'll be old D."

He puts out his cheroot against the side of the APC and waits pondering what, if anything, he is going to do. He's reasonably sure the soldiers are too busy clearing the house to notice though he does get a waved index finger from the machine gunner. "Sorry old Sport. Mistook it for a wall."

And there he is in all his blood dripping glory. Idiot probably thought the Noddy suit was bullet proof or something. Never rely on magic, never rely on ignorance.

Harrison is jumping around like a puppy with its tail in a blender. The two soldiers carrying the fallen moron are at a loss as to what to do. There's a trail of blood like you would not believe leading from the house.

"Are we clear?" he asks the machine gunner.

"Yes sir."

"Okay Harrison, get this idiot into the back of the APC and we'll see what we can do with him."

"Shouldn't we get him to the aid station?"

"Not enough time and I'm afraid he's a bit past what they could help him with bandages and blood plasma."

Way past. The man should be long dead, maybe he has some tricks up his sleeve.

They lay him out and Thespian runs flicks impatiently through the most recent set of medical protocols, written by Darwin himself for this very mission. "You know he was quite right, there have been some interesting developments. Now what has he got marked up here?"

"He's dying. Quickly!"

Thespian smiles a slow smile showing cracked teeth and receding gums, a side effect of his fifty-a-day habit. "Aha, well maybe our friend's Sadism could be the saving of him. Irony eh? I don't suppose you know what he was going to do with our treacherous pals over there, Mr. Harrison?"

Harrison looks up, the red cloud-light flashes across the NBC suit's perspex eye covers. "He said something about a puppet protocol. Someone to watch the waters."

A pause.

"Watcher protocol."

"This is the one then. Hmm, don't think we'd get too far with those fellows. They're a little too perforated and... yes. There we are. No head shots."

"Hurry hurry hurry."

"I think he's stopped breathing," says one of the soldiers. "Silly bugger didn't even clear the building properly."

"Not your fault. You'll get a lot of that from his sort, Lieutenant. Remember that," Thespian is carefully drawing out sigils along the dying man's face, his eyes flickering down to the notepad to check the exact shapings. "There's a trick to most things and the most important thing to remember is that for all the clever stuff we can do we're still ignorant as a hippo in a mud bath just like everyone else. No matter how high and mighty some among us may appear to be on our good days."

"Right, Sir."

"Nearly there, but lacking a little. He's still… leaking and some of him's plain not there." Thespian looks about and then a moment of inspiration. Repurposing. "Could you take his gloves off please Harrison, I need the… there we go."

The trick to the new protocols is to catch the soul before it can move away. Or what you could.

"Like catching a fart in a bag."

"What?"

"A tribute to our blunt friend."

Thespian fears that he may have been a little lax in his ministrations, there is a first night for every show and often there are minor changes to apply, scene settings to switch, lines to be delivered with a firm emphasis someplace else.

And this was more of a rehearsal. He remembers when he first learnt to fix slot machines. Wonderful trick but he'd accidentally had every damn slot in the casino pay out simultaneously. The methods in the notepad stink of Sandy and her lackadaisical approach. Those two. Terrible team. He even preferred whatshisname. Lawrence. Least he only hated Witches not all living things.

Hey diddle diddle, straight up the middle. Power for subtlety. He's almost glad he's getting away from the whole steaming bunch of them for a while. The continent was a clean war.

"Well I think I got…" The noise that escapes from the former Darwin is inhuman. A long drawn out moan from deep in his chest. Pain and emptiness in such measure that it brings a tear to Thespian's jaded eyes.

"Fuck. What's gone wrong…"

"Yeah that can't be right. Nothing should sound like that."

Thespian thinks quickly. It's a strength of his. The ability to adapt.

Well if he's lost some of the former Assistant or it's dropped out, then he has to use something else in its place or what's left is not going to be pretty. He casts about, there's still traces of the civil servants, not much but something. A dying man up above the shop choking out a last few breathes, a dead man in the hairdressers from a couple of days ago. A man in a car…

An old sailor still clinging to Darwin's soul. How odd.

Okay. He collects the fragments and works a minor miracle to cram them all together into something resembling a person, adjusting the sigils to catch them in place with carefully considered finger strokes. Aligning sigils before they can evaporate from the dead man's skin.

Tricksy.

"Is he?" Harrison and the soldier are just watching, he can't tell what they think due to the noddy suits but if they understood that he was working off the cuff here they would be astounded.

His work is finished. He steps back.

The thing that was Darwin shudders and draws a breath. It mutters something, words, and sensible ones. Nearly coherent.

"I think this gentleman is cold. Let's get him all bandaged up and work out what we've saved and how we might use it." He sighs. Coughs. "Watcher protocol sounds unpleasant. I'll leave that to you, Harrison."

"Thank you Thespian." Says Harrison.

"Hmm." Thespian snorts. "Well it may be a bit of a jerry-rigged botch but I suspect that whatever comes out the other side will be a damn sight more pleasant to deal with than Mr. Darwin was."

He steps out into the dust and cold leaving the new man with Harrison and the gawping soldiers, he picks out another cheroot and sighs as his lighter fails to catch.

"Up here." The machine gunner reaches down.

"Thank you my good man."

"You fuckers are nuts," says the soldier. "I'm glad you're on our side."

"Some of us, anyway." Thespian smiles, stroking the square block on his armband, and walks off down to the port. The dust clouds fizz against his static barrier and the clouds above are heavy with potential.

He has a boat to catch.

About the Author

Jack Holloway very much enjoys seeing the back of this one as it's the second book he wrote in the Ice Age in Scarlet, and you would not believe how difficult it was to beat it into any kind of shape.

In fact it's a bit too much like the protagonist for its own good.

Onwards and upwards!

https://authorholloway.com

Printed in Great Britain
by Amazon

86238044R00198